D1103847

# THE HOUSE OF
# LOVE AND DEATH

# THE HOUSE OF
# LOVE AND DEATH

## A CAMERON WINTER MYSTERY

# ANDREW
# KLAVAN

THE MYSTERIOUS PRESS
NEW YORK

THE HOUSE OF LOVE AND DEATH

Mysterious Press
An Imprint of Penzler Publishers
58 Warren Street
New York, N.Y. 10007

First Mysterious Press edition

Interior design by Maria Fernandez

Library of Congress Control Number: 2023908392

Cloth ISBN: 978-1-61316-446-4
ebook ISBN: 978-1-61316-447-1

10 9 8 7 6 5 4 3 2 1

Printed in the United States of America
Distributed by W. W. Norton & Company

*For Ellen Treacy, who makes our house a house of love.*

*Other lessons were impressed upon me even more deeply. I heard of the difference of sexes, and the birth and growth of children, how the father doted on the smiles of the infant, and the lively sallies of the older child, how all the life and cares of the mother were wrapped up in the precious charge, how the mind of youth expanded and gained knowledge, of brother, sister, and all the various relationships which bind one human being to another in mutual bonds.*

—Mary Shelley
*Frankenstein; or, The Modern Prometheus*

# PROLOGUE

The burning mansion rose above him like a great beast of flame. The flames roared red from its high windows. They pranced and jabbered behind the picture pane on the ground floor. Above the lovely wooded lane, patches of the pale blue dawn caught the glow and turned a feverish pink. Swaths of the meridian, meanwhile, were smothered under the black smoke that flooded up out of the raging heart of the conflagration.

Later, Guerrero would say he sensed Death standing inside that burning house, sensed Death standing like a hooded phantom, very still amidst the dancing fire.

Lenny Guerrero was Search and Rescue, Truck 48, the first truck. A broad, strong, boyishly handsome man in his mid-thirties, he was at the truck's side near the curb, near the lawn. The light arrays from the truck and the nearby engine, Engine 39, flashed scarlet and shadow over him as he worked to get himself game ready. Strapping his air pack on, his mask on, his hood on, his helmet.

Around him, there was movement, action, everywhere. The pipeman was "making" the hydrant by the curb while the heelman kept the line clean behind him as the water brought the hose to life. The two-man entry team was already at the mansion door, one man hacking at the jamb with an axe, the other working a Halligan, trying to pry the whole structure free.

Guerrero had often noticed—a lot of the guys noticed—how such moments—these moments just before you went in—could become bizarrely quiet, bizarrely slow—slow and graceful and almost silent, beautiful even, like some kind of strange ballet without the music. Supposedly it was because your brain was working so fast, the images and noises of the world couldn't keep up with it. That's what the captain said anyway.

It was in that moment—that slow, quiet, graceful moment, with the pipeman setting off the first blast of water as the door came free, as the flames exploded outward into the dawn light, as a second engine pulled up with its array leisurely turning and its siren sounding weirdly far away—it was in that moment that he felt Death—Death like a phantom—standing in the house, waiting in there, waiting for him, Guerrero, to come and discover the work of his skeleton hands.

Then he was racing up the rolling lawn, under the autumn trees beneath the smoke-choked sunrise. He followed the hose through the gaping door and suddenly everything was fast. The black smoke swallowed him fast. The heat washed over him fast, heat but no light. He dropped to his knees for safety.

He started crawling in the dark. Searching, blind, deaf except to the click of the regulator, the thump of his own heart. His heart—that was fast too. And the flames were fast to the right and left of him.

Guerrero worked to calm himself. At best, he had forty-five minutes of air in his pack, but breathing this hard, he'd be "on bells" in fifteen minutes tops. A Catholic, he drew himself down into the quiet of his faith and handed his life to God. Experience had taught him he could do this, and it worked. His breathing slowed. The world slowed and grew quiet again.

*Good*, he thought. *Good*. It would make the air pack last longer.

He began to make his way, crawling through the roiling darkness, searching for the fallen.

You found them just inside the doors usually. They tried to get out and couldn't work the knob or couldn't locate it. Then the smoke overcame them and they went down right there, sometimes blocking the door so you had to shove it open to get to them. Kids, a lot of times, you found hiding under a bed, or in a bathroom in the bathtub, any place that felt safe to them in the panic of the moment.

But Guerrero found the first woman at the foot of the stairs. Crawling on his hands and knees, blind in the black smoke, he felt the yielding softness of her hand beneath his heavy glove. His heart seemed to stop and darken because he knew at once there was no chance for her. Swiftly, expertly, he worked her limp body over his shoulder. It was still too hot in the house, too black for him to stand straight. He found his feet, but kept low, very low, and charged back toward the doorway with the woman slung over his back.

It wasn't until he laid her on the grass that he saw she had been murdered. Even when he did see it, he could barely comprehend what he saw. He brought her body forward and released it, cradling her head in his hand to soften her landing.

She floated gracefully down to the grass, her arms slanting out to either side of her. She seemed to him oddly untouched by the smoke and flames.

She was a woman in her forties or early fifties, blonde and slim and attractive. She was wearing an elegant powder-blue nightgown. There was a bullet hole in her, right in the center of her torso. It flashed through Guerrero's mind that she'd been killed with a deer rifle, something like a thirty-ought-six slug. The hole in her was almost the size of a fist. For another second, he still considered starting CPR, but there was no point. She was way, way dead.

Guerrero noticed another fireman's legs in front of him. He raised his face to speak his shock to a brother. It was Captain Flanagan. Guerrero saw the captain's mouth moving in the shape of a curse. Then he saw the captain turn his eyes, so he turned too.

There was Jack Morton, also S and R, also from Truck 48. He was carrying a full-grown man over his shoulders. When he laid the man down, Guerrero could see his face was gone, a tangled, gory mess. A rifle wound for sure.

A sense of urgency took hold of Lenny now. Before he thought it through, he was charging into the house again. Something in his mind had clicked and the sound of the scene had come back on. The air was full of sirens—sirens and shouts and the hoses blasting and the angry roar of the flames.

There were more engines arriving now. More trucks. Another hose.

Guerrero crossed the threshold and saw at once that the smoke inside was turning from black to gray. Some patches were already white. The teams were winning their battle with the flames.

Now Guerrero could make out shapes moving. He could see the outline of the staircase up ahead, a wide, majestic rising path going straight up, then branching to the left and right.

A ghost of a figure was descending toward him through the smoke. It was Bernard, another S and R man. He was carrying a body in his arms. As he came closer, Guerrero could see it was a young woman, small and delicate, her hair spilling back behind her, waving with the motion of the descent. Guerrero thought Bernard was moving too heavily, too slowly to save her. Then Bernard came closer. He came clear of the smoke, and Guerrero saw why he was so slow. The bullet had struck the girl in the middle of the chest. There was no chance to save her. She was gone.

Guerrero felt himself falling away inside. He felt he was in a hellish dream or maybe a dreamlike hell. He heard glass shatter, as if in another country far away. He turned toward the noise.

Now that the smoke was white, the entry team was breaking the B-side windows, the southern windows, to clear the air. In his daze, Guerrero experienced an odd, unnatural moment. Bernard was just walking past him with the murdered girl in his arms, and Guerrero thought he saw his double, a second Bernard, through the broken window, walking across the lawn. But then he realized: no, it was Brown. Brown from Truck 32. Brown was also carrying a young woman in his arms, and she was also dead.

Gaping, Guerrero looked around him. In the moment, he couldn't have named his emotion, but later he called it horror. Horror and awe. Horror because . . . well, how could this be happening? Who were these people? What was this place? And awe because . . . because now he knew that his intuition had been right, that Death was here in fact, Death in person, hooded Death, standing like the king of the shadowlands amidst the coils of smoke.

That's how dazed he was, how far gone. Then all at once he heard urgent shouts from outside, one shout followed by several others. He snapped back to full attention. Something important was happening.

He found himself back at the doorway. He was standing beneath the splintered lintel. The smoke was clearing from the house and the sun was rising outside. It was becoming easier for him to see. He looked around and spotted the source of the commotion.

There was a little grove of trees across the street, maples, elms, and oaks, with their leaves red and yellow and pale green. A little boy was just now stepping out of the shelter of the woods. He was wearing pajamas. There was a stuffed bear dangling from his hand. Several firefighters were running toward him, Captain Flanagan among them. Guerrero realized he himself was running toward the boy, as well.

He saw the captain pointing at the house. He heard his voice on the dawn breeze: "Is that your house? Is that your house?"

The boy was nodding, dazed, staring past him, staring at the fire.

The captain was on his knees now. He was holding the boy gently by the arms.

"Son, son, can you tell me," the captain said. "How many people are in the house? How many more people are in there?"

It was a long moment before the boy shifted his gaze, turned it from the smoking ruin of his home to the captain's broad, lined, friendly face.

"Who's in the house, son? Can you tell me?" the captain asked again. "Who's in the house?"

Guerrero was close enough now to hear the boy's quiet reply.

"Everyone."

# PART ONE

# THE MISSING MAN

*I'm going to tell you the worst thing I ever did. I've been thinking it over. It's time.*

*I had been in the Division about eight months. Eight or nine. Less than a year anyway. But I had already been on several major missions. I had sent a troublesome Russian diplomat to his death by luring him into a plot against his president, then making sure he was found out. I had led an Iranian terrorist into a Saudi trap—and he was never seen again. And so on. There were a couple of other assignments of that nature, but you get the idea. I had become an assassin. Not the fictional, cinematic sort, not the sniper-on-the-rooftop sort. That makes no sense as an undercover operation, once you come to think of it. It raises too many questions. No, I had been trained, instead, to arrange murders, to maneuver our country's enemies into a position where they fell afoul of those who would do them in. It was a secret, undetectable business. That was the whole point of it.*

*And listen. I'm sure I don't have to remind you, Margaret, but let me remind you anyway: Don't make notes. Don't try to hide it or put it in code or anything like that. Just don't. Don't make notes.*

*So. Early in winter, just after the holidays, I was called to the Division offices. They were in a three-story brick and brownstone building on a corner near Capitol Hill. By its looks, it could have been any sort of place: a private library, a private home. A sharp eye might have noticed that there were a suspicious number of white sandstone neoclassical government temples nearby. But then, you know, it was D.C.*

*My chief, the Recruiter, had a small office on the top floor. Very simple setup. Wooden desk. Chairs and a two-seat sofa against the wall. A flag and some framed prints. The* Mayflower *landing. Washington resigning his commission. A small El Greco:* Christ Carrying the Cross.

*It was always the same when I came in. He would be sitting there, very still, with his hands clasped on the desktop. As if he never did anything else but sit and wait for me to show up. He was always dressed in crisp khaki. The broad shoulders squared. The block of a head shaved and tilted forward so that that his deadpan black face was pointed at you like one of those flat-fronted RPM machine guns that fire something like a million rounds a minute.*

*To say the Recruiter was my mentor at this point would really be to say too little of him. There's some line in the Bible somewhere, Paul probably, where he says, it's no longer I who live, but Christ who lives in me. It was more like that. I had given my inner life over to him completely. Not Christ. I mean the Recruiter.*

*I had changed in the time since Roy had died. I think that's what I'm trying to get at. Since I'd killed Roy, arranged his death, however you want to say it. I now moved from mission to mission with a sort of blank-minded certainty I'd never felt about anything before, and possibly since. I won't say I had no misgivings about my work, not exactly. But the voice of my conscience had become the Recruiter's voice. And he was certain about what we were doing, or he seemed to be at any rate.*

*The second I sat down across from him, he said, "So, Poetry Boy, here you are. And you'll be awestruck to learn that with a single glance through the glassy surface of your idiot gaze, I can see straight into the black heart of nothingness that is your godless and therefore soulless experience of this our only mortal life. And on that evidence of my own senses, I feel safe in saying you have now become morally dead in the service of your country and are therefore ready for your next government assignment."*

*"Uh . . . thank you?" I asked.*

*He continued as if I hadn't spoken. "Up until now, you've elimi-nated the enemies of this the last best hope of earth by stratagems and at a distance. And mesmerized by your own expertise and the atheistic philosophical idiocy that has denied you access to Christ's forgiveness for the sins you've committed while battling the monarch of this fallen world in his various guises as different sorts of foreigners, you have allowed what you once might have called your conscience to turn to stone, metaphorically speaking. Which means you are now fully capable of putting a bullet in a man's heart directly so that you can watch the life bleed out of his eyes and know for certain what you have allowed yourself to become."*

*I nodded slowly. "I'm ready to do whatever you need, Chief."*

*"I know you are, you poor, sad bastard. And may the God you don't have the sense to believe in have mercy on what remains of your soul."*

*The target was an assassin code-named Snowstep. The name was a reference to something lawyers say when they're explaining circumstan-tial evidence to a jury. If you go to bed and it's snowing, they say, and you wake up and there's snow on the ground and there are footprints in the snow, that's good circumstantial evidence that someone has walked there. You don't need to see the person for yourself. The circumstantial evidence is clear. You know.*

*Several dissident expatriates crusading against a ruthless foreign autocrat had died under not-very-mysterious circumstances. Obviously, I'm pixelating the details here, Margaret. They don't really add anything, and it's safer for you not to know. But here's the gist. A journalist hiding out on a Mediterranean island off the coast of Italy had ingested a kind of hemlock with his Pinot and was found dead in his easy chair, grinning horribly. The leader of an opposition party in exile in Switzerland had driven her car off the Chluse Gorge Road into the Kander valley. And an oligarch with a grudge had woken up dead one morning, having* developed a sudden case of bullet-in-the-center-of-the-forehead despite a full security detail.

These killings were the footsteps in the snow from which our man got his name. They were warnings from his employer, the evil autocrat, meant to be recognizable as murders. And while the forensics pointed to a single operator, nothing else was known about the killer except that he was probably male and right-handed.

I flew to London. There was a documentary filmmaker there whom we suspected was Snowstep's next intended victim. About five years earlier, there had been a terrorist bombing campaign in our autocrat's home country. The autocrat had used the campaign as an excuse to round up a certain minority group and sling them into concentration camps. The filmmaker was in the process of compiling video footage suggesting that the terrorists had in fact been acting at the orders of the autocrat himself. British intelligence had heard enough convincing chatter to have the filmmaker placed under heavy guard.

To lay it out briefly, I arrived in town under cover as an emissary from a Hollywood studio. I made it known that I was willing to fund the filmmaker in his work and give the finished documentary the sort of publicity and distribution that would bring him the audience he wanted. We set up a meeting. I then leaked details of the meeting to agents who would certainly bring the information back to the autocrat.

What was, if I may say so myself, particularly clever about the whole enterprise was that, the way the meeting was set up, there was one and only one perfect place and time for Snowstep to make his move. We had a female agent rent the location, a small unrenovated flat in the warehouse district. From there, the assassin would have not only a perfect sniper shot at his target, but also an excellent escape route. He'd be able to pull the trigger and vanish through the tangled, cobbled streets before his victim's body hit the floor. Our female agent then went on vacation, leaving the flat empty and ready for Snowstep's use.

*It was—again in all modesty—a work of art. The fine art of murder, as de Quincey might have said. The setup was tempting but not so tempting as to make Snowstep suspicious. Difficult but not so difficult that he wouldn't give it a try. It was just the sort of thing in which the Division specialized, exactly what we'd trained for. But with one difference. Because Snowstep was a complete unknown, there was no way to arrange for anyone else to finish him off. So, having deftly set the invisible trap, my one remaining job was simply to wait in the flat until Snowstep made his appearance and then shoot him in the heart. After that, a cleanup team would eliminate every trace the thing had ever happened.*

*As the time drew nigh, my team kept the flat under video surveillance. A day before my meeting with the filmmaker was scheduled to take place, our preparations paid off. We saw a man enter the flat. He did a search of the rooms. Examined the eyeline from the windows. We would have moved in then and there, but we couldn't be sure it was Snowstep himself and not one of his agents. We decided to wait until he turned up on the day with his rifle in hand.*

*After he left, I took up my station in the flat, fully equipped with a couple of sandwiches, some iced coffee, and a Glock 19 modified to hold a suppressor.*

*How did I feel as I waited? Calm, actually. Calm enough, at least. If you're wondering, there was no moral struggle going on inside me. The Recruiter had been right. I was past all that. And yes, it was because of Roy. It was because I had set up my best friend, the only true friend I'd ever had. When you do something like that, something that morally catastrophic, there are really only two ways to deal with it. You can acknowledge the horror of it—the guilt—the mortal sin as the Recruiter would've said. You can roast yourself over the fire of your shame, or ask God for forgiveness if you like, if faith is in your intellectual repertoire—which, for me, it wasn't. Or you can take the other path.*

*You can tell yourself there is no shame, no sin, no guilt. It was just a job that needed to be done so you did it. Then, to keep that feeling as real as possible, you have to double down on your commitment and intensity. You have to try your best to justify the work through the ferocity of your enthusiasm. You have to celebrate the unconscionable, if you see what I mean.*

*That's the path I took, that second one. So when I say I was calm, I was more than calm. More than just ready to kill a man in cold blood. I was eager to do it. Eager to prove to myself how eager I was.*

*The Recruiter had me figured out down to the ground, didn't he? Well, he was like that. A great psychologist. Like your own dear self, Margaret.*

*Anyway . . .*

*The hour came. Late afternoon—which is dusk in London at that time of year. I sat in an easy chair I had pulled into one windowless corner. I watched the door. The flat grew dark around me. The shadows folded over me and hid me. I heard the killer coming slowly up the stairs. I took hold of my pistol.*

*Snowstep had picked the lock the first time he visited, but he'd made a key now. He came in easily, as if he lived there. He was a small, unprepossessing man. Squat, chubby. And yes, he was the same man who had cased the place a few days earlier. He was carrying his rifle in a discreet gray bag, the strap over the shoulder of his cheap, black woolen overcoat. When he shut the door and turned toward me, I saw he had a red tartan scarf around his neck and an old-fashioned fedora pulled low on his brow. His face was flabby, weak, and acne-scarred. He sported a lush brown chevron mustache, which I think was meant to distract the eye from his weak chin.*

*He took two steps into the room and spotted me. I saw him sigh with resignation. He slid the strap off his shoulder and set the rifle bag on the floor. He moved to take off the overcoat, but when he saw my gun arm tense, he hesitated. He held his hands out to show they were empty. Then he slowly brought them in to himself, pinching the lapels of his overcoat delicately so I could see he wasn't going to draw a hidden pistol.*

*He draped the overcoat over his gun bag. He was wearing black jeans and a black turtleneck underneath. His round belly bulged through the cloth. He gestured to the small sofa, and I answered with a gesture of my gun. He went over and sank onto the cushions, his shoulders slumped.*

*"I had an inkling," he said. He had a faint accent. Austrian, I thought. "Just a small one, but clearly I should have paid attention to it."*

*"You should have," I agreed.*

*His bushy eyebrows rose. "American." He smiled sadly. Shook his head. "There was a time I would have been more surprised. Back when I started out, your people were still a bit hypnotized by the idea of your own virtue. But we all must play the Great Game eventually, eh? The world is the world, after all."*

*I didn't answer. I was a bit puzzled. I didn't know why I hadn't shot him yet. It wasn't conscience. It wasn't fear. I was thinking about pumping him for information first, but it wasn't that either. I couldn't tell what it was.*

*"I don't suppose . . ." Snowstep began quietly.*

*My finger had been tightening on the trigger, but I held off now in order to hear the rest of the sentence. At least that's what I told myself.*

*"I don't suppose I could offer you a trade of some kind. Information in exchange for my life. It's very good information, I promise you that. You'll want to hear it."*

*"You can try me," I told him.*

*"And—forgive me asking—what guarantee do I have that you won't kill me in any case?"*

*"None—not that I can think of," I said.*

*"You could put the gun away. That would be reassuring."*

*"There's no chance of that."*

*He nodded thoughtfully. "You can't blame a fellow for trying, eh?"*

*"If you have something to say, you better say it."* I wanted to sound hard, you know. Certain. Seasoned. Because I had hesitated so long now, I'd begun to doubt myself.

*"There is a spy, a Chinese spy, planted at one of your universities,"* Snowstep said. *"Well, in fact, there are many spies like that, as I'm sure you know, but this one has got himself involved in the development of a technology that is essential to your nation's future defenses. If he were to pass on what he knows to his masters, your latest weaponry would be compromised even before it's installed—doubly compromised in that your people won't even realize the Chinese are out ahead of you."*

For the next—I don't know—two minutes or so, he told me what he knew. The name of the university. The department. The project. The team. The only thing he didn't have was the name of the spy. Still, he was right: it was good information, important if it was true. It raised all kinds of possibilities for out-maneuvering the opposition, even for sabotage.

He finished his explanation. Then, without any pause, he suddenly said, *"You are very young, aren't you? Inexperienced, if I may say so. Myself, I would have pulled the trigger right away. I suspect you have never done this before, am I correct?"* He smoothed his mustache down with the thumb and finger of one hand. I watched the other hand, but he kept it in plain sight, lying motionless on his thigh.

The shadows darkened around us.

*"I should tell you,"* he said. *"It's not a small thing, this thing they have sent you to do. However well they have trained you, whatever else you've done before, this—"* He nodded toward the pistol in my hand. *"This is different, as I well know. It's decisive. There is no going back from it. Once you have done this, it is who you are, who you always will be until the end. Indeed, I myself was just as you are once. And here I am, as you see."*

What was so disturbing was that I knew he was right. More than that. I knew it was precisely this, the knowledge of this, that had made *me hesitate all this time. He had explained what I had not until then understood. I was standing at the edge of a moral precipice. Once I stepped off, there'd be no going back.*

*The truth of this paralyzed me. I felt frozen now. I wanted him to say more, to tell me more. I wanted him to describe my future for me, or at least as much of it as he could deduce from his own past.*

*"I did not think I would miss my soul so much," said Snowstep. "But I do, you know. You should understand that. You do miss it when it's gone. As I say, it is no small thing what they have sent you to do."*

*The thought was awful to me, as he must have known it would be. His words revealed to me the chasm at my feet. I could feel my will weakening by the second.*

*So, I pulled the trigger and shot him dead.*

# 1

For a long moment after Cameron Winter stopped speaking, Margaret Whitaker said nothing. It was not just his words she found shocking. *I pulled the trigger and shot him dead.* It was not just that. It was the disparity between the words and the man who spoke them.

Margaret was sixty-seven. She had been a therapist for nearly four decades. She had grown accustomed to her clients being wholly different in their secret selves than they appeared on the surface. She had treated many a solid, successful, high-functioning citizen who was an utter mess inside, a complete disaster zone. But Winter was something else again. He was a conundrum. A vexing mystery. No matter how much he told her of his former life, his spy life, his assassin life, she could not quite put it together with the man she saw sitting in the chair in front of her.

He was a middle-sized man, well-made, narrow-waisted, broad-shouldered. He had a handsome, ethereal face framed with long, wavy golden hair. With his wire-framed spectacles and his tweed jacket, he looked exactly like what he was: an English professor at the local university. Thoughtful, scholarly. Yet from their very first session, she had sensed the violence in him. She had spotted the knuckles misshapen by martial arts training, the tense Asiatic control of his movements, the sad and ever-watchful eyes.

Now—now that she knew as much about him as she did—he seemed to her almost like a double image, as if he wore his present superimposed upon his past. And the complexity of that was made all the more complex by this: despite the fact that he was thirty years younger than she was, she had fallen wistfully and hopelessly in love with him over the short course of their treatment.

He had been a neglected child—a poor little rich boy—and she knew he had adopted her as a kind of mother figure. She did her best to play that role, to nurture him and mentor and advise him. But the girlish wistfulness remained there inside her. As a result, she felt that she had become a double image too. And with the both of them always wavering—between past and present, between obligation and desire—whenever she was with him, everything seemed to her somehow undefined and out of focus.

Now, added to that, there was this brutally casual revelation of his. *I pulled the trigger* . . . As if he had said: *I went out for a walk.* She knew he needed to confess these things to her. He needed Mother Margaret to understand them and forgive him. That was the core of their enterprise together. In his midthirties, with forty in view, he was crushingly lonely. Crippled by guilt and a sense of unworthiness, he had idealized Charlotte, his lost first love, until her pretty specter had become a barrier to any real and present romance. He was left with nothing but brief flings and missed connections. He needed Margaret to absolve him of his killer past so he could begin to feel worthy of love—so he could find love, and live.

But could she? Could she forgive him? *Should* she forgive him? Did she even have the right?

"What was it like?" she managed to ask him. She was stalling for time as she tried to strategize a response that would be both ethical and effective.

"Like?" Winter said. He looked away from her, back into the past. He sniffed. "He sat up very straight on the sofa when the bullet hit him. He looked surprised for a moment, then not surprised at all. Almost amused, I would say. Then the life went out of his eyes. I'd never seen that before. Not close up like that. He was there and then a sort of shadow passed over his face and he wasn't there, like a magic trick. Presto. He was gone. I'm not a religious man, as you know, though I keep my mind open. But it was a very definite change of spiritual condition. There and then not there."

Margaret waited. She thought he was going to say more. When he didn't, she made an amused little noise.

He smiled, confused. "What?" he said. "What's so funny?"

"I once had a client who told me he had accidentally hit someone with his car. He was driving out of a public garage and the man walked in front of him. He hit him and the man rolled over the top of his car and landed on the pavement behind him. I said to my client: 'What was that like for you?' And he said, 'It was like *bump*, and then *bumpety-bump-bump*.'"

Winter gave a soft laugh. "Oh. I see. You were looking for more—feeling tone."

"Well, after all . . ." she said.

They sat in a companionable silence for a few moments. Margaret found herself very aware of the vibrant colors outside her office window: the bright orange of the elm trees lining the lively street that led to the majestic white dome of the state capitol, all the colorful autumn jackets of the students and government workers making their way in and out of the brightly lit taverns and shops. She felt the contrast of that scene with this so-brown room of hers, the rug and walls and even pictures all brown and tan. Winter's chair, the client chair, and her therapist chair, also brown. It was meant to leave her clients free to bring their own color to the neutral setting.

But with Winter, it was always as if the whole gaudy world blew in with him on a wind of feeling. There was always color and passion swirling around them when he was here. These wild, violent stories he told her. The anguish of his guilt. And his love for her, their love for one another. Because there was a lot of love going in both directions, though not the love either of them was after. And that—the out-of-sync frustration of that—that had its bright color too.

"Do you ever see your parents?" she asked him suddenly. She had been looking for another way to approach the moment, and this is what had come into her mind.

"That's an odd question," he said. "Given what we're talking about, I mean."

She merely gestured.

"Not my father, no," Winter said. "He spends most of his time in Italy now with his new wife. My mother's still back east. She and I talk on the phone sometimes. I see her maybe once or twice a year. It's the same as when I was a child. She always looks surprised to see me, as if no one has explained to her that she has a son."

"Have you forgiven her for that, for being that way? And your father for the way he was? Have you forgiven him?"

He shrugged. "I don't know. I think I have. I think I look down on my father somewhat for doing the whole younger-woman thing. I'm a bit of an old-fashioned moralist about it. I think a man ought to do what he says he'll do. Stay if he promised to stay. That's what marriage is, after all: a promise. But for the rest—the way they were with me—I'm not sure I ever blamed them really. I find it sad, that's all. It's part of this oppressive loneliness, that they were never emotionally there for me. But I don't think I'm a particularly angry person overall. Do you think so?"

"No, I don't think you are."

"So, I imagine I have forgiven them in some sense, yes. If that's what you call it. Yes."

Margaret glanced at the clock on her desk. She let out a silent sigh. She didn't want to end the session. She liked him as well as loved him, and she knew he liked her. It made her sad when he went away.

"We're about out of time," she told him. "How are you feeling now?"

"Strange," Winter answered at once. "I'm not sure how I feel actually."

"Well," she said. "I think it's real progress. I think it's a very positive thing that you trusted me enough to tell me this: the worst thing you ever did."

Only her years of experience and training kept her from revealing her astonishment and embarrassment when he burst out laughing at her.

"What?" he said. "Killing Snowstep? The worst thing I ever did? Oh God, Margaret. If ever a man needed killing, it was him. He was a monster! You thought that was it? No! No, it wasn't that at all. That's just the beginning of the story. I'm only getting started."

# 2

That afternoon, just before he found out about the murders, Winter had what, in his life, passed for a mystical experience.

He was not really the mystical type. The opposite, if anything. He could be dreamy sometimes. Lost in his own thoughts of the past and its poetry: the absent-minded professor. But he was a hard character for all that, down-to-earth and practical. It was these sessions with Margaret that stirred up this other, airier side of him.

And he was stirred, all right. He had never told any other civilian about Snowstep. Never shared his true emotions about that or about the mission that followed. Plus, he loved Margaret. She was the mother he had never had. He desperately wanted her good opinion. More than that. He desperately wanted her forgiveness for what he'd done. And what if she should deny him that? What if she should hear these terrible things and condemn him and turn him away?

He left her office that morning in something of a daze. He delivered that afternoon's lecture in a daze. It was all about the fraught relationship of Percy Shelley and Lord Byron, and he delivered it almost by rote, thinking nothing, feeling nothing.

When the class was over, he drifted across campus to the Independent, the quaint little coffee shop where he was an afternoon regular. He sat at a small table against one wall and munched on one of their excellent croissants. He read the news of the day on his laptop but he didn't pay much attention to what he was reading. He did not care about politics anymore, not unless it was the politics of Europe in the eighteenth and early nineteenth centuries, the era of his literary specialty. He was distracted by a thousand other thoughts. Margaret, his past, Charlotte, Molly Byrne.

After a while, he looked up with a vaguely troubled sigh—and he noticed a young woman sitting across the room.

She was a student most likely. She was reading from a tablet set on her table. Just as he glanced at her, she straightened in her seat and flipped her lush black hair back from her face, brushing it out of her eyes with one hand. The feminine gesture bewitched him—both the gesture and the beauty of her strong, intelligent features. For a moment, he lost track of himself and was wholly immersed in the sight of her.

When the moment was over, he began to return his eyes to his monitor. Ruefully, he shook his head. He wished he could see everything the way he saw women—and, yes, pretty women especially. He wished he could see trees and sunsets and wispy clouds and litter blowing down the street with the same complete, rapt focus of concentration that women could produce in him simply by being themselves.

And then, suddenly, for a moment, he did. This was the mystical part, mystical, at least, by his not-very-mystical standards. Suddenly he saw everything in the room as if it were a woman, with the same kind of intensity. The paisley mural on the coffee shop wall and the colorful trees outside the big windows and the patterns made by the tables where the people sat and the people themselves all became vividly present to him, just as the reading student had been when she flipped back her raven hair.

It was the people who struck him most powerfully. The students at their work. The professors reviewing material. The strangers from who knows where doing who knows what. All at once, he saw them utterly. He seemed to see their souls in their faces. Their thoughts, their money worries, their love hunger, the fantasy lands through which they wandered impossibly. All their inner monologues seemed to fill the air around his head with anxious murmuring. How thoroughly alive they looked! How weirdly beautiful!

Literary type that he was, he remembered the words of Coleridge: *A spring of love gushed from my heart and I blessed them unaware.* It was true. When you saw people like this, this completely, you almost could love them, couldn't you?

The whole experience lasted for about a second, maybe less. A second later, the coffee shop and its customers were all a blur to him again. He returned to his own thoughts, his own interior monologues and anxieties. His returned his attention to his laptop screen.

And he saw the headline: *Firefighters Discover Murder House.*

The story was datelined from the wealthy suburb of Maidenvale, near Chicago.

*Maidenvale firefighters battling a dawn house fire in the gated community of Tulipwood Court yesterday discovered the bodies of four people whom police say were murdered by rifle blasts before the blaze was set.*

For some reason Winter could not have named, the story's lede immediately piqued his interest. But before he could read more, he was startled out of himself by the familiar and also irritating voice of Lori Lesser.

"We need to talk."

He looked up to find she had plunked herself down in the wooden chair across the table from his. She was leaning toward him fiercely as if she expected him to give her all his attention right away. Which was, he realized, exactly what she did expect.

Lori was the dean of student relations. Her job, as Winter saw it, was to fill the hearts of students with a sense of unending dread at the idea they might have somehow violated the university's Byzantine code of conduct—which, students being students and the code being the code, they almost surely had. Winter's relations with Lori were complicated, to put it mildly. She had repeatedly tried to get him fired for his old-fashioned cultural attitudes. She had repeatedly tried to get him into her bed for other reasons he couldn't parse. He had heard she was now on an obsessive quest to end his career. She had complained to her colleagues that the university's dean, Howard Copely, was protecting him. Why? she kept asking anyone who would listen. Winter was only an associate professor. He had no tenure. He had once upon a time had an affair with a student, which had since become a firing offense. Yet Copely had all but ordered her to leave him be. Why? Why?

If all that wasn't complicated enough, there was also the disturbing fact that Winter found the woman oddly attractive. Partly this was due to the cuddly figure under her rumpled thrift-shop wardrobe. But there was also something appealing about her wild reddish hair, the fanatical expression on her otherwise pert little features. Even her ferocious desire to destroy him somehow tickled his fancy. He couldn't explain it to himself. *Out of the crooked timber of humanity, no straight thing was ever made.*

"I'm serious, Cam," she said. "We need to have a conversation."

"Do we?" He was annoyed at being interrupted. In a minor act of rebellion, he let his eyes drift back to his laptop screen.

*The bodies of Norman Wasserman, 48, a local psychologist, his wife, Marion Belle-Wasserman, 47, their 16-year-old daughter, Lila, and their 25-year-old live-in nanny, Agnes Wilde, were all pulled from the 8-bedroom luxury home even as firefighters struggled to contain what investigators say was an arson fire set at various locations within the house.*

"You and I are friends, Cam," Lori went on absurdly. "And I don't want to go behind your back, so you need to know that I have serious concerns about your employment at this university."

Winter heard her voice as if from far away. In that strange area of his brain that seemed to light up when confronted with certain unsolved crimes, the story on his laptop was being received like a dose of an addictive drug. He could not quite bring himself to tear his attention from the monitor.

*After a preliminary examination of the bodies, police say the cause of death in each case seems to have been a single gunshot wound, likely from a rifle. The county medical examiner has not yet released his findings.*

*Firefighters found the Wasserman's 7-year-old son, Robert, alive and unharmed outside the house . . .*

*Alive!* thought Winter. His heart beat faster.

"It's not just about the sexual transgressions with students," Lori went on. "Although, really, in this day and age that ought to be enough. But Cameron, I'm sorry to say this, your resume does not hold up to scrutiny."

"What do you mean students?" said Winter, finally forcing himself to engage with her. "I had a relationship with one student before the code of conduct was rewritten. We ended as friends. She's happily married now."

Lori rolled her eyes as if this were an idiot irrelevance.

"And what do you mean my resume doesn't hold up to scrutiny?" He muttered this. He was distracted. He was thinking: *How did the boy get out? How did he survive?* He glanced down at his laptop, looking for an answer.

*Police say Miss Wilde, the boy's nanny, had lowered him to safety from his bedroom window on the mansion's third floor, allowing him to escape the carnage taking place downstairs.*

Really? Winter thought. Why hadn't the nanny gone with him then? Was it too far to jump? No. Not with a rifle-wielding madman slaughtering the family one by one on the floors below. Who wouldn't risk the jump?

"Why are there no records of your military service?" Lori demanded.

Winter was normally a man of even temperament, but he was growing irritated with her. What he called his "strange habit of mind," his meditative immersion into certain criminal events, was relentlessly tugging him into the world of these Maidenvale killings. In his imagination, he was already there. In the mansion. With the firemen. Amidst the flames. He could make out the bodies, ghostly through the smoke . . . To aid his imagination, there were photos of the dead on the news site. Dr. Wasserman, a serious, narrow-faced man, graying, bespectacled—arrogant, Winter thought. Mrs. Wasserman, a reluctantly fading beauty of the more elegant sort. Their daughter, Lila, smiling and pretty with youth, but sad around the eyes. And the nanny, Agnes Wilde, with a plain face circular as a pie plate, tumbling corkscrew curls, and a kindly smile that made her lovely.

Winter wanted to study these faces—but what was Lori yammering on about now? She was trying to get his military records? What the hell? Not only had the Division in which he had served his country as an assassin ceased to exist, but it had never existed officially to begin with. Nosing around about it was definitely not a good idea. It could even be unsafe, if some fathead politico decided his career depended on keeping the business secret.

And another thought occurred to him. He forced himself to emerge from his own imaginings about Maidenvale. He said to Lori: "What did you do exactly? Did you file a Freedom of Information Act request about me?"

Her cheeks flushed. Winter's lips parted at the sight of it. She had! She had actually filed a FOIA request about him.

Even she seemed embarrassed by this. It exposed the depth of her obsession with him. Scarlet-faced, she dropped back in her chair. "I told you," she said sullenly. "I mean to get to the bottom of what's going on at this university. Something doesn't make sense here. I mean, I don't even really know who you are, Cam."

Winter pinched the bridge of his nose and shut his eyes. Despite his attraction to Lori, he had refused her advances so often he felt like a virgin in an eighteenth-century novel. Somehow, he just couldn't bring himself to like her much. Like most university administrators, she was, he felt, a useless irritant. But all the same, he didn't want to see her ruin her life. Never mind the danger of her angering some self-important government nabob, she could easily find herself on the wrong side of Dean Copely. Winter knew things about Copely that Copely did not want known. He would never have blackmailed the man, of course, but Copely didn't know that. If Lori tried too hard to get Winter fired, Copely would likely fire Lori instead. Any way this worked out, it was going to be a mess if she didn't knock it off.

He drew a deep breath to restore his patience. Then he looked at her wearily. "Lori," he said. "This is ridiculous. I'm an English professor. I teach Romantic poetry. What's my military service got to do with anything?"

Lori's response was startlingly vicious. She pressed toward him across the table again. Her mouth twisted. Her face grew even redder. Her eyes blazed with wrath and her voice became a harsh and furious whisper. "It's not just that! It's everything about you!"

She went on, but by the second sentence he had stopped listening. He didn't really care what bee was in her bonnet, and the draw of the article on his laptop was just too powerful for him to resist.

*Police are currently seeking to interview Mateo Hernandez, 17, as a person of interest in the killings. Hernandez and Lila were both students at Briars, an exclusive private high school in Maidenvale, and Hernandez is believed to have been Lila's boyfriend. Police say 7-year-old Robert heard Hernandez's voice before escaping the house. Hernandez has reportedly been missing since the murders.*

By now, through that strange habit of his, Winter could see the scene as if he were there—and it wasn't making sense to him. It didn't fit together, not the way the news site told it. It was like a jigsaw with some of the pieces forced into the wrong places. If the killer had come in on the ground floor, if the nanny had dropped the little boy out the third-floor window when she heard the rifle shots, could the boy have heard the voice of the killer? Oh, he supposed he could find a way to explain it to himself. But in his heart, he knew it hadn't happened that way. The child was lying, or someone was. What did that mean? The family of a seven-year-old boy had been wiped out. Only the boy himself survived. And the boy was lying to put the blame on his sister's boyfriend? What could that mean?

Winter glanced up blankly at Lori's angry yet strangely attractive face. Her mouth was still moving, but not one of her words came through to him. He was that far gone. He was in the house. He was in the fire.

He was already wandering among the dead.

# 3

Winter never consciously decided to drive to Maidenvale. Yet, over the next few days, almost without planning it, he found himself watching the funerals of the murder victims.

There was video, of course. There was always video of everything nowadays. Most of it was news footage from local TV stations. In one report, solemn men and women filed into a Chicago synagogue. They had distant gazes and lips pressed thin as they passed beneath the carved, arched entryways.

A middle-aged man identified as Norman Wasserman's brother Isaac stopped to give an interview.

"Norman and Marion were two people who cared deeply about their community and their family," he said. "I keep asking myself: what sort of—animal . . . ?" Winter heard the pause between *sort of* and *animal*. He wondered what adjective the brother had left unspoken. Racial? Obscene? On the screen, Isaac Wasserman shook his head. "The America I grew up in is gone. I don't know this country anymore."

In Maidenvale itself, there had been a large gathering in the park one evening. This was for the girl, the daughter, Lila. The students from her private school, Briars, crowded together on the grass.

They held candles and brushed streaming tears from their cheeks with open hands. Girls hugged one another and sobbed. The boys hung their heads solemnly. The video was shaky, as if it had been taken by one of the kids with a phone. It showed the dean of the school in the distance. She was a reed of a silver-haired woman, introduced as Harriet Grimes. She spoke to the students through a microphone.

"It's moments like this when we remember how fragile everything is. How hard it is to build a life, a community, a country, a world, how easy it is to pull a trigger and destroy those creations."

Finally—this was phone footage again—there was a church service of some kind for the nanny, Agnes Wilde. Watching this last, Winter noticed that the pews were filled with as many Latinos as whites. Given the surname of the chief suspect, Hernandez, this struck him as interesting.

The people in the church sang a hymn together. Then a young bespectacled priest with sandy hair spoke from the pulpit: "You all knew Agnes. You knew her story. How far she had traveled to become who she was. There was no fear in her, no anger, no hate. Therefore, we can't truly remember her through fear or anger or hate. We can only honor her memory with our love—for her and for one another."

That Saturday, at dawn or thereabouts, without making any decision at all, Winter seemed simply to find himself cruising toward Chicago in his Jeep SUV, heading toward the place of the mass murder through a landscape of almost uncanny beauty.

The lake water glittered in the first light. The pastels of the forest by the shore were so lush and glorious they baffled his heart with yearning. When the blue and sparkling water caught the colors of the leaves and rippled them and smeared them over its own surface, even his wordy mind went mute. *No tongue their beauty might declare.*

That was his beloved Coleridge again. Which reminded him of that mystic moment in the coffee shop when he saw and heard the souls all around him. For the first time, it occurred to him to wonder: What the hell was going on in his mind? Why was he doing this? What was it about these murders that was drawing him on?

He arrived at the gates of Tulipwood Court just as the dashboard clock blinked to nine A.M. He had told the community's chief of security he would be coming. The wrought iron gates swung open as his Jeep approached.

The chief of security was named Stephanie Breach. She was a short, square-built, broad-shouldered woman, forty or so. Her face was squinty and hard-bitten but not necessarily hostile, Winter thought. In fact, she'd been surprisingly friendly and welcoming when he'd phoned her the day before. She sounded almost eager to have him come.

As he nudged the Jeep through the open gates, she emerged from the glass security booth to greet him. Wearing a gray guard's uniform and a cop-style peaked hat, she approached his window with a mannish swagger, thumbs hooked in her belt.

He lowered the window. She leaned in. She squint-eyed the backseat the way a cop would, just to see what was what.

"You Winter?"

"I am."

"I'll get in. You can drive us up to the Wasserman place."

"Sounds good."

She swaggered around the car and got in beside him. Gave his hand a firm shake. "Steph Breach."

"Cameron," he said. "Cam."

He put the car in motion up a slow hill. Steph Breach made brusque conversation, punctuated by directions. "So, you're a college professor? Go left here."

"I am. I teach English literature."

"And this is some kind of—what? A story you're writing?"

"Part of an essay on murder. I wanted to get in on one from the beginning." He glanced at her as he spoke the lie. He wanted to read her expression. He could not tell for sure whether she believed him or not, but he sensed she didn't.

"Right here," she said.

Winter guided the car around a long, graceful curve. He surveyed the scenery through the windows and the windshield. It was an impressive development. The homes were magnificent: elaborate and sprawling. Gray and brown palaces faced with stone. Majestic patterns of hip roofs and gables, bay windows and turrets, each ruling over at least an acre of grassy land. Oaks, elms, and maples in their fall colors everywhere.

Oddly empty though, Winter thought. No cars on the street. No lights on in the windows. Oddly spectral, the whole place.

"Nice real estate," he said.

"Oh yeah," said Breach. "You don't live in Tulipwood without you have plenty of the green stuff."

"The residents can't be happy to have had this happen here."

"The murders? Yeah, you can say that again."

Winter didn't. Instead he asked: "Where is everyone?"

Steph Breach looked out her window as if she'd just noticed the community was deserted. "A lot of these folks, you know, these are second homes for them. They spend the spring and summer here, and when winter starts to come on, they head for warmer climes. Like the birds. Most of my job is making sure the burglars don't start sniffing around the empty houses, that's . . . Left here, go up that hill."

She hadn't finished the sentence she'd started, so Winter finished it for her. "That's why you weren't watching the Wasserman's house. They were home. There was nothing to worry about."

Breach gave a harsh sniff. A twitch of a sneer in which Winter read pain and regret. But she didn't answer him. "Turn right up ahead," she said.

Winter guided his Jeep around the next bend, and there the house was.

The extent of the ruin wasn't clear to him right away. When the mansion first appeared in the windshield, it still seemed to him stately and dignified. Brown brick with two chimneys. A hip roof with three dormers. An imperial white-columned porch before the main entrance. It took another moment, another few yards of approach, before he saw the damage. The yellow police tape, the windows broken, the front door boarded up. There were holes sawn through the roof here and there. Winter supposed the firemen must have done that for ventilation. Streaky patterns of char worked up the facade, black under the eaves. Yes, he saw it all now: it was a corpse of a place. Its life was gone, and so was its dignity. So much death shamed a house, he thought.

Speaking as if reading his thoughts, Steph Breach said, "They'll never be able to sell this place again. Might as well tear it down right now. Put a fork in her, she's done. Pull up at the curb here. We'll walk up."

As they stepped from the SUV, the walkie-talkie on her belt fritzed. She unhooked it and brought it to her mouth. "We're at the house," she said. Then she told Winter: "My guys'll let us know if the police come in. We'll have to clear out if they do. I'm not expecting them. I doubt they'll get off their butts this early on a Saturday."

Winter was surprised by this. He hadn't realized they were acting in secret.

They walked side by side up the curving slope of the driveway. The house loomed over them, very dead, very dead. Their shoulders touched and Winter glanced at her. Her face was set forward. Set hard. He couldn't help but register her aggressively masculine presentation. In fact, now that he knew they were avoiding the police, he began to register all kinds of silent messages beaming from her. All these things he stored in his heart, making his deductions.

She stepped off the drive onto a slate path that led through the grass. It took them away from the front entrance where the door had been. There was just a slab of plywood there now, crisscrossed with yellow police tape. There was police tape on most of the windows too. But Steph Breach brought him to a narrow basement window on the side of the house, a long pane set down low, close to where the wall met the earth.

"We gotta climb through here," she said.

She bent over and pushed the window open with one hand. Then—supple suddenly, like a woman is supple—she slid under the frame and was gone. Winter followed with a bit more effort, more huffing and grunting. He dropped a few feet through the interior darkness and felt the jolt of his landing in both ankles.

They were in the basement now. The security chief's big flashlight picked out a washer and dryer. Two baskets of clothes. No fire damage here, Winter noticed as he followed her.

They climbed the stairs and came out into the kitchen.

There were smoke stains on the walls and up on the ceiling, but the sumptuous outline of the room was still intact. A marble island, itself the size of a normal kitchen, occupied the center. The silver surface of the double-doored refrigerator was unstained and looked like palace gates. The enormous gas range with all its decorations and gizmos reminded Winter of the chariot that took Cinderella to the ball.

"That stove—gotta cost more than my house, at least," said Steph Breach with admiration.

She led him through a swinging door, down a hall. He could smell the smoke here, smoke and char and some general sickly odor of ruination. They emerged at the main entrance.

Here the house was ravaged. By flames and smoke, yes, but even more so by the firefighters and their hoses and axes. The once red runner on the sweeping stairs was blasted to a mushy pulp. The furniture in the front living room was scorched and ragged. Lamps and photos and one fine old mantelpiece clock lay like battle casualties amidst the glass and debris on the blackened wooden floor. A lot of these objects were piled up in the corners, pushed there, no doubt, by the blasting streams of water. The scene made Winter think of old photos of mass atrocities, except with dead things instead of people. Here, the dead people had all been removed.

"That's where Mrs. Wasserman was found." Thumbs hooked in her belt again, Steph Breach pointed with her chin to the spot at the base of the stairs. "Name was Marion. Nice woman. Sophisticated, but down-to-earth. Always offered me a cup of coffee whenever I came by. Did a lot of work for the town. Local charities. Community Center for the new people. Supported this little theater we have. I don't go there much but people seem to like it. Took a thirty-ought-six slug right under the sternum. That'll do the job, sure enough."

They climbed gingerly through the mess to the second floor. Down an expansive hall to the master bedroom, a room nearly the size of Winter's apartment.

The smell was intense here, smoky and damp and sickening. There was more than just ruin in it. There was panic, fear, death.

The flames had ravaged the room—the flames and the smoke and the hoses. What had been an enormous four-poster was now a chaos of rags and mahogany. What was left of the frame knelt on only three legs like some sort of dying beast. The walls were scored and blotted with black. The heavy window curtains looked as if giant teeth had torn them. One of the holes in the roof was here. The chilly autumn breeze came down but, fresh as it was, it seemed somehow to add to the stench, that smell of human terror and disaster.

"You can tell this was one of the origin points," said Breach.

"Of the fire, you mean," said Winter. "It was definitely arson then?"

"Oh yeah. It was arson. Gasoline. The killer must have had a can of it. He came prepared."

Winter only nodded at this, but the scenario was playing out in his mind. The rifleman had come not in a sudden rage or with some alternate motive, like robbery. This—this slaughter—this was the plan. Kill the family. Burn the house. He meant to do it from the start. It was a mission. It was personal.

"He took out Dr. Wasserman right there," said Breach. "The cops think he was asleep, then heard the gunshot that killed his wife. He was just getting up to investigate when the shooter caught him through the door. Pretty well blew his head clean off." She sniffed and made another roosterish gesture with her chin. Winter followed the move and saw the remnant of some ghastly stain on the wooden floor. It added a fresh level of realism to his mind-images of the frantic violence.

"Good man—Dr. Wasserman," Steph Breach added. "Psychologist. Very well respected in his field, what I gather. Guess he did well for himself, judging by the house. But he did pro bono work, too, treating the Mexican kids at the Community Center. Really decent individual."

With that, she was off again. Winter followed her back out into the hall, past shattered frames and ravaged canvases, oil paintings now transformed to something like *papier-mâché*. Winter felt his throat getting thick and sore from the fetid atmosphere. His chest felt airy and tremulous as the frenzied mind-movie of the murder night continued to play out in his imagination.

"The daughter died here," Steph Breach said as they came to the end of the landing. She announced it heavily, like a eulogy. "I guess she heard the gunshots, too, and came out of her bedroom. Saw the shooter, tried to turn and run. He got her in the back. Lila was her name. Sixteen, almost seventeen. Hell of a thing, kid that age. Hardly know who you are at that point. Beautiful girl. Beautiful. Lit up a room. Just getting started in life." She looked down at the floor mournfully, as if the body were still lying there.

"I understand her boyfriend is a person of interest to the police," Winter said to her.

"Yeah," said Breach with another of those twitched sneers. "The boyfriend."

They took a brief gander at the girl's bedroom. Hardly any fire damage here at all. Winter guessed the shooter hadn't torched it. Which made sense if it was the boyfriend. He was gentler with her. Still, the water from the hoses had blasted the curtains and decorations off the walls and the knick knacks off the shelves. The windows were bare to the morning, revealing a little balcony over the backyard. Everything else was piled up in corners, little mounds of fluffy white and pink girl stuff, pillows, blankets, stuffed animals, all turned to sludge. Atop one pile there was a small plastic gizmo Winter didn't recognize. It looked to him like a high-tech version of one of those old stereopticons, one of those devices you look into to see 3D pictures. Winter moved closer to the pink and white mound to get a better look at the device.

"Kids," said Steph Breach. "They go through phases."

They traversed the hall again, but this time Breach stopped halfway between the daughter's room and the master.

"Found the nanny here. Face blown off," she said. Then she strode on and disappeared through a small doorway.

Winter followed her onto a winding stair. They climbed up to the third floor to where the little boy, the lone survivor, had his room. The room was wide and long, but it felt cramped from above where the slant of the roof pressed down on it. The dormer window was on the front, looking out at the street where Winter's Jeep was parked. There were two other windows opposite, looking out at the backyard lawn.

The flames hadn't done much damage here, but the smoke had blackened everything. Movie posters and a game console, books on the shelves—all were black. Rivulets of darkness seemed to drip down the walls. The paint on the ceiling was beaded from the heat. Only the cartoon characters on the little bed's quilt were heartbreakingly bright and cheerful.

"No one heard the shots?" he said.

Steph Breach lifted her square shoulders in a heavy shrug. "It was four-thirty in the morning. Five, somewhere around there. My guys, they patrol on a staggered schedule, but in between they go back to the station. A house this far away . . ."

When she merely shrugged again, Winter finished for her. "It wouldn't have woken them. What about security cameras?"

"There are a few at the perimeter, but the residents don't like the feeling of being spied on. Most of them have their own setups. The Wassermans' went down in the fire."

"And the perimeter cameras?"

She shook her head. "Possible whoever it was knew where they were. Not a thing on them."

"Like he'd been here before," murmured Winter. "Like he knew the layout."

He went to one of the rear windows and looked out. The back-yard lawn rolled gently to a ring of yellow aspens, the border between this property and the next. There was a playground set and a gazebo with a fire pit, poignant reminders of a family's life, a life now ended. The window was intact, so he had to press his forehead to the glass to judge the distance to the ground.

"She must have half hung out the window to get him low enough for the drop," he murmured. "Brave stuff." But why hadn't she hung down herself and gone after him? he wondered yet again.

He heard Breach suck her teeth loudly behind him. He turned to her. The two of them stood in the sad room with the roof pressing down on top of them.

"You didn't like her, did you?" he said. He had noticed this downstairs. That brief dismissive *Found the nanny here*—that gave it away. "What was her name again? The nanny?"

Steph Breach shrugged. "Agnes Wilde. I didn't mind her. She was kind of . . ." She rubbed the fingers of one hand together as if she were trying to spark the word she wanted out of the air. "Stiff. Prim. Religious. Never take to those self-righteous types. She was fine though. Took good care of the kid. Bobby. He adored her. She didn't deserve this, that's for sure. None of them did."

"You think the boyfriend did it?"

She bit her cheek, considering. "I do," she said.

"Any particular reason?"

"I've got sources in the police. I'm hearing the gun likely belonged to his father. There's a Winchester 70 featherweight missing from his collection, and some kind of handgun, too."

Winter studied her for a long moment. "So—you know who I am, right? Why I'm here." He had deduced this as they'd walked and talked. She had never believed in his cover story about the report he was supposed to be writing. She had known he was lying from the start. "You researched me, I'm guessing."

She shrugged again. "Chief of Security," she told him. "S'my job. They say you had a hand in solving those disappearances during the riots a while back. And that kidnapping before that. I figured this was something along those lines. What is it, like a hobby with you or something?"

"I'm not sure really. It's this strange thing that happens to me sometimes. I'll read a news story and it will just come into my head somehow. I can see what happened as if I'm there. Sometimes when it doesn't make sense to anyone else, it makes sense to me. I try to help. That's all."

"Mm," she said. Then she sniffed dismissively.

"You don't trust the local police, is that it? Is that why you let me come? Snuck me in here like this? You think they'll mess up or cover up somehow, but maybe I'll manage to get at the truth?"

She gave a short, uncomfortable laugh. "What're you, like, some kind of mind reader or something? That your superpower?"

Winter answered with a charming smile, as charming as he could make it in that miserable blood-ruined place.

Steph Breach tilted her head toward the door. "Let's get the hell out of here."

He knew what she meant. The house was just oppressive, that's all. The murders moved in the atmosphere like ghosts—like those ghosts in stories where an old crime is played out again and again, forever. The mother coming down the stairs. The father waking up, getting out of bed. The daughter in the hallway. The nanny. *Boom. Boom. Boom. Boom.* Winter could feel not just those final horrifying moments, but the violence of all the connections being torn asunder. Husband, wife, daughter, son, sister, brother, nanny. *Boom. Boom.* All the love gone. All the loved ones dead.

"Yeah," he said to Steph Breach. "Let's get the hell out."

37

# 4

Cameron Winter was, in many ways, a man out of his era. This was one of the personal insights he had acquired in his sessions with Margaret Whitaker. His mooning over Charlotte, his childhood love. His brooding over his assassin past. His academic work on the poets of the eighteenth and nineteenth centuries. These were all essentially emanations of a core obsession with *du temps perdu*, lost time. He sometimes felt he moved among the modern world like a phantom, that he watched it like a phantom from another age, an age gone by.

He enjoyed Steph Breach from that detached perspective. He was charmed by her clichéd small-town sheriff machismo and the way it disguised her maternal care for the privileged people under her watch. He could feel how she identified with the rich of Tulipwood Court, how she saw things through their eyes, lived along with them as mothers do with their young. He was touched and amused by the way she strutted like a rooster, yet gathered her people under her wings like a hen.

"Lot of problems in this area," she told him as he drove her back to the security station. She had been silent as the Wasserman house sank away in the rear window, sank back into its solitude under that weird shadow of shame that violent death brings with it. But now, abruptly, she started speaking, and Winter understood she was answering his earlier remarks, the remarks he'd made back in the boy's room, about how she did not trust the local police.

"Feds've been dumping illegals up here for years. Mexicans mostly and some from further south. Bus 'em or fly 'em right up from the border. They break the law, they sneak into the country, next thing you know here they are in Maidenvale. Feds just drop 'em off and we're supposed to deal with it. Changes the whole demographics of the place. And what're we supposed to do, pull jobs for them out of the air? This is a nice town. Nice people here. They've worked hard to get where they are. It's not that they're being mean or anything. It's just too much, too fast. If you see what I'm saying."

Winter did see. And, of course, he remembered again that the Wasserman girl's boyfriend—the suspect—was named Hernandez.

"So this boy," he said. "The one the police are looking for . . ." He didn't finish. He hoped Breach would fill in the blanks. But she turned away from him, looked out her window at the fine mansions. So he went on: "He went to this fancy private school with the girl, right? With Lila."

"Briars," Steph Breach said. Her head bobbed, face still averted. "Yeah. Yeah. He made his move, all right. Out of the Hollow. That's what it's called, the place the newcomers mostly live at: the Hollow. He's a good soccer player apparently. That's very big down there, as we know, down Mexico way. So he gets a scholarship. The school loves that. Gives them virtue points for diversity or whatever, plus he helps the team. Then one day, he sees the girl. Fairy princess. His ticket to the next level. Before you know it, he's coming in and out of Tulipwood like a native. God bless America. Easy as you please."

Winter was listening carefully, trying to assemble her version of events. He felt he couldn't quite do it, not yet.

"Do you think they quarreled?" he asked. "Hernandez and the girl. Or did she break up with him or something? Is that what you're saying? That was his motive?"

Steph Breach faced front. Frustrated, he could see, because he wasn't getting the point. "Maybe," she said. "Hey, look, don't ask me. What do I know? I'm just the security around here. It must've been something like that, though, right?"

"And you don't trust the police to bring him to justice because . . . ?"

He was guiding the Jeep around a corner, focused on the road, but he felt her eyes on him. When he could, he glanced over. He saw that she was studying him as he had studied her.

"Look," she said when their eyes met. "I don't want you to think I'm bigoted or anything like that. I'm not. One person's as good as another to me. But I don't want to throw fairy dust at you either. The truth is truth, know what I'm saying?"

"I do know that, yes."

"Maidenvale used to be a nice town. Safe. Clean. Now? Big drug trade going on beneath the surface. Marijuana. Fentanyl. Cocaine. Meth. You name it. We're a station on the Heartland Highway. That's what they call it. A straight-shot smuggling corridor from the Gulf to Canada."

Finally, the disjointed pieces of her narrative began to come together in Winter's mind. "You think the police here are corrupt. You think the drug money has corrupted them."

"Watch out for Inspector Strange," she said.

"Really. That's his name?"

"Roland Strange, yeah. He's their chief detective. Leads all the homicide investigations. Which isn't much. At least, it didn't used to be. Even now it's mostly Mex on Mex. But ask yourself: Why is Strange always siding with the bad guys over the normal people? Giving them every benefit of the doubt? Like I said, people like the Wassermans, these are good people, legal citizens, earned what they have. Strange has all the right words. Tolerance. Diversity. Whatever you want to call it. But follow the money, Winter. That'll tell you a different story, I guarantee it."

Winter frowned a noncommittal frown. He had, of course, no way of knowing whether Steph Breach spoke from personal animus or racial hostility or simply a clear understanding of the facts. But he had no doubt she was right in this at least: self-interest is most often a better guide to human motivation than any higher ideals.

"I'll keep an eye out for the inspector," he told her. "Inspector Strange."

When he stopped the Jeep at the Tulipwood gate, Steph Breach paused before getting out. "You need anything, you have my number," she said with an air of weighty sincerity. "There are still good people on the force and most of them are friends of mine. I'll do my best to get you whatever you want."

Winter believed her. Thanked her. Looked after her as she climbed out of the SUV. She gave him a sharp salute, index finger flashing to and from her hat brim. Then she hooked her thumbs in her belt again and swaggered into the station. Winter, watching her like a ghost from another age, enjoyed the whole show. He waited till she was out of sight before he put the Jeep in gear and drove on to his hotel.

The journey took him down what the local realtors called "leafy lanes" past what they called "classic homes." Those realtors must be making out like bandits, Winter thought. It would have been a lovely town in any season, but with the leaves turning color, it was glorious. Some of the homes were old—ornate, proud, confident,

Georgian like in British TV shows about lords and ladies, or Italianate like haunted houses in American horror films. But there were plenty of new builds, too, front shovels digging up old foundations and shiny mansions nearly overflowing their lots. The place was growing and thriving. Children in their autumn outfits swung and climbed in pretty playgrounds. Cars crowded the parking lot of the Colonial Revival high school with its domed bell tower above the clock in the pediment: football practice was on, Saturday after the Friday night game. Main Street ran for six blocks, boutiques and taverns interspersed. Stylish moms and prosperous dads went from store to store, pink-cheeked in the cool morning weather.

There was only one hotel close to the center of town. He'd chosen that over the luxury lodges out by the lake because he wanted to be near the heart of the place. It was a brown brick tower, eight stories high, on a road parallel to Main.

As soon as he pulled into the parking lot, he spotted the man waiting for him. A tall, strong-looking character with broad shoulders and a gym-flat belly. The man wore a dark suit and a white shirt open at the collar. It was light wear for such a chilly day, so Winter figured he was a hard case, or at least wanted to look like one.

The man was in his forties but had a full head of hair atop a horse-long face with smooth, regular features. He was leaning loose-limbed against a dark blue Ford, a Crown Victoria, a classic unmarked police car. He had his hands in his pockets, holding his jacket open, so Winter could see the five-point detective shield displayed on his belt. Something about the set of the man's expression, the gleam in his eyes maybe, struck Winter as having an aspect of the sadistic. But who could be sure at a single glance?

He murmured to himself: "Inspector Strange, I presume."

He pulled into a parking space and cut his engine.

Sure enough, the big cop casually looked away into the distance as if he hadn't noticed Winter at all, and at one and the same moment, pushed off the Crown Vic and began sauntering toward him.

Winter had only just gotten out of the car when Strange addressed him.

"Professor Winter. You see what you came to see?"

Winter was wearing black jeans, a white corded sweater, and a khaki windbreaker. To this ensemble, he added a politely inquiring smile as he waited for the inspector to draw near. He saw no reason to be overly free with information.

Strange planted himself a few feet away. He was a good deal taller than Winter, four or five inches at least. He shook his head, grinning. Once again, he looked away into the distance to where little girls chased each other laughing through a public square. The gesture was meant to convey the idea that Winter wasn't worth his full attention. So Winter thought anyway.

"That Stephie Breach, she always thinks she's two steps ahead of me," Strange said. "She doesn't know I had the department install a couple of motion sensitive cams in the Wasserman place. Mostly to keep the kids out, keep the house from being vandalized. I'm Inspector Strange, by the way. I'm guessing Stephie warned you about me."

"I believe she did mention you," Winter said.

Strange laughed easily. "I'll bet she did." He muttered something Winter couldn't quite make out, something about Steph Breach being a racist and also a lesbian. When Strange was done, he looked down on Winter again. "And what is it you do exactly?" he asked.

"I'm an English professor."

"Uh huh. And your interest in the Wassermans is what? If you don't mind my asking."

"I don't mind. It's mostly curiosity. The story I read in the paper didn't quite hang together."

"Ah. Really?" Strange nodded slowly. "That special sense English teachers have about murder. Is that it?"

"I don't know why the police don't consult us more often."

"Yeah. And Steph is hoping you'll come in here and make sure all the right brown people get arrested."

Winter laughed. "Could be. I don't know."

Strange studied his own shoes now. He was full of these little gestures, Winter noticed. He was a whole performance of a man, acting out—what?—the idea that he was dangerous, a threat, the sort of man who might start to turn away as a feint then spin and drive his fist into your gut. Whatever it was, Winter found he didn't particularly like him.

"Professor Winter, I would like to take you for a drive," said Inspector Strange.

Winter shrugged. "All right."

"Come on." With that, Strange pivoted 180 degrees and began strolling back across the lot toward the Crown Vic.

Working from the animosity between Steph Breach and the inspector, Winter deduced Strange would drive him out to the village called the Hollow to make a sociological point. He was exactly right about that. That's where they went. And if the point was that life was grim in the Hollow when compared to glorious Maidenvale, well, the point was made. No British TV lords and ladies here. The Hollow—Harper's Hollow was the village's full name—was a collection of sorrowful trailer parks with weary crate-like structures lined up side to side on dusty lots by potholed roads. Dented pickup after dented pickup was parked bumper to bumper by the curbs outside, where children played tag on macadam and littered dirt. Even drearier were the two-story apartment buildings, one after another, set by what was either a river or an open sewer, it was hard to tell which. There was a stone prison of a school building with a rusty slide outside, and a homeless character drinking from a pint bottle as he watched the passing parade of Hollow life from under a leafless tree. Not too many other people in sight this Saturday. A few heavyset Latino men and women moving slowly outside the local bodega as if carrying a weight. Some more men at the gas station on the corner. And even now, a few fellows gathered in the saloon across the street.

"People like Steph Breach burn my ass, I don't mind telling you," said Inspector Strange. He'd been ominously quiet during the short drive over the winding two-lane out of Maidenvale. Now the words hissed out of him like pent-up steam. "Some of these people here, they went through hell to get to this country. Across the desert. Through the river. Lucky if the traffickers—the coyotes—didn't take their hard-saved money and dump them somewhere, rape their women, kill them, or leave them to die. Then getting past the border men. Trying to make a better life here for their kids, just like my people did when they came over, or your people did, or any other American's. These folks clean the homes in Maidenvale, scrub the toilets and mow the lawns. Then the minute there's something like these Tulipwood killings, everyone points the finger at the Hollow. It's just . . ." He finished the sentence with a disgusted shake of his head. When Winter remained silent, the inspector glanced at him and snorted. "What about you, Professor? You agree with Steph Breach? You don't like the brown folks either?"

By way of a response, Winter asked him: "What do you think? Was it Mateo Hernandez who murdered the Wassermans or not?"

Inspector Strange let out a puff of laughter followed by a curse. "Not likely. Matt's a good kid. Star athlete at Briars, solid student. He loved a girl from Tulipwood. That's his crime. He got above his station. Pretty little girl she was, too, Lila. Wouldn't surprise me if the Breach woman was jealous of Matt on top of everything else."

Strange's tone was ugly, yes. But in fact, the same thought, or something like it, had occurred to Winter after he'd watched Steph Breach standing mournfully at the spot where Lila's body had been found, after he'd heard her speak Lila's name as if it were a eulogy.

"But the boy has disappeared, yes?" he said. "And some of the father's guns are missing?"

The inspector's long face hardened. His pale eyes glistened like burnished steel. "That bitch does have her sources, I'll give her that," he said between gritted teeth. "Yeah, someone stole a rifle and an old .38. Eduardo, Matt's dad, he's a hunter. Total solid citizen. Legal immigrant too. Been here for decades. Patriotic. Proud American. Manages the E-Z storage facility out on 10. He didn't even know the guns were missing until I came over looking for his kid."

"And where is he, do you think? The kid."

"Well, if I had to guess, I'd say he's hiding. Probably scared out of his wits. A thing like this. People like the Wassermans. A community like Tulipwood. It's not supposed to happen here, not to rich white folks anyway. It ties people's guts up in knots, you know. 'It could've been me,' that sort of thing. 'I have a gardener from the Hollow. My maid. My nanny. Any one of 'em could slit my throat while I sleep.' A lot of pressure on the police, I don't mind telling you. 'Bring in the brown boyfriend.' And you know what? If that does turn out to be the scenario—if Matt did it—the Maidenvale people will make all the right noises. 'We don't blame the newcomers,' they'll say. 'Anyone can have a bad apple.' But they'll find ways to tell their daughters: 'Stay safe. Date the right color boys.' They won't even have to tell 'em. Not out loud. The girls'll get the message, sure enough."

All this while, they'd been cruising up and down the sad, gray streets. But there weren't that many of them, and not that much to see there. They'd pretty much finished with the Hollow. Now Strange hit the Crown Vic's gas and they were on the two-lane back toward Maidenvale. Winter gazed thoughtfully out the window at a long stretch of forest, evergreens and orange elms and yellow oak and startling scarlet sassafras.

From the moment he'd first read about these murders, he had not been sure why they bothered him or why they compelled him to come here. He was not sure now. But whatever his motivation, it was still the case that something about the story didn't hang together for him. He was not swayed in this by the inspector's racial sensitivities any more than he had been swayed by Steph Breach and her various grievances. Either the Hernandez boy slaughtered that family or he didn't. That was all. But so far, Winter couldn't tell which was true.

"What about the child?" he asked. "The one who survived?" As he spoke, he turned back to Strange—and he was surprised to see the anger on the inspector's face. It was more than anger, he thought. It was rage. Some inner monologue was taking place in the inspector's mind, a stormy one, black clouds, lightning and thunder. When Strange glanced his way, it was a baleful glance. Winter began to wonder what he had wandered into here.

"What about him?" the inspector said tersely.

"I read in the newspaper that the boy said he heard Mateo's voice during the shootings."

"Ach. Kid's seven. His whole family's been wiped out. He's in shock. He doesn't know what he heard."

Winter had had the same thought about this as well. Still—why should the boy say he had heard what he hadn't?

Winter caught his breath as, suddenly and with no warning, Strange gave the steering wheel a violent wrench to the right. With a squeal of tires, the Crown Vic left the highway and fired down a narrow road nearly hidden by tall grass. At once, they were in the woods. A few more yards and the pavement was gone from beneath them. The Crown Vic bumped over rutted dirt. Trees closed in on either side of them, the sunlight piercing the dying leaves. Winter saw a sign. "The Baptiste Woods. Trails close at sunset," it said. He glimpsed rock formations through the branches, white in the distance.

The car went fast, too fast on such a rutted road. A moment later, Strange wrenched the wheel again and they were in a small parking lot, the place where the forest's walking trails began. There were four cars parked here, but no people in sight. Nothing in sight but a couple of outhouses, a bulletin board with notices, and the trees.

Strange braked. He shoved the gearshift into park. "Get out," he said. And when Winter hesitated in his uncertainty, he added: "Get out of the car."

Winter was in the process of climbing from his seat when he heard the driver's door slam and saw that Inspector Strange was striding around the Crown Vic's front fender. Winter shut his door and stood and Strange stood in front of him, stood close and towered over him. He had now hidden his expression of rage beneath a stony stillness, but his eyes still flashed, still stormy. Winter found it hard to believe he was being physically threatened here. But he told himself he had better start believing it, and quickly.

"Leave," said Inspector Strange. "This is not the place for you, Professor. Leave."

Winter could only make a small gesture of confusion.

"The deadpan," Strange said. "I don't feature the deadpan. I don't like the whole blank face thing you do. It doesn't work for me. You're not better than anyone here. You're not the only honest observer who wants to find the truth. I've got four dead people on my hands and an orphaned child. Prominent people with money and influence want these murders solved yesterday. I got that, and I got a poor Mexican kid, who probably never hurt anyone, hiding out somewhere, scared he'll be lynched if he shows his face, and maybe he will be. I'm a law officer. This is my job. You're an English teacher. Go home. Teach English. It's three miles back to the hotel, an hour's walk. Walk it. Then get in your vehicle, and drive away."

"I don't . . ." Winter began to say.

"Shut up," said Inspector Strange. "I don't care what you think. Shut up, and get out."

Strange turned and took a step away. Winter, amazed, suddenly thought the man was actually going to do it. He was actually going to fake a turnaround, then spin and punch Winter in the gut. Again, Winter could hardly believe the violence was coming, and again, he thought he'd better believe it.

An instant later, sure enough, Strange spun. Winter tensed, drew back, put his hands up, expecting the punch.

But there was nothing like that. Of course there wasn't. People don't just go around punching each other. Instead, Inspector Strange merely grinned, his hands loose by his side. His eyes danced with angry humor as they went up and down Winter, taking in his tension, his defensive stance, his absurd expectation of violence.

Grinning, he said once again, "I mean it, Winter. Leave. Don't think to stay. Get in your car and go."

He turned again and this time walked full away. He sank into the Crown Vic and started the engine roaring.

Winter, shaken by the encounter, stood where he was as the car shot away, kicking up dust around him. The dust caught the sun through the sun-drenched trees and made yellow beams amidst the autumn colors.

Alone now, Winter breathed the chill, clean morning air.

He thought: *What the hell? What the hell was that?*

# 5

Winter had plenty of time to think things over during the three-mile hoof back to his hotel. At first, still shaken by the confrontation with the angry Strange, he walked doggedly through the pleasantly brisk autumn air. The pastel woods rose up on either side of him. The trees dipped and swayed with the wind. The leaves rattled and whispered. For a stretch, he remained alert to his surroundings, less in appreciation of nature's beauty than in watchful anxiety that Strange might circle back and attack him for real this time.

Finally, though, alone with his thoughts, he slipped into meditation. He could not help feeling how odd this situation was, and how odd it was that he should find himself in the middle of it. The grievances of Steph Breach. The anger of Strange. The stench of violence in the house in Tulipwood. What did any of it have to do with him? Why had he come here? What was he searching for—what really?

He returned to his hotel room. He had not come up with any answers. He was brooding on Strange again. That sudden, threatening turnaround. That warning: *Leave. Don't think to stay. Get in your car and go.*

Well, he did get in his car, but he'd be damned if he'd be chased out of town or out of anywhere. Instead, he called Eduardo

Hernandez, father of the prime suspect, Mateo. With his usual vague excuses, he talked his way into a meeting.

He drove back to the Hollow.

The Hernandez home was in the most expensive section of the little village, on Hawthorne, one of the three well-tended streets between the elementary school and the biggest trailer park. The house stood behind a low diamond-link fence on a half acre of sparse grass, pale green. It had two stories, brick facing on the ground floor, the second floor sided with aluminum. There was an oak tree out front, and a tilted, scraggly pine. An American flag hung beside the front door. Winter noted it and remembered how Inspector Strange had described the elder Hernandez: *Patriotic. Proud American.*

Hernandez let him in and led him to the living room, just beyond the entrance. It had a large window looking out at the front. Winter was given a cushioned chair from the dining table. Hernandez settled into a tired-looking green easy chair, Dad's chair. Mrs. Hernandez served Winter coffee and set a plate of cookies down on the low table in front of him. Then she nestled down in between their second son, Tomas, and their daughter, Sara, the three huddling thigh-to-thigh on the small off-white sofa, wooden-faced, watchful. There was a metal crucifix on the wall to their right and a picture of the Virgin Mary looking heavenward, a white aura surrounding her.

"How did Mateo and Lila meet?" Winter asked them.

The love affair had begun with the soccer season, early spring. Mateo was a striking midfielder for Briars. It was his first year there. His first game. He was sixteen.

"He's beautiful on the field," Hernandez told Winter. "It's beautiful to watch him. This is not just a proud father saying so. Ask anyone. They'll all tell you. It was like watching—I don't know—a dance. The way he moved, the way the team moved around him. He created plays out of nothing. It was like he moved, and then the team moved with him, and then the ball was in the net. Goal." He raised both hands as he said the word.

Hernandez was a short but burly man. He wore a checked flannel work shirt, the sleeves rolled up. He had thick arms and a round belly. He had distinguished-looking silver hair and a silver beard. He smiled fondly as he spoke, as if he saw his son on the field in his mind.

"That was the day he saw Lila, that first day," added Mateo's brother, Tomas. Tomas was thirteen, energetic, boyish. Built short and broad-shouldered like his father. Handsome in a stately way, like his father was.

Mateo was the lithe and graceful one in the family. He was good-looking, too, but with softer features and big romantic eyes. The image of him that formed in Winter's mind was of a confident, friendly kid. An athlete, yes, but no one knew his sensitivities, no one knew his poet's soul.

The family had all been so proud when he'd received the scholarship to Briars. It was a challenge for a boy from the Hollow to go into that exalted environment, but if anyone was up to it, the family agreed, Mateo was. He had the making of a man's man, certain of himself and ready for the slug and tumble of team life. The other boys didn't want to go after him about the whole Mexican business at first. That was because of the teachers—the teachers walked on eggshells when it came to matters of race and so on. They set the school's nervous, self-conscious tone.

But Mateo wouldn't have it. He understood boy life. He knew it was better to get ragged to your face right away than take it in the back over the long run. So he went after the others for being gringos—big smile on his face the whole time, but still, really ripping them for it. Finally, his teammates had to come back at him about being Mex. It was a point of honor. After that, it was all right. Mateo became part of the team quickly.

Still, no one knew his poet's soul.

Winter sipped his coffee and listened quietly. He didn't know much about soccer. His only sports were the martial arts. As a spectator, he enjoyed a baseball or football game, or any sort of straight-up fight, any style, one man against another. Soccer, though—he'd just never taken to it. Too much back and forth, too little scoring, plus you couldn't use the hands God gave you, which just seemed silly to him. Still, as he listened, he tried to fix the images in his mind the best he could.

The family went on rehearsing what, for them, was a famous story.

First game. Key position. Big pressure. The match had been tied at zero. For most of the first half, Quinton, a solid team from a couple of towns east, had threatened the goal repeatedly while repeatedly frustrating Briars whenever they tried to attack. Mateo—according to his family anyway—had been brilliant on defense. Again and again, he'd swiped the ball just as Quinton lined up their shot. Both the crowd and the Briars team were becoming energized by his high-level play.

As halftime neared, Quinton made their most aggressive push yet. Their top nine—their best striker—broke from nowhere to receive a pass at a spot with a clean angle into the net. He fired, fast—and in an amazing rush that brought a sigh of wonder from the home crowd, Mateo was suddenly there. He intercepted the shot midway. He not only kicked the ball to the fence, he followed after it on the run.

As the crowd took to their feet, cheering, he and the Quinton midfielder met with the ball between them. There was a blurred, rapid, balletic battle, feet flying and the ball seemingly caught between them. The combat ended when Mateo kicked the ball away to a teammate with a wild, whirling move. He connected—and then hit the fence and went somersaulting over. He came down, thud, on his back, right beneath the stands.

"He's lying there, lying on his back," young Tomas told Winter excitedly.

Hernandez was half smiling as his younger son took up the tale. Mrs. Hernandez, round-faced, sad-eyed, anxious-eyed, nodded fondly, near tears. Chubby little Sara, eleven years old, continued to huddle close to her mother, as if for protection.

"He's lying there," Tomas said, "and he looks up, right? He looks up, and there was Lila. It was like Cupid's arrow, man, right through the heart. Twang. Pow."

Lila was on the second tier of the aluminum bleachers. She was with her posse, two other girls. They were all three standing and cheering like everyone else as the Briars offense, having caught Mateo's wild pass, charged downfield toward the Quinton goal.

Lila was trying out a style then. Her hair was dyed violet and green and butchered short. Her jeans were torn, and a baggy sweatshirt hid her figure. Another boy might have missed how attractive she was.

But Mateo, with his sensitivities—it was always a girl's face he saw first. Not the hair, not the body, not the style at all. He saw the tenderness and sweetness and vulnerability in Lila's face, an oval, gentle-featured face with doe-brown eyes. He saw that, lying there on the ground after the play of his life, and he saw her on her feet cheering. The whole stadium was cheering but he saw only her. He adored her instantly.

"He didn't know who she was!" said Hernandez. He said it in a defensive tone as if Winter had made some kind of accusation.

"He didn't know she was from Tulipwood or nothing." Winter understood. He remembered the cynical way Steph Breach had told the story: *He made his move . . . Out of the Hollow . . . Fairy princess. His ticket to the next level. . . . God bless America.* "He didn't even know," Hernandez said.

"Mateo," said Tomas with a sly grin. "He's a romantic, man. I tease him sometimes, he's like a girl, the movies he watches. All love and kisses, muh-muh-mwah." He rolled his eyes. His mother lightly slapped his knee: *Stop that.* But Tomas went on, imitating his older brother: "He sees Lila and then he's all, like, 'I gotta know who she is, man! I gotta find her! She's the love of my life, man. I love her so much forever!'"

Briars was a small school. It wasn't long before Mateo knew exactly who Lila was and where she lived. And of course, she, Lila, knew just as quickly that he was asking about her. They traded glances in the school halls. Then, a couple of nights after the game, he snuck into Tulipwood.

It was a daring stunt, but not that difficult. He circled the fence, hidden by trees. Found a place far from the security station. Dodged the perimeter cameras. Then he went at the spiked barrier at a loping run, grabbed two spikes, and vaulted right over them like the athlete he was. He kept low as he ran from lawn to lawn. But even then, in the early springtime, the community was largely deserted, the houses mostly dark, the streets empty. Plus, there were plenty of trees and no moon. He was hidden by *beechen green and shadows numberless,* as Winter put it to himself.

But that was Keats, whereas the lovers' first meeting was pure Shakespeare. Mateo ducked from tree trunk to gazebo, crossing the backyard in the darkness to approach Lila's house. The rooms downstairs were dark, but he saw her in the yellow glow of her second-floor bedroom. *But soft! What light through yonder window breaks?* Her curtains were open. She was kneeling unsteadily on her bed, posting something on the wall, some picture. She was wearing jeans now and a plain green T-shirt. The sight of her electrified his skin from the inside out.

He crept close. He plucked a pebble from the grass around his sneakers. He tossed it lightly, but harder than he meant to. It cracked loudly against the pane. She heard it. He saw her lift her face, as if to sniff the wind. Quickly, he threw another pebble. He overcorrected and it tapped the glass so softly he was afraid she wouldn't hear. But she was listening for it. She climbed off the bed. Went to the window. Peered out, shading her eyes with her hand.

He stepped back. She saw him. Started. Quickly, she came out onto the balcony. Winter, still stuck on *Romeo and Juliet*, thought the moon would have been sick and pale with grief to be outshone by her—if there had been a moon, which, okay, there wasn't.

Mateo whispered her name. "Lila!" She took hold of the railing and looked down at him, trying not to smile.

"What are you doing?" she whispered back, glancing this way and that to see if there were any witnesses.

"I had to see you," he called back, too loudly.

"Ssh! Ssh! You're not supposed to be here in . . ."

But she broke off with a giggling gasp, because he'd made a run at the rose lattice on the house wall. It nearly stopped her heart because the lattice was flimsy, but he climbed up so fast it had no time to break. He gripped one slat and put his foot on another. Then he swung up to the base of the balcony. He grabbed the concrete edge with one hand, then with the other hand. He dangled a second as he hauled himself up. With his arms bare in his tee, she could see his big biceps bulging. He got his feet beneath him on the edge of the balcony and rose up before her, larger than life.

"What are you doing? What are you doing? This is crazy. Stop." She was whispering and giggling at once.

He stood at the rail with her, he on one side, she on the other, their hands close on top of it.

"Hi. I'm Mateo."

"I know who you are, stupid. I was at the game."

"I saw you there. I think you're so beautiful."

"This is crazy," she said, covering her face with one hand.

He gently drew the hand away, so that his eyes could play over her.

"Stop," she said.

He had a white, brilliant smile. "I can't. I can't stop looking at you."

"I'm not beautiful. I'm not even sure I want to be a girl yet."

"Oh," he said. "Oh. Be a girl."

And on the instant, she utterly was.

He lay his knuckles softly on her cheek.

"Don't," she said, but didn't stop him. Her eyes glowed in the darkness. She gazed at the way he was gazing at her, captivated by it, by being looked at in that manner. "Why didn't you just talk to me at school?"

"You're always with your friends. Can I kiss you?"

"No! What, are you insane? We don't even know each other."

But he leaned nearer, and she closed her eyes and tilted her head, and his lips touched hers just gently.

Winter was no sentimentalist but even he was impressed with the romance of it. Not the norm these days for teens, as far as he could tell from watching his own students. Steph Breach had been certain this boy was the killer—and the little boy who survived the murders claimed he had heard his voice—but Winter found it difficult to imagine his way from such a scene as this to the carnage in the Wasserman house.

*She heard the gunshots and came out of her bedroom. Saw the shooter, tried to turn and run. He got her in the back.*

That's the way Breach had described it. And maybe—possibly—one sort of passion had morphed into the other, love to murder. But had it? Had it really?

Eduardo Hernandez seemed to read his mind. When Tomas finished his story, the father said, "You see? It was that way from the beginning. It was like that all the time. He worshipped the ground she walked on. He would never have hurt her."

"He's a good boy," Mrs. Hernandez said, her voice breaking. "He was always a good boy." Her daughter frowned and burrowed into her side.

"Helps me out at the facility on weekends. Him and his brother both," said Hernandez. "They come down and help me out."

"And you haven't heard from him since the murders?" Winter asked. "You don't know where he is?"

Hernandez shook his head. His wife wiped her eyes. "He's hiding. He's scared," she said. "Why doesn't anyone understand that? He's just a boy."

Tomas and Sara looked solemn on either side of her.

"What about the missing guns?" Winter asked.

"I didn't even know they was gone until the police asked about them," Hernandez said. "Whoever it was, they took a rifle, and a pistol, too, my .38."

"Did you keep them locked up?"

He nodded heavily. "But just in a wooden cabinet in the basement. Someone crowbarred it open. Anyone could have climbed in through the window and done it. I haven't been hunting yet this season. The guns could have been gone for weeks. I wouldn't have noticed."

"Here, here, look, Professor," said Mrs. Hernandez. She had fetched a folded sheet of printer paper from the pocket of her dress.

She had been holding it there, waiting to show it to him. "He wrote this for me. This is the kind of boy he is."

Winter took the sheet from her and unfolded it. It was a poem. "A Mother's Love," it was called. By Mateo Hernandez. Winter scanned the lines quickly. He had to work hard to keep from pursing his lips with disdain. This sort of thing was a professional hazard for him. Young people, his students, were always showing him their poetry and asking for his "brutally honest opinion," which, of course, he was never fool enough to give them. Mateo's work was typical of the breed: awful. Heartfelt, oozing sentiment, literarily empty and technically inept.

"Lovely," he said, handing the page back to the poet's mother.

"It's so beautiful," she said, her voice breaking once again. "This is how he is."

Winter turned back to her husband.

"Could I have a look at Mateo's room?" he asked.

With a heavy nod, Hernandez told Tomas to lead him upstairs. Mateo's bedroom was the younger boy's bedroom too. It was a small room with a single window overlooking a neat little square of backyard. Mateo's narrow bed was on one side, Tomas's bed on the other. Mateo's wall was decorated with posters: one of a soccer star, one of a knight fighting a monster in a video game called *The Ring of Ventura*, plus a string of snapshots: Mateo with his family, with his friends, with his teammates, with Lila. Tomas's wall, Winter noticed, was a sort of mirror of Mateo's, the same types of images reflected back from a younger consciousness: a soccer poster, a poster of a cartoonish video game called *Wasteland*, photographs of Tomas with his friends, with his brother, his parents. From this, Winter understood that Mateo had been kind to his younger brother and that the boy admired and loved him. Tomas, he thought, would likely feel moved to protect Mateo from any suspicions.

Each boy had a small work desk, a bureau, and a shelf of school-books. There was a laptop on Tomas's desk but none on Mateo's.

"The police took Matt's computer," Tomas explained. Winter hadn't asked him. The kid was watching him, following his thoughts.

Winter picked up a framed photo from Mateo's bureau. It was a selfie, him with Lila. She was wearing a sleeveless T-shirt and Mateo had one arm around her bare shoulders, holding her close. His other arm was outstretched to position the camera. They were standing in a clearing in the woods. White rock rose behind them. Lila was radiant with happiness, her brown eyes bright. Mateo wore a big proud grin and clung to her as if she were the grand prize of life. Winter noticed the girl's hair was growing out. The off-beat colors had been washed away, leaving only a tint of violet in the natural silky brown. He noticed, too, the leaves on the trees were beginning to change color.

"How long ago was this taken?" he asked the boy.

Tomas shrugged. "Month. I dunno. Not long. Maybe two weeks."

Judging by the leaves, Winter guessed two weeks was right, if even that. Which meant that five or ten days before the murder the two lovers had been all smiles. She'd been fixing her hair, probably to make it more feminine, more to his liking. Mateo had been counting himself King of Lucky Land—Winter could read it in his proud grin. Why was Steph Breach so certain this boy had slaughtered the girl and her family? he wondered. The missing rifle was some evidence, he supposed. But was her certainty just antipathy to the troublesome 'newcomers'? Could it have even been simple racism? Or was there something else, something more she was keeping to herself?

"Were they sleeping together?" Winter asked the kid brother.

Tomas rolled his eyes, embarrassed. "Man!"

"I won't tell anyone. I just want to know."

"My mother'd die if she found out, man. She's old-school."

"Didn't the police ask you about it?"

The kid looked away, and Winter knew the police had asked him and he had lied to them.

"Mateo, you know, he would never tell me anything like that anyway," Tomas said. "Punched me in the arm the one time I asked him. Hard too. He was like, 'A gentleman doesn't talk about that, man!' Like he was some kind of knight in shining armor or something."

A corner of Winter's mouth lifted. The older boy had taught the younger and now the younger was practicing what he'd learned: gentlemanly honor and discretion.

"But you knew the truth anyway, didn't you?" he said.

Tomas shrugged. He gestured loosely toward the photograph. "That's the place, you know, where all the kids go when they do it."

"This?"

"The Fox Caverns, yeah."

Winter set the picture down. He opened the drawer to the work desk. He glanced in at the mess of utensils and books and notebooks. Then he caught sight of something else. He reached underneath a yellow pad. Brought out the white object—the same odd object he'd seen in the ruins of Lila's bedroom. He looked in the eyeholes. There was nothing there.

"What is this thing?" he asked the boy.

"That? That's the Opticon," said Tomas, as if only a visitor from another planet could not know.

"What does it do? Show movies? Oh no, wait, it's for video games, right? What do they call it?"

"VR, man. Mateo was into *Ring of Ventura*. The whole soccer team would play it. You can team up, play alone. The whole school plays it." He reached into his own desk and brought out his own device. "I got one too. But my mom won't let me play *Ventura* yet. She says I gotta wait till I'm fifteen. I play *Wasteland*. It's pretty cool too."

Winter turned the object this way and that. VR—Virtual Reality. He remembered reading the first two sentences of an article about it. He wasn't interested. He simply assumed that, like modern music and the ignorance of the young, it was one more sign of the death of Western civilization, the old civilization he loved.

He lay the gizmo back in the desk drawer, and as he did, he said, "Listen, Tomas. Do you know where your brother is?" He looked up quickly to catch the kid's reaction.

Startled, Tomas said, "No!"

Winter thought he seemed like a good kid, an honest kid, but he might be lying, kids do lie. He couldn't be sure. "You're not helping him if you don't tell. Hiding away—it just makes him look guilty."

"Mateo wouldn't kill nobody," Tomas said, lifting his chin defiantly. "Not Lila, not ever. She was his queen."

"What about her? Was she a nice girl?"

"Yeah! Yeah. She came over for dinner and everything. A few times. She was nice. Helped Mom in the kitchen. She wasn't stuck-up at all."

"Your mom and dad are worried sick, son. You know that, right? If you know where Mateo is, you have to tell them."

"I don't," said Tomas. "I don't know. I swear." A while later—Winter was not sure how long a while, probably just a few seconds—the boy said: "All right?"

Winter blinked and came to himself. He realized he had momentarily slipped into what he called his "strange habit of mind," a fugue state in which his thoughts and deductions and opinions vanished, and only the facts of the matter drifted in empty mental space until, as if gravity were suddenly restored, they fell on their own into a new arrangement, which he then assumed to be the truth.

"Yes, yes," he murmured, distracted. "All right."

He smiled blandly. He still couldn't be sure whether or not the boy was lying. But it no longer mattered. He had heard what he needed to hear.

He knew what he needed to know.

# 6

Now it was late afternoon. He was driving on the same two-lane, driving his Jeep back from the Hernandez home, back to his hotel. The sun was sinking behind the trees. The daylight was dimming, starting to die.

He had a weird sense of some presence in the atmosphere around him, something ghostly, insistent and invisible. Out of sight ahead of him, the mansions of Maidenvale stood sedate and magnificent. Out of sight behind him, the rubbled territory of the Hollow lay weary, drab, and still. Here, on the stretch of wooded highway that linked the two towns, the forest was lovely with autumn. All was quiet everywhere.

And yet . . . And yet the murder of the Wasserman family and Agnes Wilde—the raw, cold brutality of it, the madness of the rampage and (what other word could he use?) the evil—haunted the entire scene. The trees bowed and rattled in the wind on either side of him, and it seemed to him that the rifle shots of that bloody night were repeating beneath the breezes, a soundless drumbeat. *Boom, boom, boom* . . . The smell of that burned-out house returned to him, the smell of terror and rage, and a family, its human bonds, blown to pieces.

How could he get at the truth of the matter? Steph Breach might be racist, but that didn't mean she wasn't telling the truth. The newcomers might well have brought more drugs and crime to the area. A Romeo-Juliet romance between a Maidenvale girl and a Hollow boy might have been fraught with who knows what complications. Maybe the boy's passion had turned violent when Lila . . . what? Cheated on him? Broke it off? Discovered something he didn't want her to know?

He shook his head in frustration as he drove. He asked himself again: What was it to him? What was any of it to him? Why had he come here?

When he reached Main Street, he stopped at a drug store and bought a flashlight. As he stepped outside again, as he started heading to where he'd parked his SUV on the street, his eyes scanned the scene. The shops had begun to empty out as evening neared. The Saturday pedestrians in their chic fall sweaters and fashionable hats were abandoning the sidewalks. Music filtered from the taverns, where some locals had retired for drinks or early dinner. Others—as Winter imagined it—had gone home to change for gatherings with friends.

And he—he was anxious again, watchful again, looking for any sign of Inspector Strange.

It had been easy to talk his way into the Hernandez home. He had relied on his academic good looks, his elegant manner, and his cultural authority as a university professor. He himself was always surprised how often this worked, how often his vague explanations smoothed over the fact that he had no legitimate reason to be there asking questions.

But now, now that he had left the house, wouldn't it occur to the family that he had been prying into their lives with no good excuse? He thought it likely Eduardo Hernandez would eventually call the sympathetic Inspector Strange to tell him about the professor who had paid them a visit. Strange would not be pleased.

So, Winter was on the watch again. Seeking Strange's Crown Vic amidst the parked cars and the traffic on the emptying streets. That move Strange had made in the forest parking lot—that still bothered him. Sure, the Inspector hadn't actually tried to punch him, but it still struck him as a violent gesture. As if Strange were unstable in some way. Angry, capable of violence, eager to protect—something. His authority? His territory? Or something else? Winter didn't know.

For now, though, there was no sign of him. Winter got in his Jeep and drove back to the hotel.

He returned to his suite on the seventh floor. He stood at its large window. He looked out at a beautiful view: a pastel sea of trees rolling to sunlit lake water, with the skyline of the city a silver sfumato blending with the darkening blue of the October sky. He felt edgy standing there, uncertain. He wanted to wait for full darkness, but with every moment he felt more vulnerable. It would be so easy for Strange to find him here, to confront him in his room alone. And what then? If the inspector had been angry at him for simply viewing the murder scene, how furious would he be to hear he had questioned the Hernandez family after he'd been told to leave?

Still, he forced himself to wait. The sun went down. The sky turned indigo, then pale black—a starless black with the glow of the city lights washing over it. What trees he could still see were bowing and swaying. The wind off the lake was growing stronger as night fell.

At last he turned away from the window. He sat on the edge of one of the two beds. He changed out of his loafers into a pair of sneakers. His mind went back to that moment in the Independent coffee shop, that mystic moment when he'd seen the faces of the customers and experienced all the fret and hope and desire of their inner humanity. He wondered: If that mystic revelation hadn't come to him, if he hadn't seen then what he'd seen, would the news story of the Wassermans' murders have struck him as it did, so real and near, so disturbing and somehow personal? Would he still have felt compelled to come?

He had no answer. It was just one more thing about this situation that he didn't fully understand.

He stood up. It didn't matter now.

It was time to go into the woods and find Mateo Hernandez.

# 7

Soon, he was back on the two-lane with the forest on either side of him. He was still tense, still watchful. He checked the rearview moment by moment. At first there were houses, driveways, lights. But then Maidenvale fell away behind him, and there was nothing but darkness, the forest, and the wind.

The wind was strong. It buffeted the SUV and made it shudder. The dead leaves tornadoed off the pavement in front of him. They flew across his windshield like black bats silhouetted against the face of the sky. *Like ghosts from an enchanter fleeing,* he thought. The trees were shadows that bent and whipped and struggled against the force of the breeze. Winter watched all this, but he watched the rearview too. There were no headlights behind him. No lights at all.

Then, suddenly, he was being followed.

He had had a moment of distraction. He was thinking: Inspector Strange must know everything he knew. What policeman in a small town didn't know where the lovers lane was? If Tomas was right, and the Fox Caverns were where teens went for privacy, Strange must have known it was Mateo's most likely hiding place.

Either he'd already searched there—or he hadn't, for reasons of his own. Which made Winter wonder if Strange might have out-guessed him, if he might be waiting for him in the Baptiste Woods.

It took him perhaps a minute or so to think these thoughts. Then he looked up at the rearview and saw the headlights behind him. Of course, he tried to convince himself that they were just head-lights, just another car on a well-traveled road. But if they were, where the hell had they come from? Yes, the car could have been traveling faster than he was. It could be coming from Maidenvale, overtaking him. But was it? Or was it Inspector Strange?

The answer came a moment later when he looked in the mirror again and the lights were gone.

"Damn it," Winter whispered.

There was nowhere the following car could have turned off, no driveways, no intersecting roads. The follower had cut his lights, that's all. He had gone dark, to come after Winter in secret.

It was what he'd been worrying about all day. There was no smart way to tangle with a cop like Strange. You couldn't trade punches with him. You'd end up behind bars, if you didn't end up in the hospital. And maybe it wasn't actually Strange at all. Maybe it was someone else. Someone worse.

He briefly considered turning back. He asked himself again: what business was this of his? But now he saw the entryway on his left, the path into the Baptiste Woods where Strange had taken him earlier. Before he could think it through, he had turned the wheel and the Jeep was rocking over the rutted dirt road.

His headlights picked out mere yards of the broken path ahead of him. Their outglow hinted at the wild forest in the wild wind all around. He went slow. He checked the rearview again and again. But there were no more lights. If he was being followed, the fol-lower had made himself invisible.

He passed the sign: "The Baptiste Woods. Trails close at sunset."
He saw the entry to the parking lot. He turned in. The lot was
empty now, except for him, his Jeep. He parked. He killed the
lights. Killed the engine. Stepped out.

He stood listening. The wind was loud. The trees creaked and
snapped and groaned like souls in purgatory. The air hissed through
their branches. Their leaves chattered and tumbled through the
underbrush, through the lot, against his legs. He strained his eyes
in the direction from which he'd come, but there were still no
lights. If there were engine noises or footsteps, he couldn't hear
them.

He took a breath. He turned on his flashlight. He followed its
beam to the trailhead. He went into the woods.

He cursed his nerves. He was a man who had been in dangerous
places—in plenty of dangerous places in the dark. But night in the
forest was like nothing else. Nothing else was so empty and yet so
alive. No lingering hint of dusk could touch the depths of it. No
trace of human life could account for the sudden scrambling noises
or the wild, distant calls. Even if a car passed, even if a plane went
overhead, the sound would be drowned out by the constant hollow
commotion of the wind. To think that Strange might be waiting
for him . . . or coming after him . . . Strange or someone worse . . .

He needed the flashlight to see his way, but it seemed to make
the woods even darker somehow. The beam lit what little it lit, but
everything else seemed to retreat from it into a deep and tangled
obscurity. When he looked over his shoulder, when he turned to
shine the light behind him, when he paused to scan the moving,
groaning, creaking forest for any sign of someone on his trail, it
all seemed dim and alien. Leaves whirling. Vines waving. Trees
bending. Winter felt as if he was being drawn into an otherworld
of threat and malevolence.

He went on. He spotted the white of the rocks through the trees. There was a sign at a trail junction pointing the way to the caverns. He followed the path to the right. The white formations loomed over his left shoulder. In the twisted blackness to his right, something made a noise, a crash, like a big beast walking through the underbrush. He stopped in his tracks. Held his breath. Listened. The wind paused a moment—and there was a high whine, a living voice of some kind, not human. Winter grimaced, annoyed with himself. This was a suburban wood, after all, a little hiking trail outside of town. There weren't any monsters lurking here. At least, he didn't think there were.

All the same, he stood there another long moment. He passed the flashlight beam over an incomprehensible pattern of shuddering vines and shivering underbrush. Nothing evil peered back at him. Nothing he could see anyway.

He moved on.

By the time he reached the caverns, he was sick of this whole adventure. He could not recall to himself even the faintest feeling of the urgency that had brought him here in the first place. He was cold. He was nervous. He wanted to go home.

But there was a cave entrance now: a low domed opening in the base of the white stone. He ducked his head and stepped in.

At once, the noise of the wind was softer, a hoarse whisper. A step or two inside and the passage grew higher. With his head bent, he could move easily through the tunnel. Shapes leaned in from either side of him, but when he turned the flashlight on them, they were just outgrowths of the rock.

He came around a bend into a final chamber. His flashlight picked out the usual teen detritus: cigarette butts, condoms, candy wrappers. He turned back—and as he did, he heard motion again, quieter this time, more like a stealthy footstep in the duff. He clicked the light off. The blackness was shockingly complete. He could see nothing. He listened, his heart beating hard. He could only hear the wind.

He clicked the light back on. Moved low, tense, at the ready. He stepped out of the little cave, quickly swiveling left and right, prepared for an attack. No one was there. Nerves, he thought. He felt ridiculous.

Again, he searched the windblown woods with the light—and now the beam fell on a huge cave entrance, a gaping hole in the rising rock, maybe twenty feet high. It was like a great open maw waiting to swallow him. This, he knew, was the place he wanted.

He followed his flashlight into the cavern. He stepped from the windy chill of the night into a vast world of stone. Rock seemed to drip from the rock ceiling. Rock seemed to grow out of the rocky ground. A whole stone forest seemed to be rising up a little way ahead of him. He moved toward it. Again, the wind became soft and distant.

He saw two passages out of the chamber, two corridors into darkness. As he moved to the one on his right, he heard another footstep behind him. He was sure of it this time. Someone was following him, close by. He glanced back. He saw no one. But at the same moment, he caught a whiff of death. He knew that smell. His heart went sour.

It was coming from the nearer tunnel. He took two more steps and the stench became unmistakable. The knowledge of what he was about to find made him so forlorn, he forgot—like a fool he forgot—the threat behind him. He moved down the corridor, dodging low-hanging stones.

The path narrowed. He had to turn sideways to move through it. The smell of the dead pressed close to him like living fog. He pinched his nose between his thumb and the edge of his finger.

He pushed through the corridor into the final chamber. He leveled the flashlight.

There was Mateo.

What was left of the boy lay in a sad little encampment. There was a sleeping bag open on the ground, stained, as the wall behind it was stained, with blood and human fragments. Everything—the gore and the blood and the body—was alive with insects. They swarmed the mess where Mateo's face had been. Larger animals had been at the rest.

The rifle lay beside the boy, near his outflung hand. It was a Winchester with a short barrel. Winter could see at a glance that Mateo could easily have held the weapon beneath his chin and pulled the trigger himself.

The scene overwhelmed him with sorrow. But then he tensed. There'd been a sound. A scrape of stone, very close. He spun. His flashlight beam danced crazily over the rocky dark.

He saw the man's shadow an instant before a bright beam flashed back at him, stabbed his eyes, blinded him. Still holding his nose, he raised his other arm to ward off the glare.

"You son of a bitch," a low voice growled at him.

The bright beam shifted. Winter lowered his arm.

Inspector Strange was standing at the narrow entranceway. He held the powerful flashlight in his left hand. His right hand held his Glock, the black barrel leveled at Winter's belly.

The lawman's long face was twisted with wrath. He looked very much like a man about to pull the trigger.

The two men stood like that a moment, a moment that seemed to Winter to go on and on.

Then Strange's gaze shifted—from Winter's face to Mateo's body. The lawman circled his flashlight over the scene. Winter saw the anger leave him. His expression changed to one of resignation.

Slowly, Strange slipped his pistol into the holster under his jacket. He pointed his flashlight at the rifle on the cave floor.

"If that's the murder weapon," he said, "I guess this case is closed."

# PART TWO

# THE THREE GIRLS
# OF GIRL-WORLD

As soon as I got back from London after killing Snowstep, I was called to the Division offices again.

"Congratulations. If we were gangsters, I'd declare you a 'made man,'" said the Recruiter. "But since we work for the government, I'll just say you're an amoral and ruthless psychopath and offer you the thanks of a grateful nation."

He was—as he almost always was—stationary and deadpan. He sat forward in his chair with his hands clasped on the desktop, his expression set in stone. I was always on edge under that strangely droll gaze of his, but I tried to act casual. To be honest, in the wake of the mission, the wake of all the missions, I wasn't very certain of who I was anymore. Sometimes I thought I was the coolest hero outside the movies. Other times I figured I was what the Recruiter said I was: a crazed killer, corrupted by the yearning for manly heroism in an unheroic age.

I gave an easy shrug—at least, I hoped it looked easy. I said: "Hey, the guy was an assassin."

"So are you, Poetry Boy," said the Recruiter. "Yet here you are."

"Well, yeah, but I work for the good guys. Don't I?"

"Who can say? Not you, certainly. In your lunatic dream of a godless universe, good and evil can only be determined by the opinions of your fellow madmen, and morality is just a matter of democracy in the asylum. Mind you, I can work with that. The government can always find a use for lunatics as long as they're homicidal. Speaking of which, I have another assignment for you."

*A week later, I was at the university—the school that Snowstep had told me about where, allegedly at least, there was a spy embedded in a research program essential to our defense. There were four scientists working on the project, but if one of them was funneling information to his Chinese masters, our intelligence couldn't find any evidence of it. It was possible the whole story was Snowstep's invention, his way of distracting me until he could reach the gun in the back of his belt. He had a gun in the back of his belt, by the way. Did I mention that? The cleanup crew found it when they packed up his body. He was just talking until I let my guard down so he could draw and kill me. I wasn't exactly certain where that left the matter morally. Like the Recruiter said: democracy in the asylum.*

*Anyway, the point of this new mission wasn't to catch the spy. It was to identify the spy so we could use him or her to slip the Chinese false information. That way they'd still think they knew what they knew but they wouldn't actually know it, if you see what I mean.*

*Our way in was through a student named Madeleine Uno. She was something of a computer prodigy and she'd been hired part-time to provide the project with tech security. She acted as a sort of project coordinator, keeping all the data safe and under wraps. Even if you were on the project, the only way to get at the information was through her, on a need-to-know basis, so only she had the whole picture of who knew what.*

*Now Madeleine was working for us, government intelligence, but she didn't know it. The funny thing was, she was so talented at what she did, she had invented a coding system that even our guys couldn't break. The situation was crazy. We were secretly funding the whole project, but we couldn't access the material to trace the flow of information and find the spy. We couldn't just ask Madeleine for access because, for one thing, that would give our presence away, and for another, she might turn out to be the spy herself. So we had to find another way in. That's what I was sent to do.*

*Madeleine had recently gone through an ugly breakup with some creep named Gerald. Gerald had cheated on her, and not just once either. Finally, she'd caught on and ditched him. The Division figured she'd be an easy mark because she was gullible enough for this clown Gerald to dupe her, plus she was now emotionally vulnerable in a sloppy seconds sort of way. I was college age and easy enough to look at. So I was sent to romance her and get enough intel out of her to find out if Snowstep's story was a bluff or not.*

*The thing that was sad about the assignment . . . Well, there were a lot of sad things about it actually. I didn't really realize it then, but psychologically I was a total mess at this point. As I say, I'd only joined the Division for the adventure of it. It was something to lose myself in while I got over Charlotte. Well, now I was lost, all right. I'd sent a friend to his death. I'd shot a man in cold blood. Was I good? Evil? A hero? A villain? I couldn't get a clear sense of it. And now they were sending me into the field to pretend to be—what? Myself, really. I was going undercover as exactly the person I would have been if I hadn't joined the Division in the first place. A lonely student. Hungry for love. It was as if my life had become a performance, and I was playing the role of myself as I should have been. It was incredibly disorienting.*

*And it was bliss too. The entire experience was heartbreaking bliss. I loved the place. The university. It was an oasis of classical learning in the vast empty plains of the Midwest. All Gothic arches and dreaming spires. Little lawns under little trees where you could sit alone and read or sit with friends and talk about your reading. I would have loved to have been there for real.*

*The Division had decided there was no point trying to insert me into Madeleine's computer science classes. I'd've been spotted as a fraud immediately. She apparently didn't go for her fellow nerds anyway. Gerald—her cheating boyfriend—he was in the drama department. So I came in as an English major. Again, heartbreaking bliss. The last few really good literature scholars in the country all worked in the English Department there. I got into a class on late-eighteenth-century poetry that was taught by Daniel Baldrick. A genius. A famous—or notorious—bulwark against the young, faddish philistines. He looked like a pair of bushy white eyebrows on top of an empty suit: old enough to have written some eighteenth-century poetry himself. But the guy was absolutely brilliant. My first day in, I went to his lecture on* Innocence and Experience *and I was just swept away. All I wanted on earth was to be the me I was pretending to be. I sat through the entire lecture with this ache in my belly. This yearning. Unrequited love for my true self, my lost self.*

*Then, after the lecture, I went out to make my move on Madeleine.*

*I followed her from her last class. She walked alone to a secluded corner of the campus. She sat atop a grassy hill beneath a small maple. She laid her books out around her and had a notebook open on the lawn. But as I approached her, she was just sitting there gazing off into space. My guess was she was nursing her broken heart.*

*It was a pretty picture. She was a pretty girl. Long straight brown hair and graceful, precise little features. Like an old master of miniatures had carved her out of some pale wood. She had a very prim style of dressing. Long-sleeve blouses, skirts that fell below the knee. Very appealing.*

*"Can I sit with you?" I asked her.*

*The autumn sun was bright that day. She squinted up at me, a long, hard look. "There's plenty of other places to sit," she said.*

*"There are other places, but you're not in them." She rolled her eyes. I said, "All right, that was clumsy. Let me try again. I'm the kind of guy who finds nothing more attractive than a beautiful girl with a book."*

*"Oh my God! Oh my God, you are so bad at this."*

*"I know, right?" I sighed and plunked disconsolate on the grass next to her. "It's very discouraging. Still, I feel I could get the hang of it if*

*you'd give me a chance. Maybe a few pointers. A drink or two might relax me."*

*She gave a little puff through her nose that might have almost been laughter. But she said: "Look, I'm sure you're a nice guy, but I'm really not in the market. I mean it. I have work to do. I'd like to be by myself, if you don't mind."*

*I made a gesture of surrender and stood up again. I lingered over her a moment. She looked up at me, shading her eyes from the sun.*

*"He must've been a real bastard," I said.*

*"Who? Oh, I see."*

*"The guy who broke up with you."*

*"Yes. He was. But I broke up with him."*

*"Then he must've been a double bastard."*

*She sniffed impatiently. "It's been good talking to you."*

*"Guys like that," I pressed on. "It isn't fair. They get away scot-free and the sweet, lovable types pay the price."*

*"Sweet, lovable types like yourself, you mean."*

*"That was—yeah, that was the implication."*

*"You really do suck at this. You might want to try another line of work."*

*"Well . . ."*

*She waved at me: Bye. What could I do? I went on my way.*

*Still, it wasn't a bad day's work. Another meeting or two like that and I figured she'd have to befriend me out of sheer pity. Which was all I needed to get the intel out of her. I made a plan to wait a few days and then bump into her accidentally.*

*But the very next day, she came to me instead. I was sitting in the cafeteria and she suddenly dropped into the seat next to me.*

*"All right. You made me feel bad," she said. "I was taking Gerald out on you."*

*"Gerald?" I wrinkled my nose. "Even his name sounds creepy, doesn't it?"*

*"In retrospect."*

*"So, what was it about me that touched your heart? The sad eyes? Like a spaniel, right?"*

*"It was the karate knuckles actually. My baby brother has them, too. They give you this nice bullied-boy-learns-to-take-care-of-himself vibe. I can just picture your mom driving you to the mall dojo in your little gi."*

*"It's a very cuddly image. It was my nanny though. My mother never loved me. That's what makes me so irresistibly pitiful."*

*"Yeah, that is pretty irresistible."*

She was a shockingly sweet person once you got to know her. A warm, open, tender heart, all woman. Always sewing things, decorating things, baking things. Endlessly taking pictures of things she made and posting them on this app she had. Wim Wam or Zip Zap or something. She was more interested in all that domestic stuff than she was in her math, but she had an uncanny gift and she stuck with it to please her father, a stern, distant guy, workaholic.

Anyway, she took me in like a lost mutt. Loved to feed me, groom me, pick out clothes for me, scold me about my bad habits, give me tips on how to meet nice girls. Maybe it was some kind of Japanese thing, I don't know. To be honest, I was such an emotional mess at that point, any woman with an ounce of maternal instinct probably would have adopted me.

And on my side, I loved it. I loved the way she fussed over me, coddled me. Lost as I was. Neglected little rich boy that I always was, as we know. Like everything else about this mission, being with Madeleine was bliss. Heartbreaking bliss.

You know what the awful thing was? This is why the mission was successful. Madeleine wasn't ready for a full relationship yet, and I had my own professional reasons for keeping things simple, for holding back, so I was content to let her mother me. So we became actual friends. I truly liked her for her kindness and her sweetness. And since I wasn't trying to bed her, she came to trust me. That's how I got the intel out of her.

*It happened one night at her place. It was a shabby second-story apartment in one of the off-campus buildings for seniors. I was lying on her ratty old sofa with my head in her lap. She was drinking a glass of wine and stroking my hair like I was her pet. Which I guess I was. It was nice. We were happy. It was what we both needed.*

*Then, casually, out of nowhere, Madeleine mentioned for the first time that she had a part-time job. I picked up on it immediately and started asking questions.*

*One question led to another and eventually I said to her, "Wait. You mean you don't even know what these researchers are working on?"*

*"I'm not supposed to know. I shouldn't even be talking about it. I'll probably have to kill you now."*

*"That's weird though, isn't it? Not knowing?"*

*"Not really. I just encrypt the data. Even the researchers don't totally know what the other researchers are doing. Unless they need to, then they have to go through me. That's the whole idea. This way I have a record of who's done what, and if there's a leak, I'll either know who did it right away or be able to trace it pretty quickly. I've got a list of all their activities."*

*"In the files."*

*"Right, it's encrypted with the rest."*

*"What if you leak it?"*

*"Me? I don't even read it. I wouldn't understand it if I did. And who would I leak it to? The Chinese? I hate those bastards. Long story."*

*"But how hard would it be for someone to just hack into the thing?"*

*She gave a cute, cocky little smile. "Oh. Very hard, my lamb. Very hard. I'm three parts Japanese and one part Jew. Have you any idea how smart that makes me?"*

*I laughed. "What did you do?"*

*"It's hard to explain to an English major. But basically, I built a system that continually randomizes the data. It's essentially a moving code without a key."*

"But then how can even you read it?"

Now I had her on the hook. She was proud of her accomplishment. She'd wanted to brag to someone about it but hadn't been able to trust anyone—until now. "There's a Rosetta Stone built into each iteration. I'm the only one who knows how to find it, and once I do, I can read it and show the researchers what they want on a need-to-know basis. It's sort of like those old codes linked to books. You can't crack the code if you don't know what the book is."

"Wow. That's cool. Has anyone ever done that before?"

"Not that I know of. I invented it."

So, there I was, right on the brink of getting what I wanted out of her. Lying on her lap. Looking up at her. A very alluring view, up over the curve of her slim, elegant figure to that delicate face—which was looking down at me so tenderly, so happy to have someone to share her achievement with. I was just a few questions away from what I needed, just a few.

But then—then something happened. It hit me hard, a solid jolt, like being punched from the inside.

I rolled off her quickly and stood up.

She was startled. "What? What's the matter?"

"Nothing," I said. "Nothing."

But that was a lie. Something had happened, something catastrophic. I stood over her, dazed, blinking stupidly. Trying to deny it. Not just to her, but to myself too. Wasn't I on a mission? Wasn't I the cold-blooded hero who had killed Snowstep without a second thought? Wasn't I just pretending to be a lovelorn college student with a passion for old poetry?

But even as I told myself, yes, I was, I was all that, cold-blooded, just pretending, a spy pretending—even as I told myself, I knew the truth. I knew exactly what it was that had rocked me so.

Madeleine had been about to kiss me. I had seen the change come into her eyes, the softness as she shared her secrets with me. She had finally reached the point where she was ready for someone new, and she had been about to lean down and press her body against me, and put her hand in my hair and put her lips on mine. And it was going to change everything.

And I couldn't let that happen. Because I had fallen in love with her. Playing her for intel. Pretending to be her pet, her project. Her friend. I had fallen in love with her.

Trying to hide my agitation, I turned away from her and moved to the window. I looked out at the street, pretending to stretch my back. Madeleine lived on a quiet residential lane with an old-world feel to it. Stone buildings and street lamps. I saw a single student down there, walking home through the dark, a woman holding her books to her chest.

I watched her. My mind was racing. Trying to escape the truth of what was happening to me. Looking for something else to grab hold of. And of course, I had that already, didn't I? The mission.

My eyes shifted until I could see Madeleine's reflection on the glass. I could see her watching me. I could see her expression clearly enough to read her disappointment and confusion.

I tried to keep my voice casual, as if I were speaking out of idle curiosity. "How do you remember the Rosetta Stone?" I asked. I turned to face her, a half smile on my face to add to my casual air. "I mean, do you just memorize it?"

Distracted, she didn't even think to keep her secret. "No," she said vaguely. "I can't do that."

"Right. Because if something happens to you . . ."

"Right. The information has to be accessible."

"So, what do you do?"

Still with her mind on other things—that interrupted kiss—that kiss that was going to change everything—she said, "It's hidden in a bunch of music files in my desktop. A little here, a little there. You know, they gave me an office up on the top floor of Cade. It has a computer in it, but I'm never there. I do most of my work on my laptop at home. So I *just tucked the key to the Rosetta in there, in the files. If I don't check in with it once every seventy-two hours, the files automatically get sent to the project security overseer, a private firm. They'd spot the anomalous data and would figure it out from there."*

*I almost laughed. That private firm—that was secretly us, of course. Government intelligence. All I had to do now was get the music files and we could find out who was passing information to the Chinese. We'd have our spy, assuming there was one, assuming Snowstep wasn't just talking.*

*"You know," I said to her—again, as if casually. I even yawned—"I should probably go. I have some studying to do for tomorrow."*

*Madeleine set her glass aside, very purposeful, very serious. She stood up. We stood facing each other. Looking in each other's eyes. It was just for a second really, but so much can pass in silence between a man and a woman in just a second. And it did pass between us. That she wanted me to cross the room and draw her to me. That I wanted to do exactly that, wanted it even more than I let myself understand. That some unseen web of complications was holding me back from her, hemming me in. She wanted to know what it was. Fear? Uncertainty? Another woman? She wanted to ask, to speak the unspoken. I could see it as if it were written on the space between us. She wanted to say to me:* Stay. Stay tonight. Become my lover. Stay.

*Her lips parted—to say it, I think. To say it out loud:* Stay with me. *I'm almost sure of it.*

*"I have to go," I said again, quickly.*

*And I left. To get that code.*

# 8

It was only then, when Winter fell silent, that Margaret Whitaker had her first real suspicion of how bad a story this might turn out to be, how unforgiveable. The thought caused a flutter of anxiety at her center.

Forgiveness, after all—forgiveness from her—was what he needed, what he was here for. He was seeking absolution for his sins so he could let go of the guilt that barred him from seeking love and a full life. She loved him and she wanted to give him that absolution—and she also didn't want to, because she didn't want him to be free to find someone else and leave her. Of course, she knew she had to clear all those intricacies away to do her job and try to heal him.

But what if he had done something that truly was unforgiveable? How would she parse her motives then?

"What?" said Winter. He was watching her from his chair, just as perceptive in his way as she was, just as much of an empath.

"You seem distracted today," she said, covering for her lapse.

"Do I?"

"Yes. Like you're reciting a story while your mind is really elsewhere."

Margaret could see him consider that, and she felt relieved. She had managed to turn his attention back on himself.

Winter said: "After our last session I had—I don't really know what to call it. A sort of experience. It only lasted a second but . . . I was in that coffee shop I like, the Independent, and I suddenly saw everyone there very clearly, as if I could read their thoughts, as if they were present to me in full, with all their dreams and worries and prayers. Their humanity on display."

Margaret nodded. Now she was back on solid ground. This was the sort of psychological material she knew how to deal with.

"Then," he went on, "a moment later, I noticed a story on a news site. About a family that had been murdered in their home, shot down one by one."

"Yes, I read about that. A gated community somewhere."

"Maidenvale. Over near Chicago."

"That's right."

"You know I have this—strange habit of mind I've told you about . . ."

"The story intrigued you."

"More than that."

Their eyes met. She understood: he had gotten himself involved in another one of his investigations. That flutter of anxiety rose in her again. Worse this time, in fact. When Winter had first begun to come to her, he had not always been forthcoming about this secret life he led. His old life in the Division—these crime-solving jaunts of his—he'd kept them mostly to himself. He had wanted to protect her from any danger that might arise from her knowing too much. Maybe he had also wanted to hide that dangerous side of himself from her. But over the months, as the trust between them had grown—and this odd, unequal love between them had also grown—this cruel love between two half souls separated by the relentless river of time—he had begun to lose his restraint. He had begun to tell her everything there was to tell. And she—well, she was a nervous old biddy, as she frequently reminded herself, and she wasn't sure at all how much she wanted to hear about murder and spycraft and such things as these.

"Didn't I read that they found the killer?" she asked him. "The daughter's boyfriend, wasn't it? He committed suicide, I think. I saw just a paragraph about it."

"Yes. It didn't get much attention. A Latino boy wiping out a white family—a boy from a neighborhood with a lot of illegals—not the sort of story the media like. I think they feel it sends the wrong sort of message. I don't know. I would've thought it would be more of a sensation."

Margaret swiveled in her brown chair.

"But you don't believe the boy did it," she said.

"I didn't at first. I talked to the boy's family. They seemed like nice people. And he—the boy—really seemed to love the girl. But after I found the body . . ."

"You found the body?" The words came out of her before she could soften her tone of surprise.

"I did, but it was too late. He'd blown his head off with a rifle. The murder weapon."

Margaret shook her head—with what feeling even she wasn't sure. She had a sedate clientele for the most part: academics, students, state bureaucrats. Corpses with blown-off heads were not the sort of problem she usually dealt with. "All right," she said. "And?"

"Afterward—after I found the boy—I had to go to the police station and give them a statement."

At the police station, an angry Inspector Strange had escorted Winter to a storage room that seemed to double as an interview room. Strange had left him there to stew for over an hour. It was a drab, cramped room. There were cardboard boxes stacked against the wall, some thick binders, and even a sort of toy chest with some cleaning equipment stuffed in it. There was also a table in the center of the room with a plastic chair on one side of it and two more on the other. Sitting there, waiting for someone to come in and take his statement, Winter felt as if he'd been stored away with the boxes and the rest.

He bided his time reading materials for his next Shelley lecture off his phone. Then, after about twenty minutes, a patrolwoman had come in bearing a cup of coffee for him.

The patrolwoman was named Ann Farmingham. She was a burly, hard-faced character, taller than he was, nearly six feet he guessed. She had whitish, acne-scarred cheeks, and brown hair pulled back hard then tied in a ponytail. As he drank his coffee gratefully, she propped a foot on a chair, and crossed her arms on her raised knee, leaning down over him.

"I heard you were out at the house with Steph," she said.

Winter remembered how Steph Breach had told him, *There are still good people on the force and most of them are friends of mine.* So this, apparently, was one of those friends.

Ann Farmingham stayed a while and gossiped with him about the case in a knowing tone. She told him Mateo Hernandez was not at all the "nice boy" everyone said he was. His romance with Lila Wasserman was, she said, "no fairy tale." According to the kids at the Briars school, Mateo and Lila had had a big quarrel just before the murders took place. Something about a video game they had been playing together. Mateo accused Lila of flirting with one of the other players. Lila had stormed off furious and Mateo was very upset.

"Guess he didn't want anyone else to have her," said Officer Ann.

There was something else too. Officer Ann leaned down closer to him and dropped her voice. "Porn," she murmured. The police had found a ton of it on the kid's computer. Not just the usual stuff either, said Officer Ann. All the kids looked at that these days, she said. This was violent porn, really sick material. Or so she'd heard. She hadn't seen it personally herself—and she didn't want to see it either. It was apparently pretty ugly.

Winter's mind went back to the poem Mateo's mother had shown him: "A Mother's Love." He considered the mind of a boy who could pour out such sentimental slop for his mom while secretly watching violent porn. It didn't make a pretty psychological picture. Maybe this, not racism, accounted for Steph Breach's suspicions about the kid.

"So now you think he was guilty," Margaret said when Winter had explained all this to her.

Winter made a vague gesture: he wasn't sure.

"But all your original questions have been answered," Margaret said.

Winter sat back in the brown chair, an armchair. He propped his elbow on the arm and lay a finger across his lips as if to hide his expression from her. "Most of my questions," he said. "All but one really."

"Which is?"

"Why did I care so much? Why did I get involved in this case in the first place?"

"Ah," said Margaret. "Would you like me to explain it to you?"

He smiled. "Please."

"You went to the coffee shop after you began to tell me this story you've been telling me. About Snowstep and Madeleine. The worst thing you ever did, you said it was."

He nodded. He had stopped smiling. He was listening to her intently.

"You've been coming here almost a year, Cam," Margaret went on. "You've been trying to tell me this story from the first day. Whatever it is you did, you feel the horror of it has cut you off from the rest of humankind—womankind especially, because you're lonely and you long to find a woman of your own. So when you finally began to tell me the story, it was a great weight off your shoulders. Afterward, in the coffee shop, you had a glimpse—a sort of vision—of what the world might look like if you were freed from the guilt of your past and could connect with humankind again. Then, just as you were coming out of that vision, you spotted the story about the murder. It represented an alternative vision you might say, a nightmare vision of what would happen if you were to tell me this story and instead of finding forgiveness, you found only more rejection, more guilt, more condemnation. The murder story was a terrible alternative vision of the violent destruction of . . ."

She paused to search for the delicate words she wanted, and Winter murmured: "'All the various relationships which bind one human being to another in mutual bonds.'" Then, looking up to see her questioning expression, he added: "Shelley. Mary not Percy. It's from *Frankenstein*."

"Mm, *Frankenstein*," said Margaret Whitaker. "Because if our therapy should fail to absolve you, you would be doomed to life as a monster, cut off from humankind and love forever. The way you feel now. No wonder you felt compelled to solve these murders. To resolve that nightmare vision and make it less threatening."

For a moment, he remained as he was, hiding behind that finger across his lips—but hiding uselessly because all his emotions were there in his eyes anyway. They were the emotions, Margaret thought, of a much younger man, the child he'd been maybe. Which was one of the things she loved about him: that lonesome motherless child always so close to his competent, even heroic, surface self.

"When I saw them," he said after a while, "those people in the coffee shop, when I saw them with all their pain and humanity revealed, it was . . ." He let his hand drop to the chair arm. He spoke with naked fervency, his soul bare to her. "It was so beautiful, Margaret."

"It's going to be all right, Cam," Margaret Whitaker told him—told him in the tender, maternal tone she knew he needed to hear. "Really, it's all going to be all right."

"Is it?" he asked her rather desperately.

*How the hell should I know*, she wanted to respond.

But instead, she offered him a sweet and reassuring smile and said, "Yes."

# 9

There seemed to Winter a certain ironic timing to what happened next. Even in the moment, it almost felt cosmically intentional, as if the fates had had a hand in it or as if there were some god who authored human lives instead of snuffing them out for sport like a wanton boy with flies.

When he came out of his session with Margaret, he was telling himself that the story of the Maidenvale murders was complete. Not only had the killer been identified, but Winter now understood why the murders had fascinated him in the first place. Margaret's explanation made perfect sense to him. He told himself he was through with Maidenvale and could return to his own life and his own business.

True, when he was having his coffee and croissant at the Independent that afternoon, questions about the murders still did drift across his mind occasionally like a perfume either smelled or remembered. If Mateo had quarreled with Lila, why did he kill the entire family? Where had such violence come from in him? Had he been abused as a child? Was he psychotic? And why had the nanny, Agnes—whatever her name was—Wilde—why had Agnes Wilde gone downstairs after dropping her little charge, seven-year-old

Bobby, out the window? That still bothered him. Did she know Mateo? Did she think she could stop him?

But never mind. Now that Margaret had given him some insight into his own motivations, Winter was able to dismiss these questions as irrelevant mysteries. Then and there, in the coffee shop, he decided to let the matter go. Which meant he could now turn his full attention to Lori Lesser.

The dean of student relations was sitting at a table against the paisley mural on the far wall. There was a man seated across from her. Attractive, lanky, silver-haired. Dignified in a gray suit and silver tie. The two were chatting over their fancy frappes, or whatever they were drinking. Laughing a lot. Smiling a lot. Showing one another a lot of white teeth. A full flirtation.

Lori kept stealing glances Winter's way. Winter thought she wanted to make sure he saw her with this handsome and obviously successful man. She wanted him to feel sorry he had rejected her. She wanted him to feel jealous. So Winter believed at any rate.

In fact, he disliked this silver fox of hers on sight, and he couldn't tell why. Which disturbed him. The idea that he might in fact be jealous of this man was annoying to him. It threatened to spoil his coffee break. After a while, he packed up his laptop and left the place. He carefully avoided looking at Lori on his way out. He was afraid she might be smirking in triumph at his hasty retreat.

He walked across campus to the building students called the Gothic. It was a looming haunted castle of gray stone, hence the name. He plodded up the stairs to the second floor. That's where his office was. If you could call it an office. It was a cramped cubicle, hardly more than a closet. He had to turn sideways and squeeze his way between the bookshelf and the desk to get to his swivel chair.

This was where the irony came in, or seemed to him to come in. Annoyed about Lori, and with his thoughts on a quiz he had to grade, the Maidenvale mansion murders had left his mind completely. The case was essentially over for him.

Then he started up his office computer.

Someone had sent an email to his university account. It was a public account anyone could access. The email's sender was anonymous—or that is, they called themselves "Secret Maidenvale," so the account had obviously been created for just this purpose. The email was blank, but there was an attachment to it. When Winter opened the attachment, he found several pages of text. After reading the text for a few moments, he realized with a shock what it was he was looking at. It was Mrs. Wasserman's diary. Marion Belle-Wasserman, as the news media called her. It was excerpts from her diary, or at least it had been written to seem as if it was.

For a few more moments, Winter continued trying to find the source of the mail. Who had sent it to him? Finally, though, his curiosity overwhelmed him. He began to read.

*The trouble is Agnes. She's one of those people people talk to, people trust. I've felt it myself. She'll be cleaning up in the kitchen and I'll wander by and start chatting, and pretty soon, if I don't stop myself, I'll find myself telling her things about me, about my feelings, about the family. I don't know exactly what it is about her. She is very sweet-natured. And there's that religious aspect to her. Not that she ever preaches or anything. I'd've thrown her out long ago if I thought she was trying to sell my children any of that nonsense. But she has that smiley, bright-eyed, otherworldly glow these Christian-types get sometimes. I find it a little spooky-kooky myself. But it does make you feel like she's trustworthy, like your secrets are safe with her, if only because she's already living in some fantasy of heaven in her head.*

*It's not that I'm jealous of her. Or maybe it is that I'm jealous. I don't know. I guess I'm a little jealous. I mean, Bobby just adores her. He'd much rather spend time with her than me. Which is actually fine as a practical matter. That is what she's here for, after all. I have so much on my plate right now between my art and the Foundation work. Add therapy, yoga, and tennis. I can't be on Mommy Call every second. But now she's drawn Lila in too. I hear them in Agnes's bedroom after Bobby goes down for the night. Gabbing away like old girlfriends and giggling and talking in low voices. As a result, Lila's not telling me anything. Which is worrisome because I think she's getting really serious about this boy.*

*Which is also fine. It really is. I mean, look, it's a first love. It's not like it's going to last forever. And at least it's got her past her whole maybe-I'm-a-boy-in-a-girl's-body phase. And really, he seems perfectly nice. Polite. Respectful. And Lila is sixteen, after all. I never expected her to remain a virgin forever. It's just, speaking as her mother, I think it's important she feels she can come to me with any questions she has. And God knows—literally only God knows—what Agnes is saying to her. I certainly don't want Lila to get the idea that sex is "sinful" in some way or that she should feel guilty. I had enough of that when I was young. For now, she seems happy enough. I just think a mother should be the one to hear about these things first, that's all.*

*Then there's all this about the boy's father. If it's true, which I'm not even sure it is. I certainly don't want to pry. I used to hate that when my mother did it to me. And I don't want to seem to hold Mateo's background against him. I'm totally fine with his being Latinx. That doesn't bother me at all. And I'm sure Lila finds it very exotic and exciting. It's just Cindy Tilden. She's driving me absolutely crazy. Every time we play tennis, every Tuesday and Thursday, the minute the four of us sit down for our salads afterward, Cindy starts in with the remarks. Dropping all these hints about what she keeps calling the "box place," the storage facility Mateo's father runs.*

*"It's not that I'm racist. I had a very close Latina friend in college," she always says.*

*I'll bet she did. So then why is it, ever since she heard Lila was dating Mateo, every time I see her now, she never fails to make a remark about the Hollow. The crime in the Hollow. The drugs in the Hollow. The so-called "Homeland Highway," which who knows if it even exists. I'm starting to dread our Tuesdays and Thursdays, honestly. Today, she just wouldn't stop. She "hears" from a "very reliable source" the Mexican gangsters use the "box place" to store their drugs before they sell them to whoever they sell them to. Although why Cindy Tilden of all people would have any inside knowledge about how Mexican gangsters operate, I don't know. Ray, her husband, is a lawyer, I guess, but he does bankruptcies. He's not exactly involved in the criminal underworld, although I guess he might know people who are . . .*

There seemed to be a break in the text here, a passage of time between one paragraph and the next. Hard to be sure because there were no dates. Either Mrs. Wasserman hadn't put the dates in, or whoever had sent these excerpts had taken them out. Assuming the whole thing was real.

It felt real to Winter. The voice—Mrs. Wasserman's voice—reminded him so much of his own mother's that he didn't think it could easily be faked. It had certainly engaged his full attention. He had read the passage staring into the computer screen as fervently as a voyeur at a bedroom window. So far, the text hadn't added anything to his knowledge of the murders, certainly nothing that made him question their resolution. What it did do, though, was bring him back into that house, emotionally speaking. It wasn't just Mrs. Wasserman's familiar voice that did it. It was her concerns as well: the day-to-day interplay of family life—all the things that night of gunfire had blown to pieces—"all the various relationships which bind one human being to another in mutual bonds," in Mary Shelley's words—the very things that had drawn Winter to Maidenvale in the first place. The diary made them all vivid in his imagination once again.

> *Big fight with Norm. Oh my Lord, what a blowout. Agnes again. I probably should have seen it coming. He wants me to fire her. Of course he does. The funny thing is, I almost did. In fact, if he hadn't asked me to, I'm pretty sure I would have. I mean, it isn't healthy, how intimate she's become with Lila. Lila hardly talks to me at all anymore. It's not right. And Bobby—he shows her his schoolwork before he shows it to me, if he ever shows it to me at all, which he hardly ever does. I was right on the verge of asking her to go. The only thing that stopped me—Well, first of all, I didn't want to seem to act out of jealousy. There's this sort of smile Agnes gives you when she thinks you're doing something wrong, but she isn't going to say it out loud. Actually, it's not even a smile. I don't know what it is. It's just some kind of thing that you can see in her, even if she tries to hide it behind that oh-so-sweet expression of hers. "Yes, Mrs. Wasserman. No, Mrs. Wasserman." But you can just tell she thinks you're doing something immoral.*

*So that held me back. Also, Bobby—he just loves her so much. Every time I thought about how he would look when I told him she was leaving, it held me back. I couldn't bear the thought of how it would break his little heart.*

*All the same, I think I would have done it. I was gearing up to do it. I'm pretty sure I would've gone through with it sooner rather than later. Then—Norm comes into my studio. Stands there, leaning in the door, making small talk. His version of small talk, which is mostly droning on about his psychological theories, or some paper he's writing. And then! Oh my God, then he started admiring my art! Are you kidding me? He never does that. Never. I never get anything from him about my art except his stupid jokes about how lucky I am he makes enough money to support my career. Har har har. So the minute he started in with "That's quite good, you know. Very gripping use of color," I was thinking to myself:* Okay, what's this about? What's does he want from me?

*"You know, I've been giving some thought to Agnes . . ."*

*I had to bite my tongue to keep from saying,* Oh, don't I know you have! You think I don't know?

*Did he think I didn't notice him finding excuses to go upstairs all the time? To wander by her room. Does he think I don't know about the other girls too? The flirty little texts he's always sending and so on. I don't even know where he finds them. Colleagues? I don't know. Not that he's ever done anything about it—not since that one time anyway. I don't think he wants to go through that again. But maybe Agnes was just too conveniently located for him.*

*Anyway, the minute he said, "I've been giving some thought to Agnes," I knew what was coming next. I knew the whole story.*

*"I don't think it's healthy for Bobby to get too attached to a secondary mother figure. After all, you're right here, available to him. He should be able to form other bonds without weakening his primary attachment to you. I really think we ought to consider making a change."*

*What set me off more than anything was the fact that he knew exactly what I'd been thinking, down to the language, the words I'd used in my own mind. He's a great psychologist, I'll give him that. No question about it. He could always read my thoughts, even when we were young. He saw I was jealous, and he was using that to manipulate me to get me to do what he wanted. It just really pissed me off.*

*So I couldn't bite my tongue anymore. I was painting. Looking at my easel. And my hand started shaking, I was so angry. I was gritting my teeth so hard I thought I'd break a molar. And I just blurted it out: "What's the matter, Norm? Did she turn you down?"*

*"I don't know what you're talking about." Huff, huff, huff, he goes. "I don't know what on earth you're talking about."*

*Like hell he didn't. One look at him and I could see I'd hit the bull's eye. Two can play the mind-reading game. I said, "Poor Norm. The sweet little Christian virgin stuck to her principles, didn't she? That's probably what turned you on about her in the first place. But if she's going to take all that chastity stuff seriously, that's no fun at all, is it?"*

*"That's a disgusting thing to say. What the hell is wrong with you?"*

*"Oh, you mean, because you're so faithful, how could such a thought ever cross my mind?"*

*"God, that was years ago, Marion! How long do I have to suffer for one mistake?"*

*On we went from there. Worst we've had in some time, more than a year probably. Bobby was in the house so we couldn't actually raise our voices, but we were hissing at each other like a pair of snakes. And now, I was defending her! Agnes. I was like: "You're the one who brought her home from the center in the first place. And now Bobby loves her. Everyone loves her. She stays, and that's final! And you can just stay away from her from now on! How about that?"*

*Poor Norm, if only he'd kept his pompous mouth shut, I'd have fired her on my own. But there was no way I was going to give him the satisfaction of punishing her for not sleeping with him.*

*He went off, huffing and puffing in that way he has, like he can't believe the world is such a vulgar place it would deny him—the mighty him!—whatever he wants. I didn't know whether to feel satisfied I'd really let him have it for once, or disappointed I couldn't fire Agnes now. I'm stuck with her.*

*I have such a headache. I need a freaking Xanax on the double.*

Winter sat back in his chair. There wasn't much room to move in that carton of an office, but he did his best to swivel back and forth as he considered what he'd just read. The diary seemed to him to change the nature of the crime somehow. It complicated matters if nothing else. It sketched in the family dynamics, colored the sketch with hot emotions. And so many of these new perspectives seemed to swirl around the nanny, didn't they? Or maybe the person who had sent him the diary excerpts—or wrote the excerpts, for all he knew—was trying to convince him that the nanny was at the heart of things.

It bothered him. The fact that Agnes Wilde hadn't escaped out the window had already been bothering him, and now it bothered him even more. Did she have a boyfriend? A father? Someone who might have gotten angry if he thought Wasserman was flirting with her?

He could see at a glance that the next paragraph on the page was the beginning of a new entry. He could see it was an important entry too. Dramatic. On the one hand, he was reluctant to start reading it because he knew it would drag him right back into this story—like a pair of hands bursting from the monitor and hauling him head first into the text. On the other hand, he knew there was no possibility he could resist.

So he read on.

*Oh my God, what have I done? Have I done it? Have I really? Was that really me? Or did I dream the whole thing?*

*No, that was no dream. Oh my God. Dreams don't feel like that. Not my dreams. Not even my best dreams come anywhere close. It was like one of the books in my secret stash. It could have come right off their pages. It felt like I feel when I'm reading one of them too—like 'This is so wrong but I don't care.'*

*I don't know whether I wish I could make it never have happened or wish I could make it happen again and again.*

*I want it to happen again. That's the truth. It's like a door that has suddenly opened and let the light in. Like a window letting in fresh air. But it's too crazy. Too dangerous. What if we get caught? The children. Oh my God. I don't even want to think about it.*

*I've always known he was attracted to me. At the Foundation meetings, he was always finding excuses to come over and chat. He'd start with some sort of business then kind of linger for some small talk. All the while, his eyes meeting mine, looking right into mine, so that I knew exactly what he was thinking, and it made me hot under the collar. I could feel him watching me whenever I walked into Menucci's too. The truth is: I started going to Menucci's sometimes just to give him an eyeful. I didn't want to admit to myself that that's why I was going there, but let's face it, how many truffle gift crates can one woman buy?*

*Then today . . . I still can't believe this is real. It happened so fast. Like a lightning bolt out of the clear blue sky. I stepped out of the store and he must have been waiting for me. He drove right up to the curb beside me and opened the door. He didn't even say anything. He barely even looked at me. And I didn't even think. I just got in.*

*He drove off and we didn't say a word, either of us. He just headed out of town. Out on Route 7 with nothing around us but trees.*

*Finally I got over my shock. I asked him: "Where are we going?"*

*He glanced over at me. Gave me that smile of his. Like when we would be talking at one of the fundraisers and he would look in my eyes and give me that smile. His mouth doesn't even move. Just his eyes smile. It went right through me. It made my knees weak.*

*"Does it matter?" he said.*

*I sat back and shut up. My eyes must have been the size of saucers at that point. My heart was beating like a jackhammer. I kept saying to myself:* This isn't happening. This isn't going to happen. *It was too crazy. Like a movie or something. But it just went on, one moment after another, not stopping. Just like one of my books. I could almost hear the words, like someone was narrating:*

He didn't say a word. He took her into his arms. He leaned down and kissed her, his hot lips hungry for hers . . .

*He took me to this house, one of the summer houses. The owners were gone for the season, but they'd left him the key. He even had the garage door remote. He pulled into the garage so the car wouldn't be visible from the street. Then we sat in silence as the garage door rolled down again. And I was thinking, This is it. My last chance. If I go into the house with him, I'm lost.*

*"What are we going to do?" I sounded exactly like one of the women in the books.*

*He didn't say a word. He just leaned over and kissed me (his hot lips hungry for mine!).*

*And that, ladies and gentlemen, was the end of that. All my resistance drained out of me with that one kiss.*

*I keep playing it over in my mind, every moment of it. Like flashbacks in a movie. It was perfect. I couldn't have made it up. The authors of those books couldn't have written it so perfectly. We got out and he held the house door open for me. I stepped out of the garage into a hallway and he came in behind me. I heard him close the door and I turned to face him and he took me into his arms. Lifted me up against the wall. Hard but not rough. Not rough like in the books. I mean, that's fine on the page, but in real life . . . well, how would I hide the bruises, for one thing? But it was hard and he was totally in control the whole time and it was, I can't lie, absolutely thrilling.*

*I'm feeling it now, just thinking about it, writing about it. My voice, his name, in my mind. Over and over. Like I whispered it to him then.*

Winter closed his eyes and pinched the bridge of his nose. He felt . . . well, he felt embarrassed for the woman more than anything. Not just for the operatic emotion, but for the purple, fantastical prose as well. It was like Mateo's poetry: sentimental, false. Mrs. Wasserman was a sophisticated woman, clearly, and yet she could not separate the reality of what she'd done from the cheesy bodice rippers she read in secret. The writing made him cringe.

But if the diary entry was real—and he believed it was real—it added even more layers of complexity to the murders. Or did it? After all, Mrs. Wasserman could have had an affair and still have been shot to death by an angry Mateo Hernandez, distraught over his breakup with Lila. Norman Wasserman could have flirted with the nanny and it still might have been Mateo who killed him. Why would Mateo have blown his brains out if he hadn't done the crime? Unless it was fear that he would be wrongly accused. Or maybe he had stumbled on the bodies and been suicidal with grief . . .

Winter dropped back in his chair. He let his hand fall to his thigh. He was frustrated. Exasperated. He had no answers. He was just making up stories now. How could he know if any of them were true or what was true?

He couldn't. He couldn't know anything.

Except one thing. There was one thing he knew.

He . . . had to go back to Maidenvale.

# 10

A young woman, slender as cigarette smoke, drifted toward him across the lawn. A breeze blew, bearing the first biting chill of winter. An armada of cumulous clouds sailed across the blue sky. Winter could picture the smoke-thin girl borne away on the breeze and vanishing. Yet on she came.

He stood from the park bench to greet her. As she neared him, the late sun emerged and struck her slantwise. He had a moment to take stock of her. A pretty, sullen teen, thoughtful and accustomed to admiration—that was his assessment. Dressed with a studiously careless sensuality in white jeans and a white T-shirt and a white windbreaker. Her hands half hung from her front pockets with that peculiarly teenage blend of defiance and insecurity. Girls with youth and beauty were like boys with fast cars, Winter thought: they had more power than they knew what to do with.

"Savannah Green," he greeted her with a nod.

It had been easy for him to find her. She had given brief, tearful interviews to both a local website and a TV news show based in the city. Both website and TV show had called her Lila's best friend. He had tracked down her cell number and phoned her. Used his usual approach, nonsensical but somehow convincing: I'm a professor doing a study of the case. The clincher was when he told her this: "You mentioned in your interviews that you couldn't believe Mateo would ever hurt Lila. The thing is, Savannah: I don't believe it either."

She agreed to meet him in this public park near the Briars school. He did not ask if she would tell her parents. He very much suspected she had not.

"So what is this report you're writing?" she asked him.

He gave her the usual nonsense. "A criminological study . . ." and so on. He assured her he wouldn't use her name unless she gave permission. He knew it didn't matter. She wanted to talk, so she would. He hurried on to his questions before she had a chance to think too much about it.

"You were Lila's friend," he said.

"Yeah. And Mateo's, too. I was friends with both of them."

"I'm sorry for your loss."

Her narrow shoulders rose and fell. "Yeah, it sucks."

"And you're convinced Mateo couldn't have done it?"

She sighed, gazing glumly across the green grass to where a young mother was on her knees, encouraging her toddler to take steps: a little girl in pink down, rollicking like a wind-up toy out of the shade of a red-leafed maple.

Winter studied Savannah's profile. Blonde hair tied back. Blue eyes full of teen angst. The strong features of a marble Venus. He was touched by her youth. She was just a child still really. Wealthy. Protected. No real experience beyond the "leafy lanes" and "classic homes" of Maidenvale. But these murders were real. The tragedy was sudden and very real. He could see her pain ran deep. She would live with this forever.

"I don't know what to think anymore," she said. "The police say it was Mateo. And he killed himself so . . . I mean, I guess it must have been him. It was just so—not like him though."

Mateo wasn't a macho man, she said. Everyone thought he was because he was on the team. The team—they were rough-and-tumble, push-and-shove boys—nice enough guys, most of them, but they all had to put on a show for one another, big voices, fake fights, leaning on each other's shoulders to gape at the girls so that the girls had to pretend to look severe as they brushed past them. Mateo played along with all that, Savannah said, but that wasn't him, not really, that wasn't who he wanted to be at all.

"He read poetry. He read Shakespeare. No one knew it except Lila."

A corner of Winter's mouth quirked at that—at *No one knew except Lila*. Because, of course, whatever Lila knew, Savannah also knew, being Lila's best friend.

"He read Shakespeare to her in the caves," Savannah said. "He said they were like Romeo and Juliet."

Which explained the balcony scene, Winter thought.

"He even wrote his own poetry," the girl went on. "He was always giving Lila poems he wrote about her. Reciting them to her. That's what I mean. He wasn't the violent type. A lover not a fighter. That was the guy he wanted to be anyway. That was the side of him that swept Lila off her feet."

"I understand Lila was experiencing some—I don't know what you call it—doubts about her identity." Winter chose the words as carefully as he could.

But Savannah waved the matter off with a dismissive noise—*Pfft*. "I take it you don't have any teenage daughters," she said. "No sister or anything."

Winter smiled another quirky smile. "I don't."

She shook her head. "Stuff like that: it's nothing. It's just girl-world. Every crazy breeze that blows, girls try it on for size. Like dress-up when we're little. Must be some sort of evolutionary thing."

"No doubt. If young women couldn't be persuaded to believe the highly improbable, the human race would die out," said Winter.

She gave a gruff laugh. "That must be it. Anyway, the minute Lila saw the way Mateo looked at her, all that crap was over. I mean, she was *all* in." She came down heavy on the word *all* to make sure Winter got the point.

Lila and Mateo spent their afternoons together in the woods, she said. Sometimes they snuck out there at night as well. Sometimes even in the dark hours before sunrise. Tangling in the duff. Long, tender kisses. Confessing their love for one another, then finally making love in the caverns. It was the first time for both of them.

They lay in one another's arms, the cave lit by candles, the shadows of the outcroppings dancing on the rock walls. She told him all her family troubles. He poured out his heart to her, his sensitive heart, his anguished heart.

"What were her family troubles?" Winter asked.

"Oh, the usual. Mom-Dad fights. Dr. Wasserman volunteered once a week at the ComCent, free therapy for the folks from the Hollow. That's where he found Agnes, Bobby's nanny. Mrs. Wasserman kept accusing him of shtupping her."

"Was he? Shtupping."

She wagged her head. "Doubtful. Agnes was pretty religious and straight arrow. But Dr. Wasserman—he definitely had eyes."

"For girls, you mean."

"Like—young girls."

"Really. You, for instance?"

"Oh yeah," said Savannah.

"Did he ever . . . ?"

She laughed before he could finish. "Nuh uh. My dad's a big-time lawyer. Lila's dad couldn't afford that mistake."

"But he looked at you."

"If eyes were fingers, he'd have stripped me naked. They were all over me."

Winter made a low noise, something like a growl. *Girl-world*, he thought. A jungle of creepy predators, with them the prey.

"What about Mateo?" he asked. "He was anguished, you said. What was he anguished about?"

"Oh . . . I think it was his dad mostly," she told him. "He'd gotten himself involved with some of these drug dealers who come up here now."

"Eduardo?"

"Mr. Hernandez, yeah."

Every Saturday, Mateo and his brother helped his father at the storage facility. He would see the gangsters coming in. The leader first—Del Rey, his name was. A big man, powerfully built, with a fat, round face and short cropped hair. Then his two muscle-bound, beer-bellied thugs would enter, just behind and flanking him. Their necks and their bare arms were all blue with tattoos. They all had murder in their eyes, and in their sneering smiles: a taste for murder, the way some people have a taste for sweets or alcohol, always thinking about it, watching for a chance to indulge.

Mateo remembered when he first saw them, when he first realized that his father hid their drugs and guns for them. He had been in the office on the second floor one Saturday, doing the paperwork. His desk faced the interior, so when he lifted his eyes from the computer, he could see through the glass of the long window in front of him and look down on the aisles of lockers. He saw the three gangsters there. They were surrounding his father, standing too close, their smiles threatening. His father was protesting something, but even at that distance, Mateo could see he was afraid of them. Del Rey sneered down at him. He lifted a wad of cash out of the vest pocket of his suede rancher jacket. He tossed the money at Mr. Hernandez's feet and pointed at it. Mateo's father had to bend down before the gangster to pick the money up, like he was bowing to him. Mateo watched through the window. The two other gangsters grinned at one another across his father's bent back. Mateo felt a black hole open at the center of his chest, a canyon emptiness black with rage and humiliation.

Later, when the thugs were gone, Mr. Hernandez trudged upstairs and came into the office. His eyes met Mateo's, a long, silent exchange. Mateo wanted to speak. He was desperate to say a comforting word, but no words came to him. Finally, his father looked away, ashamed. He left the office in silence.

"Did Mateo ever consider telling the police about all this?" Winter asked Savannah.

The teen made a face. "Apparently that wasn't an option. Apparently the top detective in town moonlighted as Mr. Hernandez's security guard. Mateo said he didn't do anything, but Mr. Hernandez had to pay him or else the facility would be vandalized."

"A protection racket," Winter said aloud. To himself he was thinking: Steph Breach was right. Inspector Strange's all-loving social conscience was just a mask for his corruption.

"The cop already knew about the drugs and guns," said Savannah. "Mateo's dad had to give him even more money to keep him quiet about that."

Winter sighed and Savannah fell silent. They both gazed off across the little park. The young mother under the red maple was changing her toddler's diaper now, babbling down at the child as the child reached up to touch the mother's face.

When Savannah turned to Winter again, he was suddenly struck by a clear sense of the woman she would become: honest, steadfast, maybe even wise. The young man who could persuade her of the improbable would be a lucky kid, he thought.

"Mateo cried when he told Lila about his dad," she said. "They were in the caverns together. Lila held him in her arms and he cried about his father. That's a big sort of thing in girl-world. It's a big moment when something like that happens with your guy. That's what I mean about Mateo though. He had that sensitive heart, that poetic soul. Lila loved that about him. He wanted—to be pure. He wanted their love to be pure. She wanted that too. They didn't want to be corrupt like their parents."

"And yet they quarreled, didn't they?" Winter said. "They broke up. Just before the murders."

Savannah made that dismissive noise again: *Pfft.* "They didn't break up. I mean, they did, but it wouldn't have lasted. It was just . . ."

"A lover's spat," said Winter.

"Like that. Right."

"What set it off?"

Savannah rolled her eyes, shook her head to convey to him what nonsense it all was. "We play this game, the kids at Briars, we all play this Opti game. Opticon. It's VR. Virtual Reality. You know, like three dimensional."

"*Ring of Ventura.* I've heard of it."

"Right. So we all have characters. And you can clan up together to fight the monster bots, or your clans can fight each other and steal loot—treasure and powers and stuff. Anyway, there was this one guy, Pike he called himself, that was his handle, his character name. He was leveled way up, very aggressive. And he kept ganking Mateo, right?" Reading Winter's grown-up confusion, she added helpfully, "He'd use his superior skills to kill off Mateo's character and plunder his loot. Every time Mateo made some progress, Pike would send him back to noob level. Then while Mateo was gearing up again, Pike would try to enlist Lila—in the game, she called herself Princess Lily—Pike would try to enlist her into his clan."

"So Pike was flirting with her."

"Exactly. It's like: even in fantasy land, you're still in high school. You know?"

Winter gave a short laugh at that. He was beginning to really like this girl.

She went on. "So finally there was this boss everyone was hung up on, big monster, blah, blah, blah, whatever. It doesn't matter. The important thing is that Lila agreed to join Pike's clan so they could take him out. When Mateo heard she was going on a mission with Pike, he went ballistic. I mean, the thing is, he was so in love with her. He thought they were living in a poem together. Romeo and Juliet. She was supposed to be his princess and he was supposed to be her knight in shining armor. He felt totally betrayed."

"Because it wasn't just fighting this superbot monster. He was afraid Lila was responding to Pike's flirtation."

"Exactly."

"Was she?"

Savannah lifted her willowy shoulders. Her hands rose into the air and fell onto her knees. "Who the hell knows? It's girl-world, right. Probably Lila didn't even know herself. It wasn't her smartest move, romantically speaking, that's for sure. Anyone could have told her how Mateo was going to react but . . ."

She shrugged again. She was wholly engaged with her story now, gossiping about her friends with Winter as if she had forgotten the bloodshed in which the affair had ended. "I'll tell you what I think it was," she continued. "I think what Mateo loved about Lila—one of the things he loved about being with her—was that he could let down his guard with her. Put off the whole soccer-man macho routine and be himself and show his sensitive side. Cry in her arms about his father and all that. But, see, in guy-world that leaves you vulnerable. Because if the girl is like 'There, there, sweetheart,' then she cheats with some tougher specimen, now you're gimped, right? I mean, we girls definitely do that. We tell a guy to show us his softer side then we dump him because he's not man enough. So, when this Pike came along—he was this big rough swordsman with clanking armor and power-ups coming out of his ears—and Mateo's character . . ."

"Prince Romeo."

"Yeah. Sir Romeo. How'd you know that?"

"Lucky guess," Winter said.

"Well, Pike had sent Sir Romeo back to wooden-sword level, so when Princess Lily clanned up with Pike, it made Romeo . . ." Savannah gestured.

"Look gimped," Winter said, doing his best to echo the gamer slang.

"Exactly." Savannah gave him a frank look, one corner of her mouth lifting. "Guy-world, right? Being a guy may be simple, but that doesn't make it easy."

Winter lifted his chin in agreement. He might be ancient in this child's eyes—he was not far off from forty after all—but he was not without his adventures in both guy-world and the more mysterious girl-world. He understood what she was telling him.

It was a brutal scenario really. Mateo had watched his father unmanned by sadistic punks. Maybe his addiction to violent porn was a way of working through his helpless rage. But that only made him sick of himself. He felt himself becoming corrupt and small and squirrely. He longed for a pure romantic love to elevate him to the level of the poetry he read. Then, this Pike character came clanking along and stole both his manhood and his perfect princess . . .

"Do we have any idea who this Pike really was?" he asked Savannah.

"Well, we don't know for sure—I mean, he masked himself but . . . I think I've got a pretty good idea." Color rose up in her cheeks as she spoke. Her eyes filled. Her friends—who had seemed alive to her while she was gossiping about them—were gone again and her grief had returned. "There's this guy, Pete Thomson. He was the star of the team before Mateo came. A total jerk. He swore to me it wasn't him but I told him if I ever found out it was, I was gonna slap the crap out of him in front of the whole school." She choked on those last words and quickly knuckled the corners of first one eye, then the other.

Winter sat without speaking for a moment, gazing into the middle distance, trying to compute whether Mateo's video game humiliation, the argument with Lila, their breakup, all underscored by his father's subjection to the gangsters—if all that would have been enough to move Mateo to an act of violence as savage as the one that wiped out the Wassermans and Agnes Wilde. It was no use. He could feel the boy's pain, but he didn't know him well enough to conjure the possible depths of his reaction. Anyway, his thoughts kept interrupting themselves with other thoughts, thoughts of the gangsters—who, after all, traded in violent savagery—and Strange, who was as dirty as Steph Breach said he was and something of a violent character himself. Lots of suspects. Complexity upon complexity.

"Is this really for some kind of study you're doing?" Savannah asked him suddenly.

The question brought Winter out of his own meditations. He raised his eyes to hers. He was touched again by her youth. The tone of her voice now was not the worldly-wise tone she had been using. She was just a kid now, talking to someone old enough to be her father. Winter didn't have it in him to lie to her anymore.

"I want to get to the truth of what happened in that house, Savannah," he told her.

Her blue eyes moved over his face, studying him, reading him. "Yeah, but why?"

"It's hard to explain. It's something I do. Something I have to do. A sort of therapy, I guess. It makes me feel I can . . ."

When he hesitated, looking for the right words, wondering if any words would tell the story, Savannah said: "Make sense of things."

"Yes. That's it. It makes me feel I can make sense of things."

The teenager dug her hands into the pockets of her windbreaker. She shivered in a fresh, cold breeze. She gazed at the mother under the maple tree. The mother was now loading her toddler back into her stroller.

"I wish I could," Savannah said. "Make sense of things, I mean."

Winter watched her for a long time as she walked away, her wisp of a body, the wind in her hair, her narrow shoulders hunched against the autumn chill. His solitude sat heavy on him. His empty apartment. His lonely life. The remembered image of Madeleine Uno came into his mind, that moment when he had lain on her sofa with his head in her lap, that moment when he had realized he was losing control of his mission, losing control of his heart. The thought of telling Margaret Whitaker the rest of that story made him ill with dread. In the darker recesses of his mind, there were gunshots echoing, gunshots from the Wasserman house and gunshots from his own past, bullets severing "all the various relationships which bind one human being to another in mutual bonds."

Off in the distance now, hands in her pockets, Savannah broke into a run. She was soon a small figure, barely visible to him.

He drew a long breath. Stood up off the bench. His heart ached—for Savannah and for Mateo and for Lila, and for all the young, including his younger self.

He turned away and started walking back to his car.

# 11

Winter drove his Jeep to the edge of town. He was about to pull onto the highway and head for home. But as the ramp drew near, he pulled the SUV into a U-turn and pointed himself back toward Maidenvale. Suspicions and scenarios were playing through his head obsessively. So many questions unanswered. Who was this Pike from the 3D video game? Who was Mrs. Wasserman's lover? What was Mr. Wasserman's relationship to Agnes Wilde? Had Mateo or his father done anything to anger the mob? Or were all his questions just a way of keeping the mystery alive for his own neurotic reasons? Perhaps it was all just as it seemed, and Mateo had murdered his girlfriend and her family, then murdered himself in his cave.

Whatever the truth, Winter realized he was sunk too deep in the mystery to leave just yet. The whole story had become psychic quicksand for him. It was drawing him under.

He set his GPS for the Maidenvale Community Center. He drove there with a low fire of mission burning in his belly. The moment he reached the spot, though, the low fire of mission died as if a bucket of water had been thrown on it. Smoke; hiss; it was out completely. He let out an ugly curse. He quickly guided his Jeep around a corner as a way of ducking out of sight.

The center was out beyond the town's upmarket main drag, out in the open territory where the malls and gas stations were. There was a little enclave of government buildings there and shops set on a small side road parallel with the four-lane. There was a cement block of a city hall, a brick courthouse with concrete pilasters for a facade, a brick police station, and the large white building behind it—that was the Community Center. Across from these stood a tennis store, a bookshop, and a gourmet supermarket, Menucci's. That, Winter remembered, was where Mrs. Wasserman had met her lover.

Winter pulled to the curb half a block away. He killed the engine and sat a moment, staring through the windshield, trying to strategize. He had a lot of business to do in this place. He wanted to go into the Community Center to ask about Wasserman. He wanted to go into Menucci's to see if he could smoke out Marion Wasserman's paramour. And he wanted to go into the police station and convince Officer Ann Farmingham to slip him some of the forensics on Mateo and the other victims.

But more than anything, he wanted to get all that done without being spotted by Inspector Strange. Not that he was afraid of Strange, but—all right, he had to face it: he actually was. He'd rather tangle with a straight-up villain than a bad man with a badge.

He knew now why Strange had reacted with such anger to his presence. As Maidenvale's top detective and a moonlighting security guard, the cop had seen the rise of organized crime here as an opportunity to rake in some serious coin in bribes and protection money. The last thing he wanted was for some errant college professor to come snooping around and ruin a good thing.

Sitting in his Jeep, Winter actually considered abandoning the whole enterprise. After all, he kept telling himself, it was none of his business anyway.

But what the hell? He knew there was no real chance he'd convince himself to go. Eventually he climbed out of the SUV and hiked around the corner to approach the Community Center on foot from the rear. He hoped that would keep him out of Strange's eyeline.

Inside, the place was a maze of hallways and open spaces, all of them busy. There was a gymnasium with noisy kids playing basketball and running laps. There was a swimming pool with women stroking up and down the lanes. There was a theater with teenagers rehearsing a play. A room full of children at desks doing schoolwork of some kind. And so on. Most of the people using the facilities were Latino. Most of the people running the place were white. It was the middle-class folks of Maidenvale providing services for their poorer neighbors from the Hollow.

Winter read the arrows on the hallway walls: arrows of blue construction paper with writing in marker. *After-School* this way. *Pre-School* that way. *Health. Counseling.* He followed the signs for counseling.

There was an old lady volunteering at the reception desk in the waiting room. She told him the name of the woman who ran the counseling department: Gwendolyn Lord. She pointed her out to him as she walked past. Winter intercepted her as she moved from one office to another.

He liked this Gwendolyn Lord—liked her on sight. He liked her so much that his eyes flicked automatically to her left hand. He was disappointed to see the wedding band there. She was about his age, maybe a bit younger, closer to thirty than forty. Erect and serene and regal of bearing, but with a wicked gleam of humor in her green eyes. She was small and slim with a graceful figure. She had elfin features and brown hair to her shoulders. Winter liked it all and even liked her style of dress—a white blouse and a wine-colored skirt—pearl earrings and a small gold cross at her throat. There was just something about her, something elevated and ladylike, that spoke to him. It really was a shame about that wedding band, he thought.

She was not the sort of person you could con—he could see that at a glance. So he tried the direct approach.

"I'd like to ask you about Agnes Wilde and Norman Wasserman," he said.

She took her time looking him up and down. "What are you, a reporter?"

"I'm an English professor."

She rolled her tongue into her cheek. The glint of wit in her eyes grew brighter. "Perhaps you'd better explain yourself."

He asked to use her computer for the purpose. She led him into her office. It was a modest box featuring a cheap desk of engineered wood. There was a view of the parking lot through a small window and photographs between the textbooks on the shelves. Two of the photos were of children, a boy and a girl, both grinning happily. When Winter saw them, he decided Gwendolyn Lord was probably unlikely to divorce her husband, ditch her children, and run away with him. A shame.

He used her computer to call up a story about himself. It was on an obscure site, but of course he knew how to find it. The story outlined his role in solving a particularly nasty kidnapping case. He sat across the desk from her and watched her read it. He admired the way the light played on the waves of her hair.

"I have a strange habit of mind," he told her. "Stories that don't make sense obsess me. Sometimes if I think about them just the right way, they suddenly do make sense. Then I can be helpful."

After another moment, Gwendolyn Lord looked up at him. "You're talking about the Wasserman murders." And when he gestured yes: "You don't think Mateo did it." He made the same gesture, lowering his chin slightly. "Well, you're almost certainly right about that."

Surprised, Winter straightened in his chair. "Am I?"

"Oh yes. I think so anyway. I could be wrong."

"You knew him, though."

"Mateo? Yes, I did. He and his brother and sister, Sara, came here for the after-school program. We tutor kids, help them with their English. A lot of it's just babysitting for working parents."

"And you—what? Don't think Mateo was the murdering kind?"

"More or less. Could he wipe out an entire family like that? Almost certainly not."

"Were you aware he was addicted to violent pornography?"

"I wasn't," she said. "But I'm not surprised. The influx of illegals brought the gangs, the gangs brought the drug trade, and that sort of thing corrupts everything it touches. There were rumors Mateo's father was involved. When a boy's father fails to fulfill his role like that, his moral role, I mean . . . Well, it's not a good thing obviously. I could see the effect on all three kids. I don't think I'll say any more than that. Before I became director, I worked as a therapist here. I still do sometimes. The things people tell me while I'm in that role are strictly confidential. Anyway, I thought you wanted to know about Agnes Wilde and Norman Wasserman."

It wasn't just her looks he liked, he decided. He liked the way she spoke too. Directly but with an undertone of—what was it?—*kindness*, he thought. And integrity too. Plus that wry humor. He felt she reminded him of someone, and then it came to him that she reminded him of the teen he'd met in the park earlier, Savannah Green. She was the sort of woman Savannah Green might one day grow up to be, if she was very lucky and very good. An odd little thought came into his head. What if, in pulling that U-turn at the highway ramp, he had somehow crossed a time warp and this actually was Savannah grown up . . . ?

All this went through his mind in a moment, and one other thing too—something he quickly filed away to tell Margaret Whitaker during their next session. Back home, back in the coffee shop, back before he had come upon these murders, he had wished he could see everything with the intensity, the clarity with which he saw women. For a moment, he actually had seen everything like that and now—now he was seeing women themselves with a new intensity.

He suppressed a smile, thinking: girl-world. He had entered girl-world.

"I understand they met here," he said. "Wasserman and Agnes."

"Yes, that's right. Agnes was working in the after-school program and Dr. Wasserman hired her away to be a nanny for his son."

"Was that the extent of their relationship?"

Gwendolyn responded at once, speaking flatly, without intonation. "What do you mean?"

Now Winter did smile. He lowered his eyes. "I was told Wasserman flirted with her, maybe even propositioned her."

"I didn't witness that."

"But you knew about it."

"I couldn't say."

Winter looked up quickly. "You mean you were seeing her. Agnes. You were Agnes's therapist."

He watched as Gwendolyn took a long breath, choosing her words carefully. "Agnes Wilde grew up here, in the Hollow actually, before, you know . . ."

"Before it was Latino."

"Before the demographic shift, yes. She had an unhappy home, and she left at seventeen."

"So that's seven or eight years ago."

"Yes, that sounds about right."

The therapist went on. Listening to her, Winter thought, was like watching someone tip toe through a minefield. She shared the facts that were generally known while gingerly stepping around the buried secrets she couldn't tell.

Agnes Wilde had run away as a teenager. She was escaping alcoholic parents, a shambolic home life, and—Winter deduced—some kind of abuse. She headed for what Gwendolyn described as "the big city" and what Winter figured was either Chicago or New York. Chicago was closer, so it was probably that. Of course, a young, inexperienced girl like Agnes in a place like Chi-town—it was bound to go badly. Gwendolyn wouldn't say exactly how badly it went, but Winter looked in those green eyes of hers and thought: very badly.

"Agnes was young and pretty and men preyed on her," Gwendolyn said.

About two years ago, Agnes had come home—or as Gwendolyn put it, "washed up back here." She was broken but determined to change and put her life in order. "She came to the center for counseling," Gwendolyn said. Winter filled in the rest: she came for counseling with Gwendolyn Lord.

"I arranged with my church to find her housing," Gwendolyn went on. "And arranged with the center to give her work."

"I understand she was quite religious," said Winter. "Was that your influence?"

"She became religious, yes. Through the church. It was a great help to her. God helped her make peace with her past."

Winter noted that she hadn't answered his question, but he let it go. He knew she was leaving the story sketchy on purpose, but so what? He didn't think he really needed the details. It was a common enough story, easy to imagine.

"And then Dr. Wasserman hired her—about how long ago?" he asked.

"Oh, maybe six months, a little less. He used to do volunteer work here, once or twice a week."

Winter shifted in his chair. He took a nice long look into those witty and yet very serious eyes across from him. He had the feeling that Gwendolyn Lord was willing him to hear telepathically what she could not say aloud.

"Used to," he said. "He used to volunteer here. How long ago did he stop?"

"About two months ago."

His eyes remained on hers, hers on his. He was thinking hard. What was the next right question?

"What else happened two months ago?" he asked finally.

Bingo. That was it. He could see the relief in Gwendolyn's expression—relief that he had hit upon a question she was willing to answer.

She responded deadpan: "Our old director retired and I was appointed in his place."

Now they were both silent, both watching each other intently. If they were moving through a minefield where secrets were the mines, they had both just pulled up short of an explosion. But the truth was plain: Gwendolyn Lord had come to power and she had thrown Dr. Wasserman out.

"Ms. Lord . . ." Winter said.

"It's Mrs. Lord, if you don't mind," said Gwendolyn. "Or Gwendolyn or Gwen is fine. In any case, I'm not at liberty to discuss the private business of the center."

"Yes, of course. Understood." Again, Winter groped for a direction. "Can you tell me though . . . when Wasserman left, were the police involved?"

THE HOUSE OF LOVE AND DEATH

"Absolutely not. There was nothing to take to the police."

"No evidence you mean."

Gwendolyn didn't answer, not right away. Winter sensed he was reaching the limit of her willingness to talk to him at all.

"I take it you've spoken to the police here," she said finally.

He nodded. "Inspector Strange."

"Inspector Strange," she repeated. That gleam of droll humor came back into her eyes—and Winter would not have been surprised to learn there was a similar gleam in his own. There was only so much they could tell one another in silence, but they managed to infuse the name of Inspector Strange with as much of the unspoken truth as they could.

"I think we better end there," said Gwendolyn Lord. She stood up so that Winter felt he had to stand as well. The two of them faced each other across the desk a lingering moment. All the truth that remained silent seemed, to Winter's mind at least, to fill the space between them.

"I feel there's something I haven't communicated to you," said Gwendolyn then. "About Agnes Wilde." Winter waited. "She was—special. A special person. A special girl. She'd been through great trials, terrible darkness. Not only did she find her way back to the light, but she became a light for other people. Everyone who knew her could feel it—or everyone who was capable of feeling it could feel it, at least."

She paused, dissatisfied. She clearly felt she wasn't getting her message across to him. She thought about it a moment. A smile played at the corner of her mouth. She said: "She was fearless, too. Here's a story. I can tell you this because she told it to all of us here. We all had a laugh about it. It wasn't a secret. There was a—what do you call it?—a peeper—a voyeur. A boy. Out at the Wasserman house. Some local teenager or something, I don't really know. But he was coming around at night, standing out in the backyard with binoculars, watching Agnes undress. Her room was at the top of the Wasserman's house, you know, so she had never bothered to draw the curtains because who would be out there? But one night, the family was away. The parents had taken the boy somewhere—Bobby—and Lila was on a date with Mateo. Agnes happened to glance out her window and there was this boy with his binoculars, watching her. Well, the boy saw her spot him and he ran off. But Agnes figured he'd come back one night when he got his courage up. She watched for him. Sure enough, one day, she spotted him, out in the dark with his binoculars. She pretended she hadn't seen him. Drifted away out of view. Went tearing downstairs, then burst out into the backyard. Well, he was still there, waiting for her to return to the window. Startled by her sudden appearance, he took off—and Agnes, she took right off after him. She chased him clean across Tulipwood, from one lawn to the next, down one street to the next, till they hit the fence and she had him cornered. So Agnes—she was just a little bit of a thing, hardly any bigger than I am. But she walked right up to the kid and she just smacked him, one good smack on each cheek. Whack. Whack. And then, she wagged her finger in his face. And she said, 'Now—you be good!' And she turned her back on him and walked away and left him there."

Gwendolyn Lord laughed. It was a musical trill, delightfully girlish. It made Winter laugh a little as well.

Then Gwendolyn sighed and the sadness of it all came over her again. "What happened to Agnes was a great tragedy," she said. "Well, of course what happened to the whole family but . . . What happened to Agnes, particularly after the life she'd lived and what she had made of it, what she would have become—well, it seemed terribly unjust. But then that's the world, isn't it?" Again, she paused to choose her words carefully. "I know you'll understand me when I tell you I had very little hope of justice being done for her at all and . . ."

She ended with a gesture. Winter understood: like Steph Breach, she had agreed to talk to him because she did not trust Inspector Strange to find the truth.

"Thank you," he said. "Mrs. Lord."

She gave him a small, sad smile—a smile that made him wonder what tragedy had given her this grace she had, this air of grace on an unjust planet. After all, if Agnes Wilde was special because she had found a path out of darkness, what was she, Gwendolyn, who had shown Agnes the way?

He glanced at her ring finger again. *Lucky bastard*, he thought.

Gwendolyn offered him a delicate white hand. He took it—and choked down a sound of surprise as she pressed something secretly into his palm. Their eyes met again. Without looking at whatever she'd given him, he slipped it discreetly into his pants pocket.

He was thinking: curiouser and curiouser this story grew. A pair of Romeo and Juliet lovers in a divided town. A corrupt psychologist doing God knew what. A wealthy wife having an affair with God knows who. A nanny with a past. All dead.

Again, he felt the panic and terror of that night. Imagined the gunshots. *Boom, boom, boom, boom.* A family dead. The nanny dead. Who was left? The wife's lover. A father involved with gangsters. A cop on the take. A security guard with a grudge. A high school student—or someone—who broke up the lovers in a video game.

What the hell happened here? What the hell happened in that house?

Gwendolyn Lord seemed to read these troubled thoughts of his.

"This was a good town once," she told him gently. "Be careful, Professor."

# 12

Late that night, near midnight, back in his hometown, Winter found himself standing more or less miserably in a dark alley. There was music playing faintly—the usual thumping modern cacophony. Hatred for such stuff burned in Winter's heart with a hard, gem-like flame. The air stank of rotten fish, which he enjoyed about as much as he enjoyed modern music.

The dirty brick wall to his right was the wall of a restaurant. That's where the music was coming from. It was probably also where the fish came from—the fish in the dumpster directly in front of him. The concrete wall to his left was the wall of a parking garage. Someone had scrawled obscenities on it. Of course they had.

It was cold too. Winter wasn't dressed for it. He stood with his hands balled up into fists, his fists shoved deep into the pockets of his windbreaker. He had his shoulders hunched around his ears and his ivy cap pulled low on his brow. All the same, he was beginning to shiver. He stared anxiously at the mouth of the alley. There was light there, the light from the street. An occasional late pedestrian passed. A car or two. Nothing else.

His mood was sour. His day in Maidenvale had ended badly. After sharing the town's silent secrets with Gwendolyn Lord, he found the murders in the Tulipwood mansion had taken on fresh life in his imagination. Mrs. Wasserman coming downstairs. All her passions and complaints, her gossip and her tennis games, her entire consciousness extinguished with a rifle shot. *Boom.* Dr. Wasserman waking in his bed, standing to investigate, belting his bathrobe as he turned to the doorway. All his philosophies and desires erased with the pull of a trigger. *Boom.* Lila, rushing from her room—seeing the killer, turning to rush back. Her adolescent love, her angst, her yearning—gone. *Boom.* And Agnes, descending the winding stair. A traveler out of darkness. She had lowered the little boy out the window and then come down to meet the figure with the gun . . . *Boom.*

Winter saw it all clearly. All the dead, all their faces. Only one figure remained in utter obscurity.

With all this in his brain, he had walked away from Gwendolyn Lord's office, eager to find out more. He wanted to visit Menucci's and see if he could uncover the identity of Mrs. Wasserman's lover. He wanted to track down this high school kid Pete Thompson and find out if he was the black knight, Pike, who'd humiliated Mateo in the *Ring of Ventura* game. He wanted to question Steph Breach and Eduardo Hernandez again.

But he had done none of these things.

Because as he'd moved to exit through the main door of the Community Center, he had looked out through the glass walls and seen—who else?—Inspector Strange.

The big, muscular cop was exactly as Winter had first seen him, leaning relaxed and dangerous against his dark blue Crown Vic in the parking lot. As then, so now, he seemed to Winter to be surrounded by an atmosphere like a putrid cloud, a green mist of sadistic meanness coming off him like steam.

Winter had pivoted on his heel, hied himself to a fire exit in the back of the building, snuck out, and slunk away on foot to where he'd parked his car.

Driving out of town, he assured himself that this had been the right thing to do. A direct confrontation with Strange would have hobbled his investigations. Nevertheless, all the long way home, he felt an invisible monkey sitting on his shoulder, antically slapping the top of his head and crying *eee eee eee*, which is monkey-talk for *coward, coward, coward.* It annoyed him. He was still annoyed now in the dark alley. Plus he was cold. Plus the alley stank of fish. And that crap music . . .

Just as he was about to mutter a well-chosen obscenity and abandon his post, he saw a figure appear at the alley's entrance. Hunched and skulking and silhouetted by the light behind him, the figure reeled off the sidewalk and began zigzagging more or less in Winter's direction. As he came, he mumbled, then shouted, then mumbled again, in conversation with some powerful Someone who wasn't actually there. His words were slurred as if he were drunk; disjointed and fantastic as if he were mad. One way or another, he was clearly out of his mind.

But then Winter already knew that. The man was an undercover federal agent, and in Winter's experience, every single one of them was batshit crazy. Stan Stankowski—"Stan-Stan" to what might laughingly be called his friends—was famously a master of disguise precisely because he lived almost entirely in his own demented imagination. He saw each new assignment as another episode in some sort of television series about himself, and he immersed himself in the part of himself so completely that his real self, if there were such thing, vanished into his cover.

It had been months since Winter had seen him. Stan-Stan had been a businessman then. Fit, precise, boring to the point of invisibility. Now he was little more than a pile of rags, a mass of sores, and a stench. As he came close enough for Winter to make him out clearly in the dark, he continued his half-mumbled, half-shouted conversation with whatever hallucination he was pretending to have. His eyes gleamed white and red as they rolled around atop the walking jumble of himself.

"Good God, Stankowski," Winter murmured. He wrinkled not just his nose but his entire face at the smell of him.

"Why do you torment me?" Stan-Stan growled. Then he shouted, "I can't get your voice out of my head! What do you want from me? I have nothing to do with you! Leave me alone!"

Since this was something a schizophrenic might say to his demons and also something Stan-Stan said to Winter almost every time they met, Winter had to admire the subtlety of it.

"I need a favor, Stan-Stan," Winter said.

The reeking mass of rags and sores leapt at him, jamming his unrecognizable features to within an inch of Winter's tortured nose.

"Arrrgh-gnarr-ach," Stan-Stan remarked.

"Be that as it may," said Winter, struggling not to gag on the stench of him. "It concerns a town called Maidenvale. There was a murder there recently. Four murders in one house, to be precise."

Stan-Stan bared his rotten, blackened teeth. A gust of breath poured out of his mouth so foul it seemed to thicken the air between them. The federal agent's voice became a hoarse whisper. "You. Are. An. English teacher, Winter! Your business is little rhymy, girly verses on pretty little pages for rhymy, girly pansies like yourself. You risk blowing my cover whenever you dabble in reality. Rhymes. Not murders. That's your game."

"I sympathize, Stan-Stan, I do. But would you mind contacting our mutual friend and asking him to dispatch his Invisibles to hack into a video game being played by the students at Briars, a local private school? The game is called *The Ring of Ventura* and I'm interested in anything on record that pertains to a character who calls himself Pike, especially if it can be traced back to the identity of his creator. It's tech stuff. You understand. It's not in my line."

Stan-Stan let out another wordless cry of anguish, accompanied by another cloud of green-smelling breath. He was not happy about any of this. Their "mutual friend" was the man Winter always referred to as the Recruiter, because he had recruited him into the Division where he'd plied the assassin's trade. The Division had ultimately been dismantled by a government shocked to discover its existence after having funded it and received its classified reports for years. The Recruiter now lived in obscurity in the Arizona desert. It was rumored that a government Black Ops team would one day come to eliminate him as a security threat. It was an open question whether this Black Ops team would succeed in their mission or be reduced by the Recruiter to a pile of dismantled weapons surrounded by a haze of Kevlar dust. In the meantime, the Recruiter's old associates—former Division assassins and techs—his Invisibles—remained loyal to him unto death. He could summon them at will and trust them to act without being seen—hence their nickname.

"Winter," Stan-Stan growled low, "while this little meeting could result in my being duct taped to a chair, doused with gasoline, and set on fire, I'd prefer that to going to visit the Recruiter and having one of his booby traps plant a curare dart in my eyeball. How about we trade places and I read poetry while you die a lingering death?"

"I appreciate your help," said Winter.

"No, really. I'll write a poem about it. Roses are red, violets are blue, Winter is dead . . ." The rest of the rhyme was both predictable and unsuited to polite conversation.

With that, Stan-Stan reeled away and began to stagger back up the alley in a lunatic pattern. But he paused. Looked back over his shoulder. The red-striped eyes in his leper-white face appeared as gelatinous orbs in the rags that surrounded them.

"And by the way, rein in your girl, Winter," he said.

Winter blinked, confused. "What? What girl?"

"She's asking all the wrong people all the wrong questions. This is not the time. Things in D.C. are unstable. People are sensitive."

"What do you mean . . . ?" Winter began to say—but then he understood. An icy little wind of fear blew through the pit of his stomach.

"Lori?" he whispered.

But Stan-Stan was already zigzagging up the alley toward the street. He tilted his head back and howled at the sky: "Turn your lasers off me, space Jews!"

Then Winter was once again alone in the darkness.

# 13

By the time he returned to his apartment, Winter felt like a corpse with a hangover. It had been a long, long day of trials and anxieties. But he had one last chore to do before he could go to bed.

The computer drive—the little rectangle that Gwendolyn Lord had pressed into his palm. With the Tulipwood murders replaying in his mind, with the obscure figure of the killer overshadowed by blackness, Winter knew he would not be able to sleep until he had seen what it was exactly that Gwendolyn had given him.

Still feeling the chill from the alley, he poured himself a small whiskey. He carried the drink and his laptop to his armchair by the terrace. Beyond the glass of the terrace's sliding doors lay the city under the night. The white dome of the state capitol was brilliantly lit, and the graceful structure was reflected in the water of the lake, which was already shimmering under the autumn moon.

Winter set his whiskey on the lampstand and his laptop on his lap. He plugged Gwendolyn's drive into the machine's port. He was expecting to see documents of some type. He was surprised when a video began to play on his monitor instead.

It was video from a doorbell camera: black and white, the picture distorted by a wide-angle lens, the focus poor. There was audio, too, but the people in view were far off and wind-made static rendered most of what they said incomprehensible. There were two of them, a man and a woman. They faced each other in the parking lot outside the Community Center under an overcast sky on a blustery day. Winter recognized both of them from their photographs in the news sites, from the stories about the murders. Both of them had died that terrible night.

The man was Norman Wasserman. Tall, fit, stiff and superior in corduroy jacket and jeans. He was looking down at the woman from his much greater height, pinning her with a doctorly gaze over the top of his black-framed glasses. The woman was Agnes Wilde. Just a little bit of a thing, as Gwendolyn Lord had described her. Small and thin, her round white face turned up to the man, the corkscrew curls spilling out from under her baseball cap. Her figure was more or less shapeless under a rumpled green utility jacket. Her hands were stuffed into the jacket's big pockets.

It was odd—eerie—to watch them there, talking, engaged with each other and with life, knowing they were ghosts, they were gone.

Winter could see at once that their conversation was ferocious, antagonistic. A confrontation, with the woman insistent and accusing and the man impervious behind an infuriating calm.

It was she, Agnes, who caught Winter's attention first. He was struck right away by her high poise in the midst of the conflict. She was clearly on the attack, but not angry. She smiled and even laughed once, self-certain, unafraid.

*She was special. A special person. A special girl.* So Gwendolyn Lord had said of Agnes. Maybe that had affected Winter's perception, because he thought he could see that in her, even in the blurry, distorted video. She seemed to him to contain a powerful moral force. It seemed to animate her, as if she were less a person than the vessel of some nameless imperative, the nature of which he did not know. It was mesmerizing to look at nonetheless—and it occurred to him that this was the third woman who had impressed him today. There was the girl Savannah, and the regal therapist Gwendolyn, and now Agnes. The three mighty girls of girl-world, Winter thought.

The video was brief, fifty seconds. In that time, the two spoke to each other quickly, first one, then the other, but he could not make out the words. He could see that Wasserman was attempting to intimidate Agnes with his stern, calm responses, his intellectual demeanor and his air of superiority, not to mention his height. But she did not look intimidated in the least. Finally, Wasserman made a gesture of dismissal and walked away. She called after him, the words unclear. Then the video was over.

Winter set the laptop aside. He got up and went into the kitchen, where he had left his computer bag. He rummaged in the bag among the wires and scraps until he found his earbuds. Then he returned to his chair.

He played the video again, this time with the earbuds in and the sound turned up louder.

". . . hardly . . ." he heard Wasserman say under the steady sough of the wind.

". . . irrelevant . . ." said Agnes Wilde.

There were crackling noises. Ambient sound.

". . . abortions and . . ." Wasserman said.

". . . what I am . . ." said Agnes. ". . . you are . . ."

That was when Wasserman made his impatient gesture. Then he turned his back on her and walked away.

She called after him, "Those are your only choices."

But he was gone. Agnes stood still a moment, looking after him. She closed her eyes. To steady herself? Winter thought. Or—since she was religious—maybe to pray?

The video ended.

Winter watched and listened to the video three more times, but that was all he got out of it. Finally, he set the laptop aside and picked up his whiskey glass.

He sipped the malt and tried to imagine what Agnes and Wasserman had been saying. Something about Wasserman's guilty activities obviously—whatever he had done that caused Gwendolyn Lord to expel him from the center. That had to be the subject. Why else would Gwendolyn have given him the video?

He felt frustrated. He felt as if he almost understood the conversation he had just witnessed but could not quite bring his understanding into full consciousness. He tried to induce his strange habit of mind—that meditative state in which dark actions began to make sense to him. It didn't work. He was too tired. Anyway, it wasn't something he could call up at will. It came to him when it came.

His mind drifted. He leaned back against the chair's headrest. He closed his eyes. He thought about Gwendolyn. Savannah. Agnes Wilde. The three girls of girl-world. He saw them, bright figures in a swirling murk—a murk of corruption. He saw a winding stairway in the dark, an angel of light descending. Agnes.

*She knew,* he thought distantly. *She knew she was going to meet her death.*

For a moment, he blinked out of a dream. Lifted his head and looked around him. He thought of Stan-Stan. His slurred crazy voice again: *Rein in your girl, Winter.*

Lori, he thought. Lori Lesser. He had to warn her. Protect her.

But his head sank back against the chair again. Darkness folded over his mind, all the bright figures gone. Nothing left but shadows and the unseen ghosts within them. A far-off sound, steadily repeating.

*Boom. Boom. Boom. Boom.*

# PART THREE

# A FOOL FOR LOVE

*I remember running across the campus through the dark. To get to Madeleine's office. To get that code off her computer so the Division could protect our weapon, uncover the spy. It's very vivid in my mind to this day. I can feel the cool autumn night even now as I tell it. I can smell the changing leaves. See the Gothic campus buildings in the lamplight all around me. Spires and arches looming black against the starry sky. I remember the sound of my own feet, fast on the winding pathways. My breathing, the sound of my breathing, also fast.*

*But you know what? For the life of me I can't think why I was running. Why it all seemed so urgent, I mean. I mean, no one knew I was there. No one knew I had a lead. There wasn't much chance of anyone else getting to the code before I did. Why was I running?*

*I wonder, Margaret . . . Maybe this is being too deep, too psychological about it. But I can't help wondering if I was running away more than toward something. You know? I can't help wondering if I was running from that moment in Madeleine's apartment, when I was lying with my head in her lap, looking up at her. That moment when the look in her eyes changed and everything shifted inside me.*

*I knew it was dangerous to fall for her. It was dangerous to have any feelings for her at all. For one thing, I thought I was immune to these kinds of emotions. I thought I was too busy nursing my torch for Charlotte to fall in love again. That was part of the story I told myself about myself, part of the reason I had become what I was. Me and my broken heart—that's what had made me the man who shot Snowstep, who had killed him in cold blood. Yet here I was under cover, pretending*

*I was the man I would have been if none of that had happened. Was it possible I was also that man somehow, that I was also the man I was pretending to be?*

*Crazy, right? Madness. The make-believe and the reality all swirling together. What is madness if it isn't that?*

*Maybe that's what I was running away from.*

*I ran to the building where Madeleine's office was. A massive forbidding castle of a place on one end of the quad, with two square towers lowering on either side of its central wall.*

*I glanced around quickly. A pair of students went walking by, boy and girl, her twittering voice trailing behind her like a night bird's song. Then I was alone. I hurried up the front steps, stone steps. The doors of the castle were locked, but locks were nothing. I was trained to get past them. I was through the door in a moment.*

*Inside, the place was dark, vast, empty. Creepy—because dim security lights were on in the high ceiling and threw long shadows across the yellow tiles on the wall. My footsteps echoed as I moved to the stairs, echoed on the stairs even louder as I went up one flight, then another, then another to the top floor. The echoes seemed to come from all around me. More than once I stopped to listen, to make sure there was no one else there, no one following me in those long shadows.*

*The door to Madeleine's office was locked, but again, I had it open in seconds. I looked up the long, dark hallway and down the long, dark hallway. There was no one in sight. I felt the cavernous spaces of the place, deserted everywhere. The emptiness felt like a living presence. I slipped into the office.*

*It was a bare, functional room. No shelves. No books. Just a desk with a computer on it. A chair. A sofa against the wall. A closet. A small window. I saw it all clearly for a moment in the light from the hall, then the door swung shut behind me and it was dark—very dark for a moment, but with the glow of streetlamps coming in from the quad, I could soon see my way again.*

*I plunked myself down in Madeleine's chair. I turned on the computer. It seemed to take a long time to boot. All that while, I was listening to the silence in the building around me. The silence was deep. Complete.*

*Finally, the monitor brightened. There was the entry screen. I typed in Madeleine's password. The Division had supplied me with that. Now all I had to do was isolate her music files so the tech boys could find the Rosetta code.*

*I started to work the keyboard, searching—and I heard a door slam.*

*My breath caught. I went absolutely still. The sound had been far away but it was unmistakable. Someone had come in from outside and let the door fall shut behind them.*

*I told myself it was a coincidence. It had to be. How could someone come here now, at the exact same time as me? It had to be some student or teacher who'd forgotten something somewhere else in the building. They'd come back to retrieve it, that's all.*

*That was what I told myself, but my heart was racing. My throat was tightening. I sat frozen at the desk. Waiting. Listening. At first, I could only hear my own pulse, hammering in my ears. But then—were those footsteps? Yes. My God, they were. Footsteps echoing just as mine had echoed. Just like mine, they seemed to be coming from everywhere. I couldn't pinpoint exactly where they were or where they were headed.*

*I forced myself out of my trance, forced myself to move. Got up from the chair. Hurried to the door. Cracked it open as quietly as I could. I peeked out. I was dizzy with the rush of blood to my head. I listened.*

*The footsteps were clearer here. Someone was coming up the stairs. I heard the change in the sound as the steps reached the second-floor landing, then I heard the sound change again as they began to climb the next flight.*

*I brought the door closed with infinite care. Raced back to the computer. Shut it off. This had to be a false alarm, a student looking for a lost wallet, a professor who'd forgotten a file. But even so, I didn't want anyone to see the light from the computer leaking out from under the door.*

*The footsteps kept coming, kept climbing, higher, closer, louder. And now they crested the final flight, reached the final landing. Then they stopped. Not far. A few yards down the hall.*

*Another long moment passed in that silence. I couldn't move. I couldn't make myself believe the footsteps were coming to Madeleine's office, to me. How was that possible? How could that happen?*

*The footsteps began again. Coming down the hall. Toward the office. Closer. Louder. For one last second, I was frozen where I was, unable to believe what was happening. I kept thinking over and over: How? How was it possible?*

*The footsteps stopped right outside the door.*

*There was only one place for me to hide: the closet. I went in. Pulled the door shut silently. I was in deep darkness, total darkness. My breath seemed very loud, deafening. I held it.*

*I heard—very clearly—the office door come open. I heard it swing softly shut.*

*I stood in the dark. I could hear the intruder moving quietly, breathing quietly. I heard him sit down in the desk chair. I heard the usual beeps and whirrs of the computer booting up again.*

*There was no keyhole, no way to look out. There was nothing I could do but stand in the darkness and listen while the intruder started tapping away at the keyboard just as I had.*

*I felt an urgency in my chest and realized I was still holding my breath. I tried to control the flow of air as it poured out of me, and I did control it, but it was not silent, not quite. When the whispered rush came through my lips, I heard the noise of the keyboard stop all at once.*

*The office outside was still, silent. My nerves pulled tight as I listened to the intruder, who was also listening, listening to me, like* the living shadow of myself. I lifted my hand, ready for him to come find me—him or her—ready to strike the instant the closet door opened.

Then my whole body slumped with relief, my back aching as the tension passed. The sound of the keyboard had started again. The intruder had apparently decided no one was there. I stood in the pitch dark. Listened while the noises continued. It seemed to take forever. All the while I was thinking: How was it possible that the two of us came here at the exact same time?

Then, just like that, the answer occurred to me. I straightened. My lips parted. I understood.

I heard the computer shut down. I heard the desk chair move. The intruder was up, walking. The footsteps passed outside the closet door, inches from me. I went tense, poised to attack again.

But then the footsteps continued on. The office door opened. Shut.

The intruder was gone.

I waited a long time before I came out. Long enough to make sure the office was really empty. Then I returned to the desk. To the computer. Worked for the next ten or fifteen minutes or so collecting every music file I could find. I sent them to the Division using my phone.

Finally I was out, hurrying down the stairs again.

I walked into the night and headed back across campus. I was moving slowly now. I was troubled in mind. I needed time to think. I could imagine only two ways that the intruder could've arrived at the same time as me. One, there was a bug in Madeleine's apartment. Someone had been listening to us talk and the intruder had heard about the hidden code at the same time I had. Two, it was Madeleine herself. Coming to her senses, realizing I had wheedled the Rosetta Stone's location out of her, she had hurried over to remove it from the computer before I could steal it.

But whether it was Madeleine or someone else who had been in the office, one thing was absolutely clear to me: the intruder was the traitor I was looking for. The intruder was the spy.

*I decided to go back to my place, file a report with the Division and wait for morning. The next day, while Madeleine was at class, I would go to her apartment and search for a bug. Meanwhile, the Division techs could take apart her music files. If I found the bug, or if they found the Rosetta Stone was still there, at least I would be able to eliminate Madeleine as a suspect. I wanted to do that. I wanted to do that very much.*

*I lived about a block from north campus. When you came off the campus, there was a line of shops, then a rising hill lined with brownstones. Mine was the fifth brownstone on the right. As I emerged from under the campus trees, I scanned the shops ahead of me. Most were already closed for the night, but a few last customers were straggling out of one small restaurant, and there were still lights on inside the local bar.*

*I walked to the corner. Headed up the hill toward my place. The street was dark. There was only a single streetlamp midway between one corner and the next. The crown of a plane tree obscured the lamp and the spindly shadows of the branches played over the sidewalk. As I walked through those shadows, I looked up and saw a black figure rise from the stoop in front of my brownstone.*

*I stopped where I was. The figure descended the stoop. It stood on the sidewalk facing me, waiting.*

*"Madeleine?" I said.*

*I went toward her. She let me draw close. I was standing over her when she spoke.*

*"What took you so long? I thought you had work to do."*

*"I took a walk to clear my head," I told her. "Why are you here?"*

*She lifted a hand and touched my cheek. She studied my face. Her eyes were soft, as they had been when I was lying on her lap, looking up at her. I remember I told myself then that I didn't love her, and I believed it, more or less. I told myself I was just playing a role, just doing a job for the Division, and I believed that too. More or less.*

*"I didn't like that you ran away from me," she said sweetly.*

*"I didn't run away."*

*"Oh," she said—like scolding a child for a silly lie, an obvious lie. "You got scared of what you were feeling. I could see it on your face."*

*"I wasn't scared," I said.*

*She said again: "Oh," in the same tone as before. Her hand was still on my cheek. She moved closer, so close that I could feel the shape of her against me even though we weren't touching. "You weren't scared?" she said—still like she was coaxing a lying child. "You didn't feel anything?"*

*My mind was racing. Trying to figure the right move. Should I play along? Was she the intruder? Was she the traitor I was after? "You know I do," I said.*

*"I do know," she said.*

*She drew me down to her and kissed me, kissed me deep, one leg climbing up the side of me.*

*What was I thinking then? I can't reconstruct it now. It was too confusing. More than anything, I think, I wished this kiss was real. I wished I really was who I was pretending to be.*

*Anyway, it didn't matter. Whoever I was, there was nowhere to run this time.*

*For the sake of the mission, I drew her into my arms.*

# 14

Winter's voice trailed off and he gazed into the middle distance, lost in the memory of that kiss. Margaret Whitaker studied his profile. She was, as always, struck by the vividness of him. In that brown and tan room, built for reflection and analysis, he always seemed so alive with suffering and color and passion.

"She stayed with you that night," she said finally. She wanted to be sure she understood.

Distracted by his own thoughts, Winter nodded vaguely.

"You made love to her under false pretenses," said Margaret.

He glanced at her, smiled a little. "Were they? False? That's just it. I wasn't sure. I'm not sure now."

Margaret took the time to choose her next approach carefully. She wanted to bring him back, back into the present with her. She didn't want to push him too far too fast. This story had been like a wall between them from the beginning of their work together. More than that, it was a wall not only between the two of them, but between him and any connection with anyone, any chance of love, of life. She didn't want the wall to crumble all at once. She thought the shock of intimacy might be too sudden. It might scare him away. Let him take his wall down brick by brick, she thought, as fast or slow as he felt he could tolerate.

"What's going on with those murders you were looking into?" she asked him finally.

The question brought him out of his memories, brought him back into the room with her, which is exactly what she'd meant for it to do.

"I went back there the other day, in fact. To Maidenvale. I saw these three women . . ." His brow furrowed as he considered this, as if there were some puzzle to it. "Very impressive women, each in her own way. One just a girl really, a teenager, then a married woman, and the third was one of the victims. I watched a video of her."

"Tell me about the second one," Margaret said.

Startled, he laughed. "How do you do that?"

"Practice," she told him.

"No, really."

"Well, you're not going to moon over some teenager. That would be creepy. You're not the type. You might moon over a dead girl. You are that type. But when you describe someone as a married woman, I can't help thinking that perhaps she has other character traits as well, but that's the one you're stuck on."

"Amazing, Sherlock."

"Elementary, my dear Winter," said Margaret Whitaker.

"Yes. I was taken with her, I admit. Disappointed by the wedding band and the pictures of her children and so on. But I manfully set all that aside and got on with my business."

"Hm," said the therapist.

"It's just . . ." Again he had to puzzle something out. She waited for him. "I'm closing in on forty, but suddenly the world is as full of womanhood as it was when I was seventeen. Women seem very present to me, more present than anything else. They come off the page of life, three-dimensional, the way nothing else does. Maybe it's just my own loneliness. I expect that's it. The loneliness is . . . well, it's like this dark figure standing over me. A vampire in a cape, sucking the joy out of existence. I keep thinking about these murders, all the bonds that were broken by those rifle shots—husband, wife, mother, father, children—boom, boom, boom, boom—I can hear the gunshots in my mind—and I keep thinking how I have no bonds like that, no bonds with anyone, nothing to even break. Except maybe my bond with you." They smiled gently at one another. Winter said, "She was a therapist, you know. The married woman. She was a therapist at the local Community Center. That was her job."

"Ah," said Margaret Whitaker, flattered. "A younger therapist I hope," she added, and then was annoyed at herself because it sounded like fishing for compliments. Like she wanted him to say, *Oh, you're not so very old as that, Margaret.* Which she did want.

"She was younger, yes," he said. "Too young to have those children, I would have thought. What was she thinking getting married at such a tender age?"

"I'm sure she's repenting at leisure, now that she's met you, dear."

Winter managed a rueful chuckle. His affection for Margaret was warm and clear in his eyes, but so was his frustration with his own longings.

"Explain me to myself, Mrs. Whitaker," he said.

"I'm not sure how much explanation you really need. You're a boy, you like girls. It's the general way of things."

"Guilty as charged," he murmured.

"But I take you at your word. Something has changed. Your perception of women has become more intense. And I'm sure you're right, the loneliness is part of that. Every meeting with a woman has a subtext of possibility."

"But . . . ?" he said.

"But your loneliness isn't situational. You came to me in the first place because you were locked up inside, afraid to open yourself to love, to accept love. You kept telling me about Charlotte. Your childhood crush. You still tell me about her from time to time. But I think it's become pretty clear now: it's not that you can't connect with someone new because you're hung up on Charlotte, it's that you're hung up on Charlotte because you can't connect with someone new."

At that, Winter dropped back in his chair. He gazed at her, open-mouthed, as if she had performed some marvelous sleight-of-hand. "Is that true, do you think?"

"I do think it. It is true."

"I don't know. I think about Charlotte—still—all the time, every day really. She wore this perfume. That one time I kissed her. This sweet perfume, like a girl would wear, not quite a woman's, it . . ." He stopped himself. She could see his body slacken as he surrendered. "But you're right. Of course. It's all so long ago at this point, twenty years almost. We were children. It can't be—sane to go on and on about it anymore."

Margaret Whitaker swiveled slightly in the leather—the brown leather—therapist's chair. She let him sit with his insight for a few seconds.

"We talked about this last time," she went on then. "This new intensity started right after you began telling me the story you're telling me now. The story about this spy mission of yours, and what happened with Madeleine Uno."

His chin lowered only slightly in agreement—as if he were barely there, as if he were hearing her, but from somewhere far away.

"This—this story—is why you can't accept love," she went on. "Your guilt over this, over what you did to Madeleine."

His chest rose as he breathed deeply, returning to full presence in the room. "Yes. That was the beginning of it anyway. A turning point."

"And not just this part of it, I'm guessing," said Margaret. "Not just this part you were telling me now. Going to bed with Madeleine under false pretenses."

"No."

"Any man might do that. Almost every man has done it, at some point. Gone to bed with a woman under false pretenses. Even if it's only his own wife."

Now, at last, their eyes met, gazes locking with a force of intimacy and trust that nearly melted her with the heat of yearning. She had had a long marriage until her husband's death, but it was a mild relationship, friendly, intellectual, comfortable, a bit distant. She had a son but he was estranged from her, a troubled man who lived far away. Had she ever really loved anyone? Had she ever loved anyone as she loved Cameron Winter? Winter, who was out of reach, separated from her on the irreversible flow of time. Was that the *reason* she loved him? Because he was impossible? Because she could make a dream of him and leave it at that? Was that why she felt an underlying sense of dread as she listened to this story of his, this story about Madeleine Uno. Because she feared what she heard would destroy even her dream?

"I'm assuming," she told him, "that that's not the end of it, that the story isn't over yet, that there's much worse to come."

Winter's lips pressed together as he fought down his emotions. "Oh yes," he answered. "Oh yes. There is much worse to come."

# 15

By that afternoon, it was clear to Winter that Margaret Whitaker was absolutely correct. As she so often was. Almost always, in fact. She had a genius for this therapy business, as far as he was concerned. For therapy with him, at least. It was unnerving. Sometimes, when he was sitting across from her, he felt as if he were made of glass and she was looking right through the surface of him into his emotional works.

*It's not that you can't connect with someone new because you're hung up on Charlotte, it's that you're hung up on Charlotte because you can't connect with someone new.*

Where did she come up with that sort of thing? How did she know it? It put the whole story of his life in a new light, didn't it? He had thought that losing Charlotte to that fascist troll what's-his-name—oh, he knew his name, all right: Eddie—Eddie-my-boyfriend. He had thought losing Charlotte to Eddie-my-boyfriend had been the heartbreak of his life, that everything else grew out of that: the Division, his isolation, and the depression that had driven him to Margaret Whitaker's door.

But no, Charlotte was just one small part of the story, one link in the narrative chain. Losing her had caused him to seek fresh purpose in his young life. That search had led him to the martial arts and his friendship with Roy Spahn. Roy Spahn had led him into the Division. Which had led to the final catastrophe with Roy. That had turned him into the man who killed Snowstep, which had led to Madeleine, which was, as Margaret said it was, the foundation of the prison of his solitude. And now that he was sharing the hellish story with this therapist he loved, this woman who had become—as he sneered to himself—his make-believe mommy, the nice mommy with whom he was replacing the icy and uncaring mommy of his childhood—now the cell door of his loneliness was swinging open and something in him was coming to fresh life.

What confirmed the truth of this observation to him was the lunatic lecture he delivered a few short hours after his therapy session. The subject was Byron and Shelley again, only this time, the lecture was as hilarious as it was professionally dangerous, a wild romp of ideas that carried his prepared notes away like a satyr carrying off a nymph at a bacchanal. The whole brain-rumpus came pouring out of him before he had a chance to check himself, and when he did have a chance to check himself, he didn't.

He heard himself suddenly speaking about the eighteenth-century movement of "Free Love," sex without restraint for male and female both. Shelley preached it. Byron practiced it. And because of it, they left wreckage and tragedy for women everywhere in their wake. Shelley's abandoned first wife drowned herself and her unborn child in the Serpentine in London's Hyde Park. Byron tore the daughter of his lover from her mother's bosom and sequestered her in a nunnery, where she died at age five. Mary Shelley was forced to grieve her own dead children in a cloud of male indifference. The males in her life were too entranced with the philosophy of their own wing-wangs to give much of a damn about the lost fruit of her womb.

Winter went on and on in this vein. His students listened, gaping at him. Even in his wild intellectual ecstasy, he was careful to say nothing that would suggest some sort of comparison between the Romantic era and the Free Love philosophy of the present day. But, oh, he could see the unhappiness in the eyes of his female students and he knew they were making the comparisons themselves.

These young ladies would be writing angry emails of complaint to Lori Lesser before the sun set, Winter thought. They would tell her how sexist he was. How offensive he was to make them feel as miserable about the current state of things as they were, but were not supposed to be. He thought this even while he was still speaking. But he could not stop speaking. Because talking to Margaret had unlocked some antic something in him and his mind was running naked and babbling down the hallways of his brain, dangerously free.

When he finished, he strode out of the lecture hall with the baleful glances of unhappy young women following him out the door. He headed for the Independent for his afternoon coffee and croissant. His mood was still so hilarious that it was only when he pushed through the coffee shop door, when he spied Lori herself sitting at her table against the wall with her silver-haired gentleman caller—only then that he remembered that student complaints were the least of his Lesser problems. First and foremost were the words of Stan-Stan Stankowski: *Rein in your girl, Winter. She's asking all the wrong people all the wrong questions.*

That brought him down to earth like the Hindenburg. He cursed under his breath right wearily. He gave Lori a quick sour-pickle smile as he passed her on his way to the counter. He ordered his snack, then found himself a table where he'd be able to keep a discreet eye on the dean of student relations and her silvery suitor.

That was his plan anyway. But he promptly forgot all about Lori the moment he opened his laptop and discovered he'd received a new email containing some more pages from the diary of Marion Wasserman.

*My head is spinning. Spinning? I feel like I'm in that game Bobby has where all his tops do battle with one another, where they spin around bumping into each other and bumping off the walls until one of them topples over. That's what my head feels like.*

*I spent two hours with my—what do I call him?—my lover, I guess—I spent two hours with him this afternoon. Two hours—and we made love three times. Rough and hard. Then gentle and tender. Then just quiet with our eyes on one another. It's so wrong. And he's so wrong for me. I keep thinking: well, it's just physical. It's not like I love him or anything. But isn't it? Isn't it almost exactly like that?*

*I floated home on a little cloud of sexual satisfaction. But the second I stepped into this house, the second the door closed behind me, it was like the cloud vanished, poof. That door swinging shut—it was like a cell door slamming. I wanted to turn right around and get out of there, escape from my own house. But where would I go? My life is here. I had things to do.*

*I went upstairs to check in with Agnes and Bobby. But I was too agitated. When Bobby wanted to show me the plastic tower he'd built, I could barely work up the focus to look at it. "That's so great, Bobby," I said. "But mommy has to go."*

*I hurried to my home office downstairs and locked myself in. Tried to do some yoga. Couldn't concentrate. Wanted to pop a Xanax just to turn off the electricity, but also wanted my head clear so I could feel the electricity and remember that first time he took me. And the second time. And the third. I thought about pouring myself a vodka. But Norman would know and become suspicious. They say vodka has no smell, but Norman doesn't have to smell it. He just knows. He always knows.*

*So, I stood there. Hating him. Hating my husband. For an hour. Pacing and hating Norman and staring out the window at the garden and hating him. The dying colors of the late zinnias. My domain. This kingdom he pays for. This kingdom prison he's put me in.*

*I sat down and typed all this. I heard Lila come home. I heard her call for Agnes. Well, let her. Let her run to Agnes. Let both my children run to Agnes. They can have her. All I want is freedom—freedom and these ecstasies.*

*Later. Calmer. I feel like I've been practically insane these last ninety minutes. Now comes the guilt. The confusion. I don't hate Norman. Not really. I don't hate this house. My kids. I adore my kids. I adore my life. If ever a man was wrong for a woman, this lover is wrong for me. I know that. I'm not stupid.*

*I came out of my office. Went down the hall to Norman's study. Shut myself in there. Just to—I don't know. Be with him. Be with him without, you know, the him of him, that big harrumphing smarter-than-thou him with his insufferable calm and his hundred-syllable words. I just wanted the steady leather smell of him, the man-smell. The leather chair and the big wooden desk and the framed picture of some baseball star he had his picture taken with. And the walls of books. All his collector edition leather-bound favorites.*

*Nietzsche. Freud. Marx. Singer. Harari. Didn't I admire this about him once? Even love it? How smart he was. The way he'd talk. His theories. His high ideas.*

*Whereas, on the other hand . . .*

*My lover told me a story today. As we were lying together, as I was lying in his arms. Between the second time we made love and the third. He told me this story about the storage place where he works. How these Mexican gangsters use it to hide their drugs in the lockers. How they not only pay him, they pay him twice, because he skims some of the drugs out of the lockers and sells them in the city for "a bundle," as he put it. He snickered when he told me. "I'm making a bundle off these guys," he said, and he snickered.*

*It's weird. While he was telling me all this, while we were lying there, while I was still, to be corny about it, glowing—and there was definitely a lot of glowing going on—this story he was telling me didn't seem bad to me somehow. It didn't seem ugly or corrupt. It was comical. I laughed too. It made him seem dashing to me. Like he was having an adventure, outsmarting the gangsters. That's what I told myself anyway. Glowing as I was.*

*But then later, here, home, in Norman's study, as I was sitting there in Norman's great big leather chair, swiveling back and forth, and smelling Norman's smell, remembering how he was when we were first going out together, I saw things differently. I thought about what I'd been told, about stealing the gangster's drugs and selling them—and how he'd snickered when he told it—and I don't know, it just seemed sleazy to me suddenly. Low.*

*After a while, I got up. Went out. Went upstairs. Stopped at Lila's room. She wasn't there, but I paused in the doorway.*

*Looking in. God, it's all so girly suddenly. Where did she get those posters with the gag-me platitudes?* "Believe!" "Life isn't perfect, but your outfit can be." *Eesh. And the rose bedspread. I thought we'd thrown that thing away. She's even dug up her old dollhouse and put it on top of the bookshelves. I didn't know that was still around. All of this since Mateo came on the scene. How easy we are, we women. How eager we are to remake ourselves in their image of us. But who am I to talk? When I snickered, too, over the story about the drugs, snickered just like he did. I probably fluttered my eyelashes too. My hero!*

*I trudged upstairs to Bobby's room. He was there, on his bed, his face glued to his handheld game machine. He barely looked up from it when I came in. Grunt. That's all I got.*

"*Where's Agnes?*" *I asked him.*

*He kind of gestured with his head toward her room, and murmured,* "*With Lila,*" *like he was talking in his sleep.*

*I went down the hall to Agnes's room. The door was closed and I heard Lila's voice inside. I know, I know, I should have knocked. But I couldn't help myself. I stood outside. I listened. Eavesdropping on my own daughter. Well, because I knew if I came in, she'd clam up. And Agnes would look at me with that poisonous sweetness of hers. And I'd know she was keeping my daughter's secrets. Which would have been awful. Unbearable. So I eavesdropped instead.*

*Well, friend diary, it seems Lila and her Latin lover have had a bit of a lover's quarrel, doncha know. Mateo apparently thought she was flirting with this boy named Pike. She swears she wasn't. But, and this is a direct quote, "It's just that sometimes, Mateo can be so romantic, you know. He writes poetry about me. He says I'm like some angel. It's embarrassing. It's like, I think he wants me to be more than I am. I feel this pressure to live up to this perfect picture he has of me. And I kind of want to live up to it even. But I'm not some princess in a fairy story, I'm just a person, and sometimes I just want to clown around or be stupid, like the way I can be sometimes with other guys who don't want me to be so pure and everything. I mean, Mateo doesn't even want me to curse! I mean it! He says it's not ladylike! I guess it's some kind of Latino thing or something."*

*I couldn't hear what Agnes's answer was. That little-girl whisper of hers: it didn't come through the door. But when she was done talking, Lila answered her. She said: "Oh, I know we'll make it up. He already texted me to say he was sorry he got mad and that he knew I would never cheat on him. And I wouldn't. I mean, I love him. When I'm with him, you know, I feel I could almost be like he wants me to be. It's just: I've never been in love with anyone before, not really, and it's a lot to deal with. I'm going to sneak out and see him first thing in the morning, before everyone is awake. We'll make up. It's just confusing, that's all."*

*At this point, I lifted my hand to knock. But then I didn't. The truth is: I didn't feel worthy. Because of what I'd been doing all day. And the idea of seeing the two of them together, Lila and Agnes, sharing everything. I thought the shame would kill me.*

*So, I just went back downstairs. Back to my office. Took that Xanax I'd been hankering after. Writing this while I wait for it to kick in.*

*What am I doing? What are you doing, Marion? I'm so unhappy. I sit here. I look out at the garden. The zinnias.*

*Red and purple and yellow and orange. They'll be gone with the first frost. Like the children will be gone. Like love. Sex. Life. Everything is so fast and then it's over.*

*I keep swearing to myself I'll never cheat again.*

*But I know I will.*

# 16

Winter had become utterly immersed in the diary. As he read, it occurred to him: this must have been her final entry. Her last words. Her last emotions. Death must have come to the Tulipwood house in the predawn dark of the very next morning. *Boom. Boom. Boom. Boom.* "Everything is so fast and then it's over."

He finished reading, sat back in his chair. Reached for his coffee cup. As his consciousness returned to the present moment, he had a growing awareness that something was wrong. What was it? The ghostly voice of the diary? The story about the gangsters? The idea that the breakup between Mateo and Lila would have soon been mended? What was bothering him?

It came to him suddenly. Not the diary. Not the murders at all. It was Lori. Lori Lesser. She was gone. She and her silvery boyfriend—they were both gone.

Winter had positioned himself so they were in front of him, so he could glance up and see them without seeming to spy. But he had not glanced up. He'd been too absorbed in his reading. Now, as he came back to himself, a movement caught his eye. A young man with a backpack and a cappuccino was hurrying to the empty table, the table where Lori had been. The boy was grateful to find somewhere to sit in the crowded café.

Lori must have just left. Winter looked over his shoulder. He thought he spotted her wild copper locks and her tartan scarf wafting out of view at the edge of the shop's long window. Quickly, he snapped his laptop shut, stuffed it in its bag. A young woman—also with a backpack and a cappuccino—rushed to take his place as he hurried out into the street.

Yes, there they were. Lori and the silver-haired man were walking shoulder to shoulder in the flow of pedestrians. Lori was gesturing and chattering, her hair bouncing and her thrift-shop scarf sailing behind her on the autumn breeze.

Winter hung back and followed them. He paused and pretended to look in a tavern window as they reached the edge of the campus. Out of the corner of his eye, he saw them kiss goodbye. A brief kiss, not a passionate one. Which could either mean they were just friends or that they were already sleeping together and had no need to do their kissing on the street.

Lori continued away under the autumn leaves, amid the stately stone and brick structures rising from the grass of the campus. She seemed happy, judging by her jaunty step.

Silver Fox, meanwhile, turned south. Winter went after him. The fox headed toward the area where the off-campus housing was. Soulless towers for the most part, trashing the autumn scenery. But foxy man went past them and arrived at an older brick apartment building, more attractive than the others, three attached wings, each a mere three stories high.

By then, Winter had come to a decision. He had decided the silver man was nefarious. He could not have said why he was so certain, not exactly anyway. There was his own immediate dislike of him. Stan-Stan's warning: *Rein in your girl.* There was the way the man's expression changed the moment Lori was out of sight, the way all the warmth went out of his face and it became grim and watchful and business-like. All those things, plus Winter's own experience with men of this nature, men with this training, men like himself.

As Silver Guy went up the steps to the central door of the brick building, Winter quickened his pace. He set his computer bag down at the base of the stairs then trotted up behind the man as he was opening the door. It was only as he closed in on his target, only at the very last second, that Winter realized he had made a terrible mistake.

Silver Guy hadn't seemed to see him coming, but it was clear in that final moment that he'd been aware of him for some while. It was afternoon, a bright blue day with the late sun angling in from the west. Silver Guy had known, in other words, that if Winter made his move from behind him, his shadow would fall forward and give him away.

Just as Winter stepped in to strike, Silver Guy drove his elbow straight back toward his face with the force of a high-speed piston. It was a much-practiced blow, expertly done. If Winter's face had been where it should have been, the elbow would have driven his wire-rimmed glasses so deep into his brain that poetry, melancholy, and a wistful sense of cultural nostalgia would have come flying out the back of his skull in great bloody gobbets.

But in that same final second before the strike, Winter saw his own shadow fall and realized what a fool he'd been. He dropped low. The elbow sailed over his head, bringing Silver Guy halfway round to him. Winter sprung up from his crouch and drove the stiffened fingers of his right hand into Silver Guy's Adam's apple.

Silver Guy gagged painfully. Winter lifted his knee almost to his chest, and then snapped his foot into Silver Guy's midsection.

The kick sent Silver Guy flying through the open door into the shadowy foyer.

With a quick look around, Winter saw that, by some fortunate alignment of the planets, not a single student had taken video of or even witnessed the incident. He slipped into the building and shut the door behind him.

He had hoped—and even expected—to find Silver Guy sitting on the floor clutching his throat and gasping for breath. But no such luck. The agent was silvery but he was tough. He had kept his feet. He was turning to meet Winter as he entered. There was a folding tactical knife in his hand, black and nasty, with the blade fully sprung. Winter read the man's eyes and saw he was furious, ready to whittle him into a decorative figurine.

"Really?" Winter said. "You're going to kill me?"

"You hit me in the throat," said Silver Guy hoarsely.

"You tried to elbow me in the face," Winter countered.

"You were sneaking up behind me," Silver Guy snarled back.

Winter wagged his head. "All right, you have a point. But you'll make a hell of a mess."

By that time, Silver Guy had mastered his anger and could see Winter was right. How would he explain such a killing? Or if he couldn't, how would he get rid of the body and clean up the blood? Plus it would completely upend his assignment.

He sneered, annoyed. "All right, I'll just kick your ass then," he said. And he folded the knife and slipped it back into his jacket pocket.

Whereupon Winter seized the moment and punched him so hard in the face that blood exploded from his nose and he staggered backward, both arms wheeling. Then, at last, he dropped onto his backside and sat there, clutching his face as blood streamed down under his hands onto his chin.

Winter took the opportunity to retrieve the knife from the man's pocket—just in case the broken nose annoyed Silver Guy enough to make him return to his original plan of killing him. After slipping the weapon out of reach in the pouch inside his windbreaker, he rubbed his sore knuckles. Silver Guy nursed his nose.

"Is there somewhere we can talk?" Winter asked him.

"Yeah, yeah, yeah," muttered Silver Guy.

"Let me get my bag."

Silver Guy's apartment was on the third floor. It was a service place with the sort of blond-wood, white-cushioned furniture that comes ready-to-assemble with a handy Allen wrench. There was a living room with a balcony overlooking the street and a bedroom in back. Silver Guy, who gave his name as Ted Caesar, went into the bathroom to wash his face.

Winter put down his computer bag and dropped onto the blond-wood, white-cushioned sofa with a sigh. He waited, listening to the water run. He assumed there was some possibility silver Caesar would come out with a pistol in his hand, but he still didn't really think he'd kill him. Broken nose or no nose, it would still be too messy, too difficult to explain.

Apparently, Caesar had come to the same conclusion. He emerged from the bathroom holding a washcloth to his face. There was murder in his eyes for sure, and in his heart, too, probably, but it would have to wait for another day.

He dropped into the blond-wood, white-cushioned chair across from Winter. He called Winter a filthy name.

"Oh, come now. I was only planning to push you through the door," Winter protested.

"You're a liar. You were going to kidney punch me."

Winter made an embarrassed gesture. In fact, he had been planning to kidney punch him.

"You didn't just spot me either," said Caesar bitterly. "Someone tipped you off."

"You can have House Intelligence form a committee to investigate. Meanwhile, what the hell, Caesar? Lori Lesser? Really? What the hell? Are you people drowning in tax dollars? Have we no enemies foreign or domestic for you to ply your trade on?"

"She was asking questions about the Division."

"So what?"

"I need to know what she knows."

"She doesn't know anything. She's just trying to find some way to get me fired. Leave her alone."

"People in Washington are nervous."

"People in Washington are idiots. She's a harmless functionary at a more or less obscure institution of erstwhile higher learning. Her job is to terrorize teenage boys who were never taught to behave like gentlemen for taking advantage of teenage girls who were never taught to behave like ladies. What are you going to do if she does know something? Assassinate her for being a fool? Where would it end?"

Caesar grimaced. "Yeah, I thought it was kind of ridiculous myself. What do you want from me? I caught the assignment."

He dabbed at his face, then inspected his washcloth for blood. Which gave Winter the chance to see that his nose was purple and beginning to swell. Winter found the sight gratifying, though he was ashamed to admit it to himself. Still, he really had disliked this guy from the start. On consideration, he still disliked him.

"Did you sleep with her?" he asked.

"What's it to you?" said Caesar. "You in love with her or something?"

"No. I don't even like her particularly."

"Yeah. Who could? Nice body though."

Winter grunted. "Look. Go back to D.C. Talk to the bosses. Tell them it's nonsense. What could she possibly find out? You think she's going to file a FOIA request and some blinky bureaucrat is going to send her a government pamphlet that says, 'Yes, we once had a Division that arranged the deaths of evildoers?' I think we can all have full confidence that our government hasn't lost its ability to lie."

Even Caesar chuckled at that—then flinched and dabbed gingerly at his nose again.

"Really," said Winter. "Tell them to stop."

In pain, Caesar sneered. "Or what?"

"Oh, please, what are we, ten years old? Or I'll kill you. All right? I mean it, Caesar. If Lori Lesser so much as strikes her foot against a stone, I will hunt you down. Not the president. Not the director. You. And then I'll come after whoever gave you the order. Ask him how well he thinks he'll sleep at night if I become invisible."

Caesar gave a mirthless laugh. "You're living dangerously now, Poetry Boy."

Winter's only answer was a sour glare. Caesar tried to return it for a moment or two, but finally averted his eyes. That *Poetry Boy* crack had given him away. If he knew the Recruiter's derogatory moniker for Winter, he also knew Winter's reputation. And the Recruiter's reputation. And the reputations of the Invisibles, the former Division agents who were still willing to put a girdle round the earth at the Recruiter's command.

"So that's your message?" Caesar muttered. "This nobody babe stubs her toe, and it's all-out war between your Invisibles and the might of the empire?"

Winter didn't answer.

"Maybe you do love her," said Caesar.

"Trust me. She's just a colleague. Killing you would be a professional courtesy."

"Uh huh. You're, like, what? Her white knight? Is that it?"

Winter burst out laughing.

"What's so funny?" said Caesar.

"I'm glad Lori didn't hear you say that. She only uses the term *white knight* as a pejorative. To her, it's a bad thing."

Caesar smiled derisively. "But not to you," he said.

"No," said Winter. "Not to me." He stood up out of the chalky depths of the sofa cushions. "I'm sorry I broke your nose," he said.

"Oh, bullshit."

"Yeah, you're right. I enjoyed it. But really, Caesar. Go home. Tell them it's nonsense."

He was glad to get out of that place. With its blond-wood, Allen-wrench furnishings. Its anonymity. How many rooms like that had he occupied? And for what purposes? All that talk of death and assassination had brought it all back to him. As if he were sitting in the darkening room with Snowstep again, about to pull the trigger as he had so many years ago. As if the past were a rolling mist he had once outrun but which now had caught up with him and engulfed him. More grist for Margaret Whitaker's therapeutic mill. Would he ever be free of his bloody sins?

He walked back to his apartment building lost in random meditations. For some reason, his mind returned to thoughts of Gwendolyn Lord. Her elfin face, her stately bearing. Her ladylike outfit and the glint of humor in her green eyes. What did she think of white knights? he wondered. Her with her husband and her two kids.

As he stepped out of the elevator and moved down the hall toward his apartment door, he rubbed the back of his hand gently against the side of his pants leg. His knuckles were scraped and stinging. What had he been thinking, punching Caesar like that?

He opened his apartment door—and in an instant he was drawn out of his meditations and back into the world of his current obsession, the murders of the Wasserman family and Agnes Wilde.

While he'd been out, while he'd been busy threatening the lives of undercover government operatives, the Invisibles had paid him a visit. Sitting on the living-room sofa, in plain sight from the door, was the strange little device he had seen in both Mateo's bedroom and in Lila's. The Opticon, the virtual reality machine on which he and she and the entire student body of Briars private school had played the game *The Ring of Ventura*.

It was that game that had drawn Mateo and Lila into a lover's spat in the final hours before their deaths.

Now it was Winter's turn to play.

# 17

He gasped aloud. He had never experienced anything like it. The moment he turned the Opticon on, he was surrounded by a world of fantasy. He was open-mouthed, amazed. He had read about such things, of course, but only a little. His mind was largely occupied with early nineteenth-century poetry. He didn't have much interest in these new-fangled innovations.

But now—now, he was interested all right. Fascinated. There he was, sitting in his own apartment, on his own sofa, with this gizmo strapped clumsily to his face, covering his eyes—and the images that surrounded him were so vividly real and immersive that they laid claim to his very nerve endings. His mind protested it was all a technological trick and an illusion. But he couldn't resist it. It was as if he had fallen into the pages of a novel or been drawn through the surface of the screen into a film. He was there—there in the imaginary country of Ventura—and his heart beat faster with the excitement of it.

Somehow, the Recruiter's Invisibles had managed to collect a series of scenes that the Briars students had recorded from their games. Winter didn't have to learn how to play or maneuver, he was simply swept passively along as the videos unwound.

He traveled through a storm-darkened landscape of cliffs and ruins, distant fortresses and forests striped with moonlight and mystery. He flinched and his heart hammered as he witnessed knights with gleaming swords do battle against ravening werewolves in the silver shadows of night-shrouded groves. He threw his hands up helplessly to fend off the lightning bolts fired from the fingers of sorcerers and witches as they unleashed their magic to defeat a great beast, half scorpion, half spider. He watched, enthralled, from behind a tree as clever archers populated the branches of ancient oaks. There, they lay in wait for an enormous ogre who made the earth shake—and the Opticon vibrate on Winter's face—as he galumphed along the trail below, swinging his spiked club through the underbrush. Winter found himself growing tense as the monstrous gray creature thundered in his direction. But a moment later, the archers rained arrows down on the brute. It screamed and swung its club at them blindly. Winter helplessly pressed back into the sofa cushions as the ogre toppled toward him and fell dead.

He traveled on. He gaped at rainbowed clouds of fluttering fairies. He sighed aloud at a lady cloaked in gossamer who rose from the surface of a lake like mist to deal out weapons to the deserving. He watched the world become enchanted again. For a student of the Romantics, for one who was something of a Romantic himself, it was fearfully like coming home.

Then came the climax. He held his breath as the scene shifted and he saw Princess Lily and Sir Romeo riding white horses over an open plane.

He knew them on sight. It was Lila and Mateo, the dead lovers—but alive again in their avatars. More than the video of Agnes and Wasserman, more than Marion Wasserman's diary, this was something wildly intimate, an almost pornographic intrusion into two lost lives. These young people, now in their graves, had left behind their fantasies for him to wander through, an animated full-color three-dimensional rendering of their imagined selves.

So many mournful thoughts passed through his mind as he watched. His heart ached for them. Here they were in front of him, not as they had been but as they had dreamed of being. What, Winter wondered with half a smile, would Lori Lesser say if she could see what they'd wished they were: a princess and a white knight, she slender in her flowing pink gown, he noble in his gleaming silver armor, icons of womanhood and manhood. They rode side by side—and Winter traveled with them—over a foggy blue landscape with rocky crags and ruined pillars and a sparkling and majestic castle rising on a far-off hill.

They spoke. Winter caught his breath again as he heard their recorded voices, piped directly into his ears as if into his brain. He found it incredibly poignant. By some protocol of the game, they were trying their best to speak in character. They weren't any good at it, of course. It was way beyond their level of education. They sounded clumsy and absurd. But it was still the two of them playing out their dreams of nobility and valor. Had he been given to easy tears, Winter would have shed them.

"There's the castle now, my princess," Mateo said. "We must go there, and fast." He had a deep, mellifluous voice, with a hint of sing-song Mexican rhythms.

"The dragon that guards the place, y'know, has devoured two clans," answered Princess Lily. "Send off the, uh, y'know, the falcon there to tell the guardians that we are on our way." It sounded ridiculous in her nasal Great Lakes whine, with its choked o's and its flat, elongated a's.

"Yeah, hold on a sec, hold on. I gotta get the, the falcon here, hold on," Mateo's Romeo answered.

It was all so silly. But to Winter, picturing their violent deaths, knowing how Mateo yearned for pure romance and how he had bulled through Lila's ordinary modern-girl life to her more lofty desires, it was heartbreaking too. They had been barely more than children.

Romeo released his message-falcon and off it flapped, rising into the pale blue sky. The knight and his lady watched it head for the castle until it became invisible in the distance.

But now, from out of a grove of trees, there rode another knight, a black-armored knight on a great black charger. Winter knew at once that this was Pike.

Sir Romeo uttered an obscenity not often heard in fairy tales. And Lila said, "Damn it, Pike, leave us alone for once, wouldja!"

But Pike had now taken up his stance in the middle of the road ahead of them. He blocked the way to the path that wound up the high hills to the castle. He spoke—and it was clear that he was using some sort of device to blur and slur his voice so it would be unrecognizable.

"Hold, Romeo. Ya wimp. Before you join 'em up at the castle, you gotta face me first and prove your manhood."

"Leave us alone, Pike!" Princess Lily whined. "I mean it."

"Yeah, why don't you help us for a change?" said Sir Romeo weakly. "You could come with us, help us fight the dragon."

"What are you, like, afraid to fight me? Are you a man or a mouse?" said Pike.

Winter watched the scene with parted lips. As absurd as the dialogue was, the images were so real, his imagination was still beguiled by them. He felt a tremor of suspense as if he really were watching knight challenge knight.

"Before you join 'em, you gotta prove yourself or else you're not worthy of Princess Lily," Pike taunted.

And without another word, he charged.

"Stop!" Princess Lily cried. "Would you stop? Damn it!"

The two knights came together. The fight was pitifully brief. Winter didn't understand it all, but he could see that Pike had far more power than the smaller Romeo. Pike swung a studded mace until it blurred with speed as he galloped over the distance between them. Then their horses came together. Romeo raised his shield in defense, but the mace smashed through it with a single blow. A swift second strike clanged against Romeo's helmet, sending a splash of blood straight at Winter's eyes, so that he started backward on the sofa. Princess Lily—Lila—tried to help Romeo with some sort of spell, but the purple radiation that buzzed from her palms glanced off Pike's black armor without effect.

Less than a minute more, and all was over. At a third and fourth strike from the mace, Romeo toppled sideways from his saddle and sprawled inelegantly in the grass. The helpful message "Romeo is dead," wrote itself in blood on the bottom of the image. Adding insult to injury, Pike dismounted and kicked the white knight's body so that it flew doll-like several yards down the trail. According to another message, Pike then acquired whatever weapons and powers had belonged to Romeo.

"You so suck, Pike," said Princess Lily. "That's really mean. I'm serious."

"A girl like you deserves better than a clown who's gotta regenerate every ten minutes," Pike replied. He climbed back into the saddle. "C'mon, let's go fight that dragon. It'll be fun."

"Who are you?" said Lily. "Is that you, Pete? It's really mean what you keep doing to him."

"It's the way of the world, girl," Pike replied. "The strongest knight wins. You might as well get used to it now, believe me.

C'mon, I'll show you how you beat the dragon. The boys aren't strong enough."

"You so suck," said Princess Lily again—but she spoke with sulky resignation this time. And when Pike rode off toward the castle, she simply sighed and rode off after him. It was as if her will had been conquered by Pike's superior strength just as completely as Romeo's body had been. She was beguiled by the stronger knight. Easy to see, thought Winter, why Mateo had felt hurt and angry, especially after he'd let her see him cry.

The scene ended. The landscape lapsed into a blackness deeper than night. Winter stripped the device off his face and set it back on the sofa beside him. He sat still a moment, staring at nothing. He was aware he felt a vague sense of regret. He scoffed at it, but there it was all the same: he was sorry to leave Ventura, sorry to return to this drab and dysfunctional modernity in which he'd never quite belonged. He had dreams, too, after all, just like the children of Briars.

A few minutes later, he came back to himself as if from far away. Without realizing it, he had slipped into that strange habit of mind of his, that vaguely meditative state in which his views and opinions vanished and only fact and incident and human character remained, all the contents of a scenario floating free, until they dropped into a new configuration.

He blinked out of this wordless contemplation to find himself suddenly one step closer to understanding the scenes of slaughter that haunted him.

# 18

Stephanie Breach swaggered out of the Tulipwood security booth and moved toward the gate to meet him. Winter waited in his Jeep SUV as the barred gate swung open with a grinding buzz. He watched through the windshield as Breach strutted toward his passenger door, her short, stocky figure rolling like a sailor's, her thumbs hooked in her gun belt, her strong jaw set as if for battle.

He popped the door for her. She pulled it open and swung up into the seat beside him.

"Hey," she said gruffly.

Winter nodded and started driving.

It was a gray day. Cold. The sky was solid slate. A gusting wind stripped the trees of their dying leaves. Leaves that had already fallen rose up off the pavement in small tornadoes. Winter still wore his windbreaker. He hadn't yet shifted over to his heavier shearling. But he had a heavy cord sweater on underneath, and he wore the collar of the jacket turned up around his jaw.

"Getting to be winter," Steph Breach said.

"It is," said Winter.

"So—what's this about? You want to take a look at the house again?"

He shook his head. "Not necessarily. I think you and I should talk though."

"All right."

Winter didn't have to glance at her to read her expression. He could hear her discomfort in her voice. But then, she must have been expecting this. It was an edgy sort of game she'd been playing with him. He understood that now. She must have known he'd figure it out eventually.

After a while, though, he did glance at her—if only to meet her eyes. She squinted at him defiantly from beneath her gray cap. Her mouth was set and thin.

"I take it it's you who's been sending me the pages from Mrs. Wasserman's diary," Winter said.

She drew a hissing breath in through her narrow nose. "The pages I had, yeah. I thought they might be helpful to you."

"And Officer Ann Farmingham shared them with you?"

"Because she knew they'd never see the light of day otherwise, that's why."

"Right. Inspector Strange will do his best to bury them. Because they implicate him. Because he was Mrs. Wasserman's lover, wasn't he?"

Steph Breach gave a grunt. "That's the way I read it. Both Ann and me, that's how we read it."

"Well, it makes sense. He'd have been able to watch her as she went in and out of that fancy grocery store."

"Menucci's. That's what I thought too."

"The police station is right across the street. He'd've been able to watch her and then drive up and pick her up when she came out, just like she describes it."

"That's it."

Winter drove slowly. He took the turns smoothly. He had no reason to return to the house, but something compelled him.

"So that means Strange is in league with the gangsters. That was what you wanted me to know without getting your fingerprints on it. You can't afford to get on his bad side. Not in this town."

"It was Ann I was protecting mostly. She needs her job."

"If Strange was her lover," Winter went on, "then Strange was the one ripping off the Mexican dealers, skimming their product. That makes sense too. He moonlighted doing private security, so he was on scene at the E-Z Storage. That's also why he had access to the empty house where he took Mrs. Wasserman for their afternoons."

Out of the corner of his eye, he saw Steph Breach frown angrily. "I told you. Didn't I tell you? Since the feds started dumping the illegals here, there's been too much bad money. And Strange—well, he's just the type to dip his fingers in, isn't he?"

Winter didn't answer out loud, but he thought, yes, Strange was just the type.

"So what was your point?" he asked her. "What were you trying to tell me?"

"Just that you couldn't trust him, that's all. That he'd tell any story that kept the money flowing."

Winter nodded. "He defended Mateo when he thought that would make him look good to the gangsters in the Hollow. Then when Mateo turned up dead, he figured what the hell? Accusing him was a fast way to end the investigation before his dirty business came to light. Mateo was already gone so no one got hurt."

"That's right."

"What else did Ann Farmingham send you?" he asked her.

She looked away from him, out the window at the wind-bent trees, the leaves flying under the slate-gray sky. "Not much. Just gossip."

"Forensics?"

"Some."

"Any traces of Strange's DNA in Mrs. Wasserman?"

"If there was any, he buried the evidence. Ann and I never saw it anyway."

"Anything else?"

Steph Breach sighed into the passenger window as if the whole thing made her weary. "There were bruises on the Wilde girl. The nanny. Agnes. Breasts and torso. A black eye. Hard to tell with the body burned, but it looked like someone had roughed her up."

"Was she raped?"

"No sign of it, not that I heard about. But like I said, the body was burned pretty bad. She maybe was just banged up in a fall or something."

Winter took a moment to think this through. "But you don't think so. You think it was the killer."

Still without facing him, Steph Breach gestured: *Who else?*

Winter nodded to himself, taking it in. Another version of the murder movie to play in his mind.

"What about Mateo?" he asked. "Any forensics on him?"

Still turned away from him, still watching the world outside, Steph Breach spoke into the scenery. "He died the same night. The same morning. Probably right after the killings."

"So, he could have done the murders, returned to the scene of his love affair with Lila, and blown his brains out."

"Right."

"Any traces of gasoline on him?"

"Not that I know of."

They had reached the house, that dead house. Winter pulled to the curb across the street from it. He looked at the place, his expression grim, the house grim. The police tape was still up, but some of it had loosened, some of its ends had detached. A yellow strand or two fluttered in the high wind. It looked like ribbons on a slack-jawed corpse, sad and grisly.

"You still haven't really answered me, Steph," he said. "What were you trying to tell me, sending me the diary? You wanted me to put a story together that wouldn't come out if it was left to Strange. What was it? What was the story?"

Now he turned and she did, too, and they faced each other. She looked fierce and determined. Winter studied her expression as she spoke.

"I think Mateo wanted to protect his father, his family," Steph Breach said. "You know how his people are about that sort of thing. Family honor and so on. He told Lila about the drugs, maybe to impress her. Lila told Agnes—she told her everything. Mateo suspected. He had that violent streak. All the porn and so on. He beat the truth out of Agnes, then came here and killed them all to protect his dad. Then realized what he'd done. Went to the caverns and shot himself."

Winter smiled slightly. He had figured it was something like that. "It's good," he told her. "It's a plausible scenario. Mateo did tell Lila about his father and the mob. He was very upset about it. It wouldn't surprise me if she told Agnes too. Agnes seems to have been the sort of woman people confided in. So, yeah, it's a plausible scenario. But it's not what happened."

Her frown deepened. "What do you mean?" she said. "Why not? Why wasn't it?"

"Mateo was already at the caverns when the murders happened," he told her. "He was waiting there for Lila. She was going to sneak out to see him. They were going to make up their quarrel."

She stared at him as if he had gone blurry and she needed to bring him into focus. "How the hell do you know that?" she said.

"It was right there in the diary, Steph," Winter told her gently. "Mrs. Wasserman heard Lila telling Agnes. Lila was going to sneak out and meet Mateo in the cave and they were going to make up."

Steph Breach went on staring, frowning, her eyes filled with emotion.

"You missed it," Winter told her. "It was right there on the page. You didn't see it because you didn't want to see it."

"What's that supposed to mean?"

He sighed. "It means you were in love with her. Or had a crush on her or whatever. It was written on your face when we were in the house together, when you stood over the spot where she died. You were crazy about her. She went through that little phase of sexual, whatever, confusion—it's kind of a thing these days, I'm told. But you clutched at it. You made more of it than it was because you thought it meant you were in with a chance."

Breach stuck her jaw at him. "Who says that was the phase? Could've been Mateo. He could've been the phase. That happens."

"Oh, come on. How old are you, Breach? You look about my age. Is that right?"

"Thirty-five," she said defiantly, but Winter thought she was older.

"It was a rotten thing to do," he told her quietly. "That thing with the video game, with Pike. Getting between them like that. Humiliating Mateo like that. You disguised your voice, but you couldn't disguise the speech rhythms. Or the obsession with Mateo's manhood. Or the way you made fun of 'the boys,' which gave away that you weren't a boy yourself. They were kids. It was their first love. It was no business of yours. What were you thinking?"

"I was just trying to make a point."

"Yeah, that you were more of a man than he was."

"Well . . ." she said.

"It was a rotten thing to do."

"I never would have touched her. She was too young. I knew that. I never would have gone near her, I swear."

"I believe you. But it's not the point."

"That's why I used the game."

"It's not the point," Winter insisted. "They were kids in their first love. You're a grown woman. You should have left them alone."

He kept his eyes on her. He saw her own glance shift to the house behind him. Her square jaw trembled. Her squinty eyes grew damp.

"The heart wants what it wants," she muttered finally.

Winter answered with a sharp whiffling noise of annoyance. What an idiot thing to say that was! It was an idiot remark when Emily Dickinson made it, and was probably even more idiotic when Steph Breach heard it from whatever pop singer or movie actor had passed it on.

"The heart wants what it wants," he repeated with derision.

He turned away to give her a chance to dry her eyes. He looked out at the house again. He heard again the gunshots that had extinguished all those hearts and minds in there, and all the bonds between them. His own mind was on Lila mostly. And on Mateo waiting for her in their cavern love nest. Waiting until the killer came to finish him too.

"You were afraid Mateo wiped out the Wassermans because of you, weren't you?" he said. "Because of what you did, because he was angry about his quarrel with Lila after she went off with you, with Pike. That's why you sent me the diary pages. To prove to me it was about the drugs. To tell me a story that eased your conscience." He gave a mirthless laugh. "But you missed the fact that he wasn't there at all. It was right there in front of you, Steph. But you didn't want to see that they were going to make it up out in the caverns—the way young people do make these things up mostly. You didn't want to see that so you didn't."

After another moment, Steph Breach spoke again, her voice low and sodden with unshed tears. "So? What then? You don't think *I* killed them, do you?"

He didn't look at her. He just shook his head at that staring corpse of a house with the yellow police tape flying in the wind like ribbons.

"I don't," he said. "I don't think that. You wouldn't have sent me those pages if it was you. No. I think you really did care about her. You acted like a damn fool, butting into young people's business where you had no place. But you were a fool for love, at least. This . . ." he went on, nodding toward the house. "This wasn't an act of love. Whoever went through that house was insane with rage. Or insane with something. Shame. Vengeance. Something. Not love."

When he figured she had herself under control, he looked at her, not without compassion. "None of it was because of you, Steph. It wasn't Mateo going nuts because you humiliated his avatar. You don't have to think that anymore. It had nothing to do with you."

Steph Breach's pasty cheeks flushed. The desperate relief that filled her hard eyes was pitiable—even Winter was touched, even as annoyed with her as he was. The heart does want what it wants, in fact, and people do stupid things for love. They even kill for it sometimes, but not like this, not when there's genuine affection, not on a wild rampage like this.

Steph Breach gave a desolate sniff. "I didn't matter that much to her. That's what you're saying."

"That is what I'm saying. Of course you didn't matter. They were a boy and girl in love. Nobody else mattered to them all that much. If the last trumpet blew, they'd've spent their final hours in their sleeping bag out in the cave. That's how the world works. That's how life goes on."

"Up yours, Winter," she said.

Winter snorted. She snorted, too, a hard laugh, shaking her head at herself. However old she was—thirty-five, forty—she was too old—too old and too tough—to deny the basics, not to face them head on.

"I was a fool for love," she said, taking up his phrase, comforting herself with it.

"You were," said Winter. "But you didn't get anyone killed."

He watched as she breathed that in, gathered herself around it, grew solid again, her normal solid self.

"Do you know who it was?" she asked finally. "Who did do it?"

He shook his head. "Not yet. I could use some help with that, in fact."

She lifted her chin at him. "What do you need?"

"I need to talk to the kid. The boy. Lila's little brother."

"Bobby?"

"Yes."

Steph Breach's eyes widened. "Wow. That's a tough one. I hear he's with an aunt and uncle in Chicago."

"Can you get me to him?"

She thought about it. He could see she wanted to. He had relieved her conscience. She wanted to help him, to pay him back. After a while, she nodded.

"I can try," she said.

# 19

The autumn day grew darker still. The wind grew stronger. He drove the desolate two-lane to the highway, with the trees bowing and swaying on either side of him. Great colorful flocks of leaves flew across the road in swift rushes. They clung to his windshield, pattered the sides of his Jeep.

He reached the junction with Route 10. It broadened to a four-lane. The forests fell away and there was open country, drab, harvested croplands, rimmed with small, distant sycamores, already stripped bare.

The E-Z storage facility was a faceless three-story building between one town and another. A building that seemed thrown together, sheet metal and glass, it stood on a patch of asphalt on a stretch of nowhere. He pulled the Jeep into the parking lot. Shut it down. Walked in.

Inside, the place was tomb-quiet. A maze of storage units with red corrugated doors. There was a metal stairway up to the office on the second floor, an office with a long window looking inward, down on the maze of units. As Winter climbed the stairs, he could picture Mateo up there, looking down at his father kowtowing to criminals, humiliated, compromised, corrupt, taking their cash to hide their drugs.

The office door came open as he approached. There was Hernandez himself. He looked formidable framed in the doorway. He was wearing slacks, a shirt and tie, no jacket. Somehow the outfit emphasized his big shoulders, his powerful arms. He did not look as friendly as he had before. He had buried his son. He had heard his son accused of murder. Beneath the silver hair, behind the silver beard, his face seemed narrower than it had, worn and grim.

"I got nothing else to say to you," he said—that was his greeting.

Winter stopped on the platform a few yards away from him. He put his hands in the pockets of his windbreaker. He nodded to show he understood. Then he said: "I don't think Mateo killed the Wassermans."

The man's face twisted with bitterness and grief. "He wouldn't kill nobody. Nobody."

"Did the police recover your .38?" Winter asked. "You said the killer stole a rifle and your .38. Did the cops give you your pistol back?"

Hernandez shook his head. "Strange said they needed to hold onto it. For evidence."

"Yeah. He's lying. He hasn't got it. Because he hasn't caught the real killer."

Hernandez blinked as he took this in. Winter saw an opportunity.

"I need to come into your office," he said. "I have something to show you. Something you'll want to see."

Hernandez hesitated, but Winter knew he had reached him. The older man turned to look behind him, into the office. Winter could see a woman in there: a colorless bundle of clothing, a pair of cat-eye glasses, a gray-brown mess of pinned-up hair. Hernandez gestured to her briefly and she got up, came out, hurried past Winter. He heard her footsteps going down the stairs behind him.

Hernandez made the same gesture again, to Winter this time. He moved aside to let Winter pass.

In the office, the two men stood over one of the computers. Winter played the video—the one Gwendolyn Lord had given him. He and Hernandez watched as the fifty-second scene played out. Agnes Wilde and Norman Wasserman standing in the lot outside the Community Center. A gray day, a windy day, a day a lot like this day. The sound was turned up so they could hear all that was left of the broken voices, all the words that hadn't been blown away by the wind.

". . . hardly . . ." said Wasserman.

". . . irrelevant . . ." said Agnes Wilde.

". . . abortions and . . ." Wasserman said.

". . . what I am . . ." said Agnes. ". . . you are . . ."

Then, as Wasserman turned and walked away, she called after him, "Those are your only choices."

The monitor went dark. The office was silent. Against the rear wall, three monitors showed security footage of the storage units below. The images shifted, one to the next. Otherwise, the little space seemed very still.

Winter turned to Hernandez, expecting a reaction. But Hernandez remained exactly as he was, staring at the screen, though it was now blank. Winter could only see his profile, but the expression on that half of his face alone was fearsome enough. Winter imagined he could feel the room's atmosphere quivering with suppressed wrath and violence. He thought: *He already knew.*

"You see what it is," Winter said.

Hernandez faced him. The full blast of that expression made Winter's throat tighten. Why was it, he wondered, that whenever he was in Maidenvale, he felt some man was on the verge of punching his face into the center of his head? What made it such an angry place?

"What do you want here?" Hernandez asked him, as if continuing his line of thought. "What do you know about it here anyway? About this place? About what our lives are like?"

But that was just it. That was the whole problem. To Winter, the nature of the place didn't matter. What Hernandez's life was like or anyone else's didn't matter much to him, either, not in the overall scheme of things. To Winter, only the dead mattered here. The lives erased. The bonds destroyed. Whatever it was in him that needed to see this made right—that mattered. The principle but not the place. Because, after all, he was not a man who felt at home anywhere but in the poems of the past.

He kept quiet about all this, of course, about his own feelings—which didn't matter that much to him either. All he knew about Maidenvale was that, if he spoke the wrong words to the wrong person at the wrong time, he risked being beaten senseless.

"Wasserman stopped working at the Community Center right after this, right after this meeting with Agnes Wilde," he said finally. "He quit or was fired. I'm not sure which. I don't think it matters which. If he quit, it was because he was forced out."

Hernandez sneered. "What did she know? That woman. Agnes Wilde. What did she know either?"

Winter controlled his breathing, controlled his tone, watched for the sudden eruption, the sudden blow without warning. Hernandez was smallish, but he was burly, muscular, tough. Winter didn't want to take his punch if he could avoid it.

"I think she knew that Dr. Wasserman was a sex pest of some kind," Winter answered him. "One of the girls I talked to told me:

if his eyes were fingers, he'd have undressed her. I think he hired Agnes to be his son's nanny because he thought it would give him time to work on her, break down her defenses. He was going by her past reputation. He didn't realize she had changed her life. Or maybe he didn't care."

Hernandez's face seemed to darken visibly, as with a rush of black blood to his cheeks, a black blush. "You should go away from here," he said. "You should go away and not come back. You don't know. You're not untouchable."

Winter ignored the threat and pushed on, though his eyes did flick to Hernandez's hands, watching for that sudden blow. "She was from the Hollow, you know. Agnes. She'd had hard times."

Hernandez snorted. "It was a better place once," he said. Then he turned back to the computer, stared at the screen again as if the video were still playing there. But Winter was not distracted by that. He kept a watch on his hands.

"Maybe so," he said. "But that's probably why Wasserman thought Agnes was an easy mark—because of her hard times. She had a bad stretch of life after she left town, before she came home. He didn't realize she'd changed all that, but she had and he couldn't get his hands on her. That's all I'm saying."

Hernandez shook his head slowly, thinking his own thoughts.

"Anyway," Winter said, "when Agnes found out what Wasserman was, she went to him and confronted him. Told him he had to leave the Center. Stay away from the girls there. I'm guessing she told him a lot more than that. That she'd find a way to destroy him if he didn't stop what he was doing. She should've gone to the police, I guess, but she couldn't, could she? With Strange being what he is, tied up with Del Rey the way he is. Still, she could've destroyed Wasserman's career, knowing what she knew."

Staring down at the blank screen, Hernandez lifted his lip so his teeth showed. "She should've been afraid. That's what she should've been. Afraid."

"You're right. She should have been. But I don't think she was. I think she was a special sort of person and she wasn't afraid of much. She found out what she found out and she confronted Wasserman. He tried to game her, it sounds like. Bring up her past. That's what I think he's saying to her on the video. 'You're hardly the one to throw stones at me, having done what you did.' Something like that. And she tells him that her life is irrelevant. It's not the point. He pushes her about her sins. That's the part where you can hear him talking about abortions. And she answers, 'It's not about what I am. It's about what you are.' Finally she must've told him he could either resign his post and keep his hands to himself, or she'd go public, or find an honest cop, or get his license revoked, or whatever the threat was. I don't really know. 'Those are your only choices,' she told him. Wasserman tried to get his wife to fire her after that. Then he could discredit her. He could say she was a disgruntled former employee or whatever. I don't know what was in his mind. But his wife wouldn't go for it. Her son loved Agnes. And Agnes loved the boy. And maybe Agnes wanted to stay in the house so she could keep an eye on Wasserman, too. I don't know."

Now Hernandez turned on him so swiftly that only Winter's readiness kept him steady, kept him from striking before he was struck. Instead, he stayed where he was, planted solidly, motionless.

Even so, they were now very close together in that little room, nose to nose almost. Winter could feel Hernandez's hot breath on his face, coming fast. He could feel the air between them thrumming like a plucked string.

"He was filth!" Hernandez spat. "Wasserman. Fancy man. Rich man. White man in his mansion. Pervert. He had everything.

The sick bastard. Going after children. He had everything and he was filth."

"He was," said Winter.

"You think I'm sorry what happened to him?"

"No."

"Why should I be?"

"Why should you?"

"There's no reason. He was the scum of the earth."

"He was." Winter had reached the final part of his story, the worst part, but what could he do? He'd come this far. He had to say it. "Agnes must have always suspected what Wasserman was. Even when she took the job in his house, she must've suspected his motives. But she probably told herself he was just a lecher, all eyes, all desire, nothing else."

"He was filth."

"He was. But something must've changed for her. That's why she confronted him. Someone must have told her something. I think Lila told her something. Lila told her everything. And your son told Lila everything. I think he told Lila about your daughter, Sara . . ."

Hernandez gave a soft, strangled cry of grief and rage from deep in his throat.

"About Sara," Winter went on.

"She was eleven years old," Hernandez said.

Winter didn't answer. He didn't have to. His feelings were plain. Anyone could have seen them written on his face. His sneer of disgust seemed to give the older man some comfort, to answer the anger in his heart and take some of the violence out of him. Hernandez finally broke away, turned away, moved away until he was standing at the edge of the long window looking down on the still maze of storage units, with the security footage shifting on the screens behind him. He put his hands in his pockets and gazed on his business, Winter thought, as if he were looking down on the ruin of a once-great city. There was a long silence between the two of them.

"I came here the right way, the legal way," Hernandez said finally. "I'm an American. I made an honest living."

Winter nodded, but said nothing.

"These criminals now. These gangsters . . . And Strange, he's no better. And Wasserman in his big house. Money! That's all they care about." He made a sound as if he were spitting. Then he fell silent.

Winter, meanwhile, carefully considered his next move, his next word. He felt he was close to understanding the murders in the Tulipwood house. He felt the whole story would soon unfold in his imagination, clearly this time, point by point, gunshot by gunshot, death by death. But not yet—not quite yet. And if he spoke too much now, probed too much, pushed Hernandez too hard for whatever he knew, it would end badly, maybe even with that violence that was still thrumming in the air between them. Thrumming all over this town, it seemed.

He hadn't quite decided how to proceed when Hernandez, still staring out the window at the maze below, said again, "You should go." He glanced at Winter, then away. "I mean it. You don't know how close you are. You should go and not come back. What can you do here? What can anyone do here? Strange. Wasserman. Del Rey. Everybody wants what they want here. Nothing else matters. Just what they want. Money. Sex. Drugs. Whatever it is. Nothing else. They have no God. They have no souls. They're just meat, not people, all of them." He made that spitting noise again. "You should go and not come back. Really. You don't know how close you are."

As Winter left the place, as he walked out into the weather, under the darkening sky, through the rising, biting wind, he was wondering about those final words. *You don't know how close you are.* Close to what? he was wondering. Close to the truth? Or to a bad end? A fatal decision by Strange or the mobster Del Rey.

He climbed into the Jeep and headed away from the facility, still wondering as he drove.

But he didn't have to wonder for long.

As his Jeep rumbled back onto the desolate two-lane, as he traveled between the forests of autumn trees bent over by the wind, as the dead leaves whirled around him, reminding him, literary man that he was, of damned lovers whirling through hell on the winds of desire, he glanced up into the rearview mirror and saw a car speeding after him, its headlights gleaming in the deepening dark. He looked ahead and saw two more cars speeding toward him out of the near distance. A thought flashed through his head, the thought that murder bends the atmosphere, distorts the fabric of human relations, befuddles that human sense that seeks for justice even in this eerily inhuman and unjust world.

But he had no time for that thought at the moment. The car behind him was closing in. The cars ahead of him were speeding up. He knew the violence that had bent the bonds of community in Maidenvale was about to emerge from the atmosphere and take living shape, and that he would be at the center of it.

Hernandez was right. He hadn't known how close he was.

# 20

The wind blew harder. The trees bowed down. The leaves swirled everywhere around him. The headlights in his rearview grew brighter swiftly, larger swiftly, and the headlights in his windshield raced toward him, already blinding and huge. Winter could hear the roar of the oncoming engines over the roar of the surrounding wind. Seconds left until impact. His heart hammered. His eyes darted left and right, looking for a way out or a way through. There was none—nothing but a dirt shoulder carpeted with dead pine needles and swirling with wind-blown leaves. Could he sneak past them on that? He doubted it. The cars up ahead were side by side, taking up both lanes. Which was frightening in itself because it meant they expected no one else to come, no one who might inter-rupt them or call for help. They must have blocked off the road in both directions. Still, he watched for his chance as the headlights in his rearview grew enormous, like a madman's eyes, and the grill of the hopped-up junker grinned at him, speeding nearer.

The trap closed. Winter waited for his moment, the narrow window of time when the two cars up ahead were close enough, but not too close to cut off his maneuver, and before the car behind him could connect and drive him off the road.

The instant came. He didn't wrench the wheel. A short, sharp, controlled movement to the left carried the Jeep off the pavement, onto the soft shoulder. He dodged to the side of the onrushing cars, so that now they were rushing toward one another. He thought he might make it. He thought he might get past them while they crashed into each other. He had one wild second of hope. Then the nearest car zigged into him hard, scraping the Jeep's side.

The Jeep fishtailed. Its rear whacked a tree. Winter tried to pull away and lost control. The SUV spun off the shoulder into the middle of the road, tires screaming. More tires screamed as the junker behind him and one of the cars ahead both tried to brake and turn before they smashed together. It was too late. They were too close. The edges of their fenders collided. Glass shattered. Metal crumpled. The junker spun grill-first into the trunk of a pine and hit it so hard the airbag deployed, swallowing the driver in the white balloon. The other car, the oncoming car, a revamped Dodge, skidded into its partner, a red Corvette, and the Vette jiggered crazily onto the shoulder.

Winter's car was still spinning. He wrestled with the wheel. The SUV went off the far side of the road and the tail smacked into a sycamore with an ugly crunch. All this took place in one endless second. Winter still thought he might pull a hard turn and make a run for it.

But now his attackers were tumbling from their cars to come after him. One gangster staggered from the junker, dazed stupid by the airbag's impact, staggering like a drunken man. But the heavy-set tattooed punk who got out of the Vette was wide awake and white-eyed with fury. Winter knew at once that this was Del Rey himself. He saw the gangster's hand going behind his back, and knew he was reaching for a gun even as he strode toward him. The driver of the Dodge was angrily fighting to shove open his dented door. Winter saw this was Inspector Strange. It flashed through his mind that this confirmed it: the gangsters had closed the road. No other driver would pass by. Strange would not have acted in the open like this if it weren't so. Winter was alone out here.

Winter screwed his steering wheel hard to the right, hoping to do a screeching U-turn and blast the hell out of there. But it was no good. Del Rey had his gun out, a blunt Glock. He charged the Jeep with the barrel leveled at Winter's face. If Winter hit the gas, it would be the last thing he ever did.

Winter put the gearshift into park and killed the engine. With one hand, he took off his glasses and lay them on the dash. The other hand slipped quickly in and out of the inner pouch of his windbreaker. Then he raised both hands in surrender.

Del Rey was now right outside the door, the gun pointing straight at him. Winter gave himself only a sixty percent chance of living into the next second. But Del Rey apparently got hold of himself. Controlled his emotions, his rage. He gestured with the Glock: *Get out of the car.*

Winter opened the Jeep door and tumbled out into the wind, staggering, trying to look more dazed and weakened than he actually was.

Del Rey smacked him in the side of the head with his gun barrel.

The pain was an electric fire that erased the world. The wind, the trees, the leaves, the autumn sky were all far away while the pain was inside him and everywhere. Winter reeled to the side and dropped into the leaves. Everything tilted sickeningly, and nausea filled him in a toxic flood. He looked up through a blur of weather and hurt and saw Del Rey sneering down at him, pointing the pistol at his head. Winter still thought he well might pull the trigger, but no. The gangster gestured with his head to Strange.

He was delegating the tedious chore of beating Winter bloody to the town's top cop, his underling.

*Maidenvale*, Winter thought. Then Strange was towering above him and kicked him in the stomach.

Winter saw it coming half a second before it came. He timed his roll to lessen the impact, but the impact was hard. The kick turned his guts to water. Acid spurted into his mouth. In a blind agony, he rolled to the edge of the wind-whipped forest, the leaves like a red and yellow cyclone rising around him.

Strange stalked after him. His long face was bright with sadistic pleasure. He was wearing a sweatshirt and jeans, ready for action. His big fists were balled at the end of his tense, powerful arms.

Winter tried to climb to his feet. He was halfway there, sick and unsteady, when the big cop caught up with him and struck again. It was a heavy fist to the head this time. Winter managed to duck under it—almost. Strange's knuckles grazed the top of his skull. Winter pretended the shot was worse than it was, and staggered deeper into the woods, past the first line of trees.

Dizzy and green with pain, he stood bent over, clutching his belly. Strange stormed after him, his teeth bared. He felt confident enough now to take his time, to circle around, looking for his best position. That caused him to plant himself between Winter and Del Rey's gun.

That was what Winter was waiting for.

He knew he had only two options here. He could take the beating and hope that was all they had planned for him. He guessed it was. He guessed they were just trying to scare him off. But he could also fight back and risk things getting out of hand, risk Del Rey's anger and a quick trigger finger and a bullet to the head.

He decided to risk the bullet. He didn't like getting beaten. He especially didn't like getting beaten by a sleazy son of a bitch like Strange. He knew he was probably too angry to make a wise decision here. He knew he should probably second guess himself. But he also knew that wasn't going to happen.

He had only one thing going for him. They hadn't searched him. He still had the tactical knife he'd taken off Ted Caesar, the government agent who'd been romancing Lori back home. He had palmed the knife before he got out of his Jeep, the blade aligned with his wrist, hidden up his sleeve.

Strange swung again. It was meant to be a knock-out blow. He was overconfident. He thought Winter was hurt worse than he was. He threw a big punch, nearly a roundhouse, his hips open, his fist aimed at Winter's jaw.

Winter ducked under the blow. The shot went over him, leaving Strange off balance. In an instant, Winter was behind the detective and had him in a stranglehold, yanking his head back. He pressed the knife blade hard against Strange's throat.

He held the cop in place in front of him, like a shield. Del Rey and the other thug—Gangster Two—both tensed and pointed their Glocks at him, but neither fired. He was all but hidden behind the struggling, strangling Strange.

"I'll kill him, Del Rey! I'll kill him!" Winter shouted over the noise of the wind.

There was a momentary pause. The wind roared around them. The trees creaked and squealed. The leaves were everywhere, a cloud of moving color. Strange gagged, open-mouthed and helpless. Del Rey and Gangster Two looked on, eyes flaring.

Then Del Rey shrugged. "So kill him."

Strange's cry was cut off as Winter dug the blade deep into his neck. The detective's blood sheeted down over Winter's knife hand.

"All right, all right, all right," said Del Rey. "Don't kill him. Don't kill him. Hey, hey, I was joking. Don't kill him."

Winter relaxed. Strange made gurgling noises as Winter continued to press his arm under his chin.

Del Rey laughed and shook his head. He looked at Gangster Two as if to say: *Can you believe this character?* Gangster Two tried to smile as if he got the joke, but he didn't. He was still dazed from the airbag, and furious too. Also he was an idiot.

The wind blew and the clouds darkened, and a shadow seemed to fall over the world.

Del Rey eyed Winter sidelong. "Just who exactly are you, *hijo?*" he asked.

"I'm an English professor," Winter said, holding the knife to Strange's bloody throat.

Del Rey laughed again, shook his head at Gangster Two again. *This character!*

"Okay. So what now, English professor? You think I don't kill you? You let him go, I kill you. You run away, I hunt you down and kill you. You escape, I come to your home and kill you. What are we doing here?"

There was a sudden crack of thunder and it started to rain, one, two, three big drops pattering on the leaves and then a downpour. Winter released his stranglehold on Strange. As the big cop staggered forward, clutching his bleeding throat, Winter kicked him in the back and sent him stumbling out into the road. Winter faced the gangsters' guns unprotected.

The rain, meanwhile, grew heavier. Very quickly, it became a cold thick curtain of water. As he walked out of the forest and approached Del Rey, Winter folded his knife and slipped it back into his windbreaker. Then the two men stood together, face to face.

Del Rey was a big man, broad and thick. He had a round, fat face bristling with cropped hair on his head and on his chin. He wore jeans and a checked shirt and a suede jacket, but wherever his skin was exposed, it was covered with blue tattoos.

Winter stood in front of him, already drenched—drenched and sick and aching.

"If you kill me," Winter told him quietly. "You and all your people will be dead in a week. No one will know how and no one will care why, and even your bosses back home will find it wise to forget you."

Their eyes met. Del Rey took Winter's measure. He stopped smiling. He nodded. "An English professor," he said. He had to raise his voice to be heard over the rain.

"Look, murder's bad for business, Del Rey. You know that," Winter told him. "That's why we're here, isn't it? The minute you heard about the killings at Tulipwood, you wanted this case over and done with, right? You wanted Strange to protect Mateo to keep the investigation away from Hernandez and your drugs, then when Mateo was dead, you wanted the whole blame dumped on him to make the case go away. The last thing you wanted was the staties or the feds to come in here and start asking about the Hernandez family, finding out what I found out, their ties to you and the Homeland Highway. Now you want to scare me off for the same reason. But you don't really want me dead."

"No?" said Del Rey with a laugh.

"No. If you think the staties would be bad, the guys who would come after you if I got killed would be a lot worse, believe me."

Del Rey seemed to consider this. Then he spoke so softly it was almost inaudible under the rain. "I believe you," he said. He sounded surprised.

The wind rose and the sheet of rain slanted and lashed at them. A few last leaves blew off the high swaying branches, but the leaves that had already fallen were pinned to the ground by the steady rain. The four men stood in the midst of that downpour—Winter and Del Rey, Strange, bleeding and hangdog, and Gangster Two, grim and angry but too stupid to quite know what he was supposed to feel. The wrecked cars were all around them and the rain drummed on them noisily and made the broken glass on the pavement jump and dance. The empty, desolate two-lane stretched off into the storm-washed nowhere.

"I want whoever killed the Wasserman family," Winter said. "If it was you, then it's you I'll come for."

"Wasn't me," said Del Rey with another shrug.

"Then your best move is to leave me be. Let me do what I came here to do."

With that, Winter turned his back on the gangster. He plodded through the rain to his Jeep.

"Hey, English professor," Del Rey called quietly behind him.

Winter still half thought he might catch a bullet here, but he was in too much pain and too angry to care. He had his hand on the Jeep door but paused to listen without looking back.

"It's personal between you and me now, you understand that," said Del Rey. "I have to make this good. Not today maybe. Not for a while. But one day. Soon. I will kill you. You understand that."

Winter nodded wearily. He did understand it.

"I'll be seeing you, *hijo*," Del Rey said.

Winter labored his way into the Jeep. Pulled the door shut behind him. He started the engine and got the windshield wipers going. He looked out at the scene through the glass. Del Rey still watched him. Gangster Two was holstering his gun, disappointed. Strange was frowning, shocked at the blood on his hand as the rain washed it away while still more blood poured out of his neck.

Winter's eyes met Del Rey's. There was no doubt in his mind that the gangster was serious and would one day soon come to murder him. Del Rey lived in a world where you made threats and made good on your threats or you were no one. He would bide his time. Then he would come.

Winter, on the other hand, lived in a different world. He had not been trained to make threats. He had been trained to arrange for people to die as if by accident, or by some series of events that had nothing to do with him or with the government that had once employed him. Looking through the windshield at Del Rey—Del Rey smirking at him and making his plans—he wondered if he would ever be done with that lonely business of murder. He wished he had never come to Maidenvale. What had he been trying to accomplish? What had he expected to fix or save?

He put the Jeep in gear and drove away, through the rain, through the wind, down the empty road.

PART FOUR

# THE BLOOD IN THE DARKNESS

*It's nothing. It's nothing, Margaret. An accident. It looks worse than it is. I don't want to talk about it. Maybe later. Not yet. Not now. Now I want to tell you the end of this story. What happened between me and Madeleine Uno. I have to finish it. I have to.*

*I went to bed with her—under false pretenses, as you say, though maybe not as false as I tried to believe. In the morning, I walked her home. Early because she had an early class. We held hands as we walked. The streets were empty. The wind was high and cold. When we got to her place, we stood outside and kissed for a long time. Then we said a fond goodbye, and she went in. And I posted myself across the street and waited for her to leave so I could search her apartment.*

*I probably should have been more careful, more patient, more sure. I probably should have waited until I was certain she was gone for the day. But I was desperate. I couldn't stand the suspense. I needed to find the bug, you see. Because if there was no bug in her apartment, that meant Madeleine was the one I was after. She was the only one who could've come to the office at the same time as me. If there was no bug, if the spies weren't listening when she told me how to get the code, then she was the one who'd been selling information to the Chinese.*

*I know all about my motives now, but I didn't know it then. I didn't know how desperate I was to exonerate her. I didn't know I was still the boy I was pretending to be, and how deeply that boy had fallen in love with her. So, the minute I saw her go out again, I broke into her apartment and started searching.*

*It wasn't long before I found exactly what I wanted to find.*

*I was kneeling down by a lamp in the far corner of the room. Checking a tangle of wires in the socket there, thinking it would be a good place to hide a listening device. I was down on one knee, shining a flashlight over the wires in case there was a camera with the bug and I could see the lens flash. And it did flash and there it was. There was a bug pinned through the insulation of one cord, the pins connected to the wires so it could draw on the electricity. It was well done. Almost invisible. But not quite. I reached down and drew the thing out with my fingers. Examined it. I was grinning without even realizing it. My heart was flooded with relief. Madeleine was not guilty!*

*Then the front door opened.*

*"What are you doing?"*

*She'd come back. I never found out why. Maybe she'd forgotten something, I don't know. I hadn't even heard the lock turn. I was so absorbed with what I had found. But there she suddenly was, gaping at me.*

*You'd think I would have prepared a story in advance in case this happened, right? Or you'd think I would have been suave and expert enough to come up with something plausible on the spot. But I hadn't. I wasn't. I was completely flummoxed. And in that one second of silence when I turned and looked over my shoulder at her, when I stared at her with my mouth open and nothing to say, Madeleine understood everything.*

*I can still see her in my mind. She was beautiful. Wearing this short tweed skirt the girls were all wearing then, just down to her thighs, and a black tee and a black jacket. She had a beret on and her hair was all tousled from the wind. She was the college girlfriend I would have wanted, basically. Maybe the wife I would have wanted, I'll never know. But to see the look on her face, the look of betrayal, the pain—it sank into my heart like the blade of a dagger.*

*"Oh," she said. She held her hand up as if to make life* stop. *She pushed her palm at me repeatedly*: Stop, stop, stop. *She said, "Oh. Oh, what have you done?"*

*She moved to the sofa, the sofa she'd been sitting on when I'd had my head in her lap. With one hand she was holding her stomach as if I'd shot her. With the other, she had to reach out to find her way, because her glassy gaze was all turned inward, watching her own thoughts as everything became clear to her.*

*Her fingers touched the sofa arm, and she clutched at it, pulled herself to it, sank unsteadily into the cushions. She sat there, staring at me. She spoke my name—only it wasn't my name, not my real name. It was my cover name, the name the Division had given me for this assignment. The only name she knew.*

*"Danny," she whispered. "The Rosetta? The key code? Is that what you were after? Is that what all this was about?"*

*Obviously, by "all this" she meant everything between us, our friendship, her care for me, our conversations, our romance, our lovemaking.*

*I still couldn't speak. I still couldn't think what to say. I couldn't tell her the truth, that I loved her, because I couldn't admit to myself that I loved her. And I couldn't lie and pretend I loved her because . . . well, because I loved her and couldn't lie to her anymore.*

*I rose slowly to my feet. "Look . . ."*

*But she waved her hand at me urgently, her eyes white and wide. "Ssh!" she said fiercely. "Ssh! Ssh! Ssh!"*

*"Madeleine . . ."*

*She pulled back, recoiling into the sofa cushions, hand up, eyes wide, as if I were physically attacking her.*

*Finally, I realized I had to tell her the truth, some version of the truth. "Listen to me. Listen. It's all right. I'm the good guys."*

*She gave a high cry of wild laughter that sounded like a cry of pain.*

*"I am," I insisted. "If our enemies have these files, they can disarm us without our even knowing it. They can wait for their moment and disable us when it counts the most. We had to know who was passing information on to them, so maybe we could turn the tables."*

*She put her hands on her shoulders, her arms crossed in front of her, as if she were naked, as if she wanted to cover herself, protect her vulnerability. "You . . ." she said. That was all she said. But the rest of it unspooled in my mind:* You lied to me. You befriended me. You made love to me.

*"It wasn't like that," I told her. "I didn't mean to hurt you. We just didn't know who it was, who the spy was, or even if there was a spy. It could have been you. But now—now, it's all right. You see?" I held up the disconnected bug.*

*She didn't even look at it. She just sat there, gaping at me. Still computing the number and depth of my transgressions. Then she blinked as if she were coming out of a daze and she said, "What? Danny? God, is that even your name? Do I even know the name of the man who was inside me? Who was whispering the things you whispered to me—what—just hours ago? Do I see what, Danny? What are you talking about?"*

*"Last night. Last night, I went to your office, to get the files, the music files, so my people could trace who'd been pillaging the information. You're so smart, your code was so smart, it baffled us. But while I was there, someone else came in. I had to hide, I couldn't see who it was, but I knew if it wasn't you, someone must have bugged your apartment, must've been listening in. That's why I'm here. To search the place because if I found the bug then I would know it wasn't you and . . ."*

*Very slowly, weirdly slow, her eyes shifted, moved from me to the thing I was holding, the bug. And then, with that same unbearable slowness, her whole expression changed—from a look of hurt and heartbreak to a stare of horror.*

*"They were listening?" she whispered. It was a desolate sound.*

*I wagged the bug at her. Why didn't she understand? This was a good thing. She was in the clear. "Yes," I said. "Yes, that's how they knew what to look for. That's . . ."*

*"But," she said—said with this bizarre, hollow calm. "But then . . . But then you've killed me, Danny."*

*"What? What do you mean? I . . ."*

*"They heard," she said. "They heard me tell you." Her eyes filled. She shook her head. "Oh God. Oh God. I'm such an idiot. I thought you loved me. I thought you were who you said you were. I was just trying to show you how smart I was. I wanted you to admire me! That's all. I never even considered . . ."*

*"What? What do you mean?"*

*"It was only after I told you, after you ran out like that, I thought: was it possible? I thought: No, it can't be you're a spy. You're just a boy. You just love me. So just to reassure myself, I went to the office . . ."*

*Now it was my turn to stand and stare. To realize the extent of the disaster. Finally, the truth broke out of me. If I hadn't loved her, I would've seen it long before.*

*"It was you!" I heard the words as if someone else had spoken them. "It was you?"*

*"You've killed me, Danny. They'll think I betrayed them. I did betray them."*

*"The Chinese?" I said. "Why? Why would you do that? You said you hated them."*

*She brushed the question away as if it were trivial. Meaningless. "I didn't even know who they were. They played me. Just like you did, Danny. They sent a woman to me. Somehow, it was like she knew me. She knew everything I cared about. Like we were born to be friends. She coaxed me into giving her—nothing—a string of numbers. Some equation. I didn't even know what it was. But once I was in, there was no way out. They told me I'd go to jail. I told myself—I don't know—this college is flooded with Chinese money. They get everything we have one way or another. It made no difference. That's what I told myself. But once I was in, I couldn't get out."*

*After a frozen moment, my mind began racing. Looking for a way to salvage this.*

"Well, we'll—we'll get you out. We'll protect you," I said.

She laughed. "You'll lock me up. You know you will. Or give me over to them."

"No."

"Oh!" she said. As if one more lie from me were too much to bear. "You think they couldn't reach me? In prison? Wherever you hid me? They'd find me. I'd just have to sit there and wait for them."

"No, no," I said helplessly. "We'll work something out."

Again, the look she gave me—it went right into me. A stabbing pain. She shook her head. "Who even are you, Danny? What's even your name? Even now, you seem like . . . you seem like who you pretended to be. But then what you've done . . . I don't understand it. I don't understand who you even are."

What could I say to that? How could I answer her? I had no answer. I had no idea who I was.

"You better go, my lamb," she said gently—in her old sweet style. "You really better go."

"What will you do?"

"I don't know, sweetheart. Something. Don't worry. I'll do something. I'll think of something. I'm good at that." She was staring into the middle distance, her face blank. She seemed to have drifted away.

"Let me help you," I said. "Let us help you. Please."

She glanced at me as if she'd already forgotten I was there. "You better go," she said. "Don't worry. I'll be fine."

After a while, I did go. Why not? I was a cold-blooded assassin, after all. I'd done what I'd come to do. Mission accomplished. Let the Division handle the rest.

Immersed in that lie, I called the Recruiter from the street outside Madeleine's brownstone. I explained to him what had happened. He ordered me to clear out at once. He didn't even want me to return to my apartment or pack up or anything. He just wanted me to vanish. My *records would be gone by morning, he said. Any trace of me would be erased. I would never have existed.*

*So, I did what I was told. I vanished.*

*It was a week before I heard anything more. This was not surprising. In fact, it was standard op. Most of the time, if anything resulted from one of our assignments, we were more likely to read about it in the news than get a direct briefing on it from within the Division. No one told us much of anything.*

*But this time was different. One evening, I received a call at my apartment in Alexandria. I was told to come downstairs in ten minutes. When I came down, there was a limousine waiting for me. The driver got out and opened the back door to let me in. The Recruiter was waiting inside.*

*We sat together in silence as we drove along the Potomac. I looked out the tinted windows and watched the monuments of empire white against the mellowing sky. The Lincoln Parthenon, the Washington obelisk, and the Capitol dome passed in the distance as the daylight faded. Beside me, the Recruiter stared directly ahead at his own reflection on the black glass that hid us from the driver.*

*Maybe it was my imagination, but when I glanced at him, I thought I detected some faint sign of feeling in those dark and deadpan and unreadable features. Compassion? Pity? Maybe just irony. Like I said, I'm not even sure it was really there at all.*

*At last, as we passed into Arlington, he started talking.*

*"As you can tell by the expression on my face, I am delighted to report that because of your reprehensible behavior the people of God have been spared a devastating attack by the demonic yellow peril that threatens the freedom of mankind. I like to imagine that news would please you if you had the wit to believe in God and so understood how the powers of this world's darkness represent the spiritual forces of evil in the heavenly realms. Then at least you would be able to receive God's forgiveness for*

*your despicable actions instead of sinking slowly into denial, guilt, and a resulting sclerosis of the soul that will ultimately condemn you to a loveless and therefore joyless existence—before you face an eternity that I presume will be spent in hell, though who am I to judge?"*

*I tried, as always, to echo his deadpan tone. I did not know yet that my heart was broken. "I'm glad to hear it, Chief," I said. "I think."*

*"But we lost the girl," he told me.*

*I felt something take a vertiginous drop inside me. "Lost her in what sense?"*

*"In the usual sense that we can't find her. She's a clever little thing, isn't she?"*

*"She's a genius, yes, sir."*

*He shifted slightly in his seat, but never looked at me. "I suppose with both Japanese and Jewish blood in her, she'd either have to be sneaky and greedy or brilliant beyond belief."*

*"Those would be among the combinations of offensive racial clichés she could choose from, yes, sir."*

*"We arrived at her apartment less than half an hour after you left, and there wasn't a trace of her," the Recruiter said. "No trail. It was a remarkable piece of tradecraft."*

*I tried to hide my surprise. "Was she in the trade? Was she an actual professional?"*

*His expression did not change, of course, and he didn't move, not visibly, but I thought he gave an extra little puff of air or something—something to indicate that the idea—the idea that Madeleine was a professional intelligence agent—was ridiculous.*

*"No," he said then. "They roped her in. It was that stupid app she uses all the time. The one she posts pictures of her cupcakes on. It was one of their devices. They used it to get into her computer, steal her keystrokes, even watch her and read her facial expressions. By the time they sent someone to approach her, they knew her better than she knew herself.*

*They played to her dissatisfactions with her father, her frustrated love of the arts, culture. She probably didn't even know what was happening until she gave them the first piece of information. Then she was stuck. They told her she'd be arrested if she didn't go on with it. She probably would have been."*

*"Yes, that's pretty much how she described it to me."*

*"She's a dreamer," said the Recruiter. "A poetry girl like you're a poetry boy, except with numbers. Her head was in the clouds. I don't think she understood what she was doing."*

*"I don't either," I told him.*

*He drew a deep breath, which I took to be an expression of emotion. "That said, when she put her mind to something, she did it exceptionally well. After she found out who you were and what had happened, she put her mind to disappearing." He paused again, even longer this time. Then he turned to me, gave me the full, impenetrable Recruiter stare. "If she had been in the trade, she would have been wiser. She would have turned herself into us. We could have protected her, Poetry Boy."*

*My lips parted as I began to respond, but I didn't say anything. A sense of deep misgiving had come over me, a kind of acid dread filling me. I hadn't asked where we were going. I didn't ask now.*

*We entered a sorrowful part of the city. Once dignified suburban homes sat dilapidated on plots of unshorn grass. The car slowed as we approached a watery ditch with a fence of boards slanting by the side of it. The dark was almost full now, but the last light lingered.*

*"There was a wall here once," the Recruiter said. "To keep people with my color skin from mingling with people of your color. The Chinese occasionally like to take time out from exterminating their minorities to remind us that we Americans have also been unkind at times. Still, it was damned decent of them to call and give us a location."*

*I saw her from the window. I choked back a cry. I had the door open before the car had come to a full stop. I stumbled on the sidewalk, then ran to her. I knelt over her, my pants soaked in mud, my hands outstretched helplessly above her, my palms open to the sky.*

*She lay half submerged in the grass and water. Her nightshirt gleamed white against the evening darkness. Her face stared upward at the purple night.*

*I became aware after a while that the Recruiter was standing over me, his hands in his overcoat pockets, his face rock-hard yet somehow grave with sadness.*

*"They tortured her!" I cried.*

*"Of course they did. We fight who we fight for a reason, son. We kill who we kill for a reason."*

*I turned and looked up at him. He was the only father figure I'd ever had. I ever have had. "I did this," I said to him.*

*Sirens sounded in the near distance. He looked off into the evening toward their oncoming lights. I guess he'd wanted to bring me here first, to let me have this moment with her. I saw him nod once before I looked down at Madeleine again.*

*"You did do this, it's true," he said to me. "You saved untold lives, Poetry Boy. Maybe thousands of lives. Each one as real as she was. Each one loved, as you loved her. I know you're too smart to know this, too brainy, too sophisticated, but maybe one day you'll acquire the wisdom of a fool and you'll remember what I say to you now: this world is the kingdom of the enemy of mankind. He chooses the battlegrounds. We do what we can do."*

*"They tortured her," was all I could say in answer. I was in shock, I think. His words "as you loved her" were slowly filtering into my consciousness. As they did, the full awareness of my love was finally coming to me, opening like a great dark flower blooming. It was as if, because he'd said it, I had permission to feel it. I did feel it finally, but of course, there she lay, and what good did it do me now? It came just in time to tear my heart to pieces.*

*The sirens in the distance grew louder. They made it hard to hear what the Recruiter said next. He spoke so softly, I've never been sure I heard him right. If I did, for the life of me, I can't even now understand why he said it.*

*What it sounded like was: "Look at that moonrise. How lovely."*

*The next moment, the Recruiter reached down and took my arm in a grip of iron. He hauled me to my feet by main strength.*

*"We have to go," he said.*

*Then we were in the car again, driving away from the scene. I think I knew even then that life had closed itself to me. Love and life. I think I knew that I had become what I'd pretended to be. Now I was damned to live with it, alone.*

*I leaned against the window and stared out at what was now the night. I was on the driver's side this time, so I had the same view as when we'd come. The monuments of empire, lit by floodlights, appeared again across the river, dome to obelisk to temple. A full moon was rising. It was autumn orange.*

*The Recruiter was right. It was lovely.*

*I watched its light shimmering on the ripples of the black water.*

# 21

"What do you want me to say to you, Cam?" said Margaret Whitaker when he was finally silent. Her tone was almost severe, almost angry. Well, she was angry. She was angry because she loved him and he was in so much pain. Even now, she couldn't keep the tenderness out of her tone. Not while she was looking right at him, not while he looked the way he did.

He had a square of gauze taped to the left side of his head just above his brow line. A dark, raging purple bruise spread out from under it, staining his cheek and his eye socket. That whole side of his face was swollen and misshapen. She had always found it a beautiful face, the face of a Renaissance angel. It hurt her to see it looking like this.

She gestured at his wounds. "Explain to me what happened to you," she commanded brusquely. "I can't think clearly about anything else until I know. How were you injured?"

He drew in breath through his nose. Flinched. Even breathing wasn't easy for him. He didn't meet her eyes. He stared down at the tan rug. He was very quiet, very still. From the start of their therapy, she had been aware of his quiet capacity for violence, but this was the first time she felt—felt viscerally—that there was actually something frightening about him.

"I was beaten up by gangsters," he told her finally. He said it in a vague monotone, as if he didn't care, as if his mind were on other things, still in the past maybe, still kneeling over Madeleine's body in that ditch.

Margaret took a moment to steady herself. "Gangsters," she said. Her voice sounded thin and stringent, even to herself. She thought she sounded like an old maid schoolteacher scolding a rowdy boy she's secretly fond of. "I assume this is because of this murder you're fascinated with. This family in the house in Maidenvale?"

"Yes," said Winter. "The gangsters wanted to scare me off because they're afraid a deeper investigation might expose their business. Drugs and guns and whatnot."

"So of course, good citizen that you are, you immediately informed the police that you'd been assaulted."

He laughed once, then flinched again—and she flinched, too, this time, feeling his pain with him.

"The police were there at the time," he said.

"With the gangsters?" she said, startled. Then immediately, she wondered at herself: how had she gotten so close to seventy years old while remaining innocent enough to be shocked by something like that? Was it because this sort of thing didn't happen when she was a girl? Or was it that it did happen all the time and she lived in an old lady's self-soothing state of nostalgic denial?

Winter raised his eyes to her with a gentle affection that both warmed and tormented her. "Well, yes, Margaret," he said. "The gangsters and the police are working together. That's part of the way things unfold in Maidenvale these days."

"I see," she said tartly, still the schoolmarm. "So what will you do now?"

He made a gesture, lifting a hand, tilting his head. As if to say to her: *The answer is obvious.* "I'm going to find out who killed that family."

"Even though it could get you killed as well."

"It won't get me killed."

"Oh," she said with a harsh, fluty laugh. "And why not, pray tell?"

"Margaret . . ."

"No, I mean it, Cam. Why not?" She sounded even more severe, angrier. His nonchalance was getting under her skin. It made her want to shake him. "I mean, I assume these gangsters threatened you while they were beating you up. Didn't they? I assume they said something like, 'Stay away from this place, Winter, or we will kill you,' the way gangsters do on television shows."

"They did say something to that effect, yes," he said. "Though it was more convincing coming from them."

"Well, yes, yes, I'm sure it was. So what on earth makes you think they're not serious?"

He met her eyes. "Oh, they're serious," he said.

"But what?" she asked. "You don't think they're really dangerous?"

"No, they're very dangerous . . ."

"But what, Cameron? Why do you think they're not going to do exactly what they say . . . ?" Then suddenly, with another shock, she understood him. She said: "Oh. Oh, I see. They're dangerous, but you're dangerous too."

He smiled a little—sadly. That was his only answer.

"More dangerous," insisted Margaret Whitaker. "You think you're more dangerous than they are."

"Yes," Winter said.

She sat back slowly in her chair, the therapist chair with its authoritative brown leather and high back. She shut her eyes a moment, trying to think what to say now, where to go from here. *God*, she thought, *this man*. He was lodged in her mind like a trauma, like a lost lover, like a song you like but don't know all the words to. What was she going to do with him? How was she going to help him? She thought of Madeleine Uno. Dead. Tortured. Lying in a ditch. How could she move him past that? *Should* she move him past it?

A thought flickered in her mind. She seized it. Her eyes came open. "Tell me something," she said.

Once again, he lifted his gaze from the carpet to her.

"How did you feel just now when you told me about Madeleine?" she asked him.

He sought an answer in the empty air. Seemed to find none. Gave a slight gesture, a slight shrug. "I don't know. I was desolate. It was very sad."

"Then. When you found her."

"Yes."

"But now, I mean."

He made that gesture again, that shrug.

"You wept when you told me about Roy Spahn," said Margaret.

"Did I?"

"Cameron."

"All right. All right, I wept."

"You're not weeping now. You didn't weep when you told me about Madeleine. Tortured. Dead in a ditch."

Winter didn't like that. He didn't like this whole line of questioning. His face hardened. The sight of it chilled her but she told herself that he could turn to stone for all she cared. Him and his gangsters and his bruises. She wished she had the gangsters here. She'd give them a piece of her mind. Send them back to their television shows where they belonged. But she didn't have them.

She only had him. And no matter how stony he became, she would not allow herself to be intimidated by him because she was as sure in her heart as Sunday morning there was no power even in hell that could move him to do her harm.

"You remember when you began to tell me this story, Madeleine's story," she went on. "You remember how afterward, you had that moment in the coffee shop, that moment when you saw the other people around you? You saw their inner lives exposed to you."

He nodded grimly. "Yes. Of course I remember."

"That's what connects us to each other, isn't it, Cam? Our inner lives. I mean, our bodies connect. Our bodies, our faces, they attract us to one another. But that's not the real bond, is it? It's our inner lives that form . . . What was it you said? That quote from *Frankenstein*?"

"'All the various relationships which bind one human being to another in mutual bonds,'" he recited tonelessly.

"Mutual bonds. Right. It's our inner lives that form our bonds," said Margaret. "Everything else is just chemicals interacting, atoms colliding. Even sex. Without our inner lives connecting, sex is just a predatory pleasure. It reduces our partner to a drug, living pornography."

He gave a slow, sullen blink. "I don't understand what we're talking about anymore."

"We're talking about love, Cameron. You loved Madeleine, didn't you?"

"Yes. I told you."

"And you haven't been able to love—or to be loved by—anyone since. Because of what happened to her."

He didn't answer.

She didn't wait. She kept at him: "When you started to tell me about her, you felt I might help you get free of that problem, ease your guilt about her, ease your fear about what might happen to someone you loved or who loved you. That's why you saw the inner lives of the people in the coffee shop just then. You were seeing the possibility that you might be open to love again. We discussed this."

He shifted uncomfortably in his chair. His mouth spasmed with pain, but he shook it off. "All right," he said. "So?"

"You don't sound open to love now," said Margaret. "In fact, just now, when you were talking about these gangsters, you sounded like a cold-blooded killer—like the cold-blooded killer you were pretending to be when you were with Madeleine."

For a moment after she spoke, she did fear him. She feared he might fly into a rage. She saw the possibility in his eyes.

But the moment passed. He sighed. He pressed two fingers into one temple and massaged the spot. "Margaret," he said. "I have a terrible headache. Why don't you just tell me what you're trying to say?"

Margaret rocked a little in her chair. She steepled her fingers, pressed them to her chin. Breathed deeply to maintain her calm. "All right. When you went to Maidenvale to investigate these murders, whenever you go and investigate these crimes of yours, whenever you put yourself in the way of dangerous people, whenever you put yourself in harm's way, you give yourself an excuse to play the assassin again, don't you? Just like the old days. Just like you did with Madeleine."

He went on massaging his temple. He squeezed his eyes shut, clearly suffering. "Why would I do that? I can barely live with what I've already done. Why would I want to go back to it? Why would I want to be a cold-blooded killer again?"

Margaret Whitaker gave a little sniff of a laugh. "Because cold-blooded killers don't get broken hearts. Do they, Cam?"

# 22

Winter canceled his afternoon lecture on Byron and Shelley. The lecture was informally titled "The Road to Hell." It was an exploration of the different ways in which the two poets saw and presented themselves. Byron cultivated the pose of a delightfully wicked seducer. "Mad, bad, and dangerous to know," as one of his lovers called him. Shelley liked to believe himself a liberated sexual revolutionary, changing the world one liaison at a time. But were they what they said they were? Or were they both simply disguising the way they used other people—used other people's bodies—for their own selfish purposes?

*Without our inner lives connecting, sex is just a predatory pleasure.*

Thus Margaret. Who had ruined him for the lecture. Their session had ruined him altogether. When he left her office, the pain in his head was sharp and biting, and there was a dull throb of more pain underneath that. He could hardly think, let alone do the work it would take to explain his thoughts to a hall full of undergraduates—slouching, sullen undergraduates so ignorant that they thought they knew something. He simply did not think he could get through it. He called the department and canceled the class. Then he shouldered his way home through the wintry autumn weather.

He didn't like to take medications. There had been too much of that when he was in the Division. Medications for pain. Medications for sleep. Medications to keep him awake. Not to mention all sorts of experimental vaccines meant to protect him as he journeyed into strange and sinister places. When his stint was over, he had had to make an effort to clean out his system. Nowadays, he rarely took even an aspirin. But when he arrived at his apartment, when he plumped down on his sofa, when he fell into a deep sleep and then woke to find his head still pounding, he stumbled into the bathroom and fumbled some generic NSAID out of the medicine chest. He chucked a handful of the tablets down his throat without either a sip of water or a moment's hesitation.

He willed himself to bull past the liquor cabinet without stopping. He planted himself in his chair by the glass doors that looked out onto the balcony. He sat and stared balefully at the city, the dome of the state capitol, the iron water of the autumn lake, the dramatic green-black clouds tumbling in from the west, a storm coming. He wished he'd poured himself the whiskey when he had the chance. Now the liquor cabinet seemed too damned far away.

The minutes ticked by. The painkillers kicked in. The headache receded. But his session with Margaret—the mental images from that session—the images of Madeleine in the ditch—the body he had clung to in the warmth and sweetness of her life now cold and still and half-submerged in muddy water—all these remained. These—and Margaret's hectoring words:

*It's our inner lives that form our bonds. Everything else is just chemicals interacting, atoms colliding.*

Yes. Yes. Byron and Shelley be damned. He had loved her. Madeleine. Playing the cold-blooded killer playing the lover, he

THE HOUSE OF LOVE AND DEATH

had become the lover. The lies he had whispered to her in her bed had all been true.

"What did you have to torture her for, you bastards?" he moaned aloud. And when he said it again—"You bloodthirsty bastards!"—his voice broke. He pressed the fingertips of both hands to the sides of his battered head. Margaret was right. It was all coming back to him. His inner life. His ability to love.

It was unbearable. Unbearable.

He couldn't go on like this. The pain was just too great. In his head. In his soul. He lay back against the stuffed chair's headrest. He stopped thinking, just gazed out the window at the black clouds boiling above the Capitol dome.

At some point, the storm broke. Rain pattered on the balcony. It spotted the glass of the doors. He went on gazing at it, but he did not see it. He saw Madeleine's body in the muddy water. He comforted himself, as he so often did, with the resonance of poetry. Eliot. The last of the Romantics. In *The Waste Land*: a rock desert where spirit had run dry, where the living water of the inner life was nowhere to be found.

*If there were water and no rock. If there were rock and also water . . . If there were the sound of water only . . . But there is no water.*

*Without our inner lives connecting . . .* Margaret whispered to him.

He did not even notice when the memory of Madeleine's body morphed into the image of Agnes Wilde's body. Agnes sprawled in a pool of blood on the second-floor landing of the Wasserman house in the gated Tulipwood community. There were bruises on her, Steph Breach had told him. He saw the bruises now. On her breasts and torso. A black eye. Why had she come downstairs? She had already lowered little Bobby to safety. She could have dropped down with him, but she didn't. Why not? She was bruised. Beaten. She knew she had an enemy. Why had she come downstairs?

The mind-movie of the murders played behind his eyes in flashing snippets of violence.

Marion Wasserman on the sweeping stairway. Had she faced her lover, Strange, who realized he had told her too much? Or the gangsters who had found out how much he'd told her?

*Boom.*

Norman Wasserman, rising from his bed, turning to see the figure in the doorway. Was it Eduardo Hernandez, who found out what Wasserman had done to his daughter?

*Boom.*

Lila rushing out into the hall. Was it, in fact, Mateo there, who could not forgive her for betraying him, for betraying his image of her, for refusing to play his pure princess?

*Boom.*

Then Agnes . . . Why had she come downstairs?

*It's our inner lives that form our bonds*, Margaret Whitaker told him.

At her words, Winter came out of that weird fugue of his. He sat up in his chair with a sharp intake of breath. A revelation had begun to take shape like a specter on the shadowy border of his mind.

But the next moment, it was gone, as smoke is gone when the wind blows. The loud buzz of the doorman's intercom had startled it away.

Dazed, he climbed to his feet. He made his way to the intercom where it hung by the front door.

"A Miss Lori Lesser to see you," the doorman's voice announced.

Winter closed his eyes. Pinched the bridge of his nose. Shook his head. He cursed her. What had he just been thinking? He didn't know. He couldn't remember. How annoying could this woman be?

"Send her up," he said.

# 23

When he opened the door and saw Lori on his threshold, she looked so miserable that, for a moment, Winter forgot how miserable he must look himself. Her shock at the sight of him confused him. Then he remembered: Oh yeah, he was a mess too.

She stepped into the apartment, gaping at him. Her camel-hair coat was spotted with rain. Her frizzy hair was even frizzier under a scarf she'd put on against the downpour. She'd been crying by the look of her—crying hard and for a long time, past the point where she could hide the effects of it under makeup.

"What the hell happened to you?" she said. She sounded impatient, he thought. She had come here to attack him as usual, he thought, and the sight of his injuries was diverting her from her purpose.

"I was in a car accident," he told her. It was the lie he had been using with everyone—everyone but Margaret. "Out in the country. I lost control and hit a tree. It was nothing, but the airbag deployed and . . ." He finished the sentence by gesturing at his injuries. "It's not as bad as it looks."

"It looks bad. It looks awful."

He gave her a lopsided smile, the only sort of smile he could manage. Still, for another moment, she stood where she was, her coat dripping, her face puffed up with spent tears. Her eyes traveled over his bruises. She examined him. Studied him. The silence became uncomfortable.

"Can I take your coat?" he said.

She stripped it off and handed it to him. Even so, she went on with her careful study of his face.

As he turned away to hang her coat in the front closet, she said to his back: "Was it Ted?"

He glanced over his shoulder at her. "Sorry? Was it who?"

"Ted," she said. "Ted Caesar. My . . . The man I was seeing. Did you have a fight with him? Is that what happened?"

Winter hesitated. He was experienced with cover stories, of course. He was good at lies. But for a second or two, he felt uncertain. How much did Lori know already? Had Silver Guy told her about their fight? Had she seen his busted nose? He went on working her coat onto a hanger—a bit of business to give him time to formulate an appropriate response.

Finally, he closed the closet door and faced her. "Of course not," he said. "It was a fender bender, I told you. Nothing at all. Why on earth would I have a fight with the man you were seeing? I didn't even know him. Come into the living room, Lori. Sit down. You look upset."

He escorted her to the sofa. "Can I offer you something? Coffee?"

"Wine," she said flatly. "White if you've got it."

It was still only four in the afternoon, but he supposed with the rain it was dark enough to play at it being the cocktail hour. It must be five o'clock somewhere, he thought. He poured them both a healthy dollop of Chardonnay. He sat in one of the armchairs across from her.

They raised their glasses to one another. Each took a single sip. The wind blew rain against the glass doors.

"I just want to know what's . . . ?" Lori said, and burst into a torrent of tears.

Winter sat in embarrassed silence. Lori held one hand over her face and sobbed, her shoulders shaking. Winter took another hit of wine. He thought maybe he could use the time to try to recover the idea that had come to him before the buzzer sounded. It was no use. Like most men, he found a woman's tears profoundly distracting. The sobbing alone made it impossible to think. This was truly the dark four P.M. of the soul, he decided. A lousy day entirely.

"I just know this is your doing," Lori said when she could get a word out. She wagged a finger at him with one hand as she held a tissue to her nose with the other. "I know this is about you somehow. I know it."

"Lori, what are you talking about?" he said—though by this time he could guess. "What is it you think I've done?"

"Ted and I were getting along so well and then . . ."

She wept again. He felt compelled to ask: "And then what?"

"He ghosted me. He just—vanished."

Ah, thought Winter, not without satisfaction. Silver Guy had taken the hint and left town. He and his broken nose were back in D.C., where he was explaining to his masters that silencing Lori Lesser—who knew nothing—would incite the anger of not only Winter, but of the Recruiter and his Invisibles—who, in fact, knew everything. The game was not worth the prize.

"He's just gone," Lori said, with a pitiable squeak in her voice. "Like he never existed. He just vanished. Like that student you slept with."

Winter didn't bother to protest that he hadn't slept with a student, or at least not with the student she meant. His head was beginning to throb again. He didn't have the energy for an argument. Also, he felt sorry for her. He knew she was lonely and unhappy. She must have hoped "Ted Caesar" was romantically interested in her. It had been unfeeling of Silver Guy to play it that way. Winter was glad he'd punched the son of a bitch.

"It's like I'm in some kind of nightmare," Lori said, sniffing noisily. "People disappear off the face of the earth. Ted's apartment is empty. His phone number doesn't work. His company isn't listed. No one's ever seen him. I feel like I'm going crazy."

She waited for him to answer. He didn't answer. He thought it would be unwise.

"But I'm not going crazy, am I?" she said accusingly.

"Lori, I don't know. I don't understand any of this," Winter lied.

"Stop lying to me," she said—but what started as a furious outburst dissolved into more tears. "Really, Cam. Stop. I feel so lost!"

He said nothing else. He drank more wine. He wondered if it would be wrong to pour himself a second glass.

"Something's not right about you," she said tearfully. "I know it. I'm not stupid, Cam. I know you have no respect for me, but I'm not stupid."

He made a polite noise, but what could he say? She was right. She was right about all of it. She wasn't stupid. And he didn't respect her, at least not very much. And something was going on. But what good could come of talking about any of it?

"Nothing about you is what it should be," Lori said. "Nothing about you is normal. Students complain to me about the things you say. About sex. About men and women. It's unacceptable. I pass the complaints onto the dean. Any other professor here would be penalized. Suspended. Fired even. But with you, the dean does nothing. I see you going home with a student, but when I report it, I find out she doesn't exist." This was an accidental admission on her part. In her obsession, she had followed him, spied on him, though she swore she hadn't. "I start asking around about you, about your past, and out of nowhere a man shows up and starts romancing me. He's interested in everything I'm interested in. He's read all the books I've read. He's perfect for me," she said, her voice cracking. "Then he's just gone? Just like that? And you with your face all banged up? Just—tell me, okay? Tell me what's happening so I don't feel like I'm going insane."

"I don't know what to tell you. It was the airbag," said Winter helplessly.

"Oh!" she cried.

She fetched a fresh tissue from her purse and blew her nose loudly. She dabbed carefully at her tears, but smeared her mascara anyway, so that she looked even worse than she had when she first came in. What a pair they must make, Winter thought. Him with his purple bruises and her with her running black tears.

"Are you some kind of spy?" she asked him suddenly. "Is that what it is? Did I stumble onto some kind of, I don't know, government conspiracy or something?"

This time, Winter raised his wine glass more to hide his face than anything else. Hard as he was trying to protect her, the woman was going to get herself killed if she kept this up.

"Lori . . ." he said.

"No, really. You're ruining my life. Just tell me the truth so I know what's happening."

Winter did his best to look baffled and innocent. "I don't know what you want from me, Lori. I don't know how I became your enemy."

"What do you mean you don't know?" she cried out. "It's everything about you. You defended a rapist."

"He wasn't a rapist."

"You slept with a student."

"She wasn't a student."

"The things you say, the way you act, the way you think, what you teach. You're living in the past."

Winter made a mild gesture. "You're not the first person to say so. But really, living in the past—is that a sin in your religion?"

"Yes! Yes, of course it is. This is a new day. Everything is changing. You can't just go on doing the same things, saying the same things, teaching the same things people used to teach, the same disgraced poetry with its outmoded notions. You can't just expect me to sit by while you do that. It isn't right. I mean, who are you? Just tell me that. Who are you really?"

"Lori . . ." Winter raised his glass, but didn't drink. "I'm an English professor."

Lori cursed him in a manner he found most unladylike.

"No, really," he said. "I mean it. I know things are changing. Things are always changing. But I teach poetry—because when everything is done changing, everything will be exactly the same, and the poetry will still be here, in the midst of other woe than ours, a friend to man."

"I don't know what you're talking about."

"It's a quote," Winter told her. "From 'Ode on a Grecian Urn.' By John Keats. One of the poems I teach. You should read it. In fact, you should go home right now and read it. Or at least go home right now. This conversation is not going to get us anywhere." He set his glass down decisively on the nearby lampstand. "And I have work to do."

She glowered at him, but he was determined to outlast her. He couldn't let this go on and on. He was tired of lying and he couldn't tell her the truth. Not about anything and certainly not about herself. She wanted to play the powerful crusader. How could he tell her she was really a maiden tied to a tree, lucky the white knight she despised had slain the dragon she didn't even know was there?

Finally, she got to her feet. She made a show of storming out, though she had to pause so he could hold her coat for her while she angrily struggled into it. At the door, on the threshold again, she turned to face him. Her frown was fierce but her eyes were pleading.

"Just tell me, Cam. Please. I need to know. Was it you? Did you fight with Ted?"

"Why would I, Lori?" he said.

She was about to spin away and storm off in a rage. But he touched her arm midstorm. She paused to face him again.

"No, really," he said. "Really. Why would I?"

He waited until he saw the faintest gleam of understanding begin to come into her eyes.

Then he shut the door.

# 24

The door swung open, and Winter recognized the man he had seen on the video: Isaac Wasserman, Norman Wasserman's brother. He was a tall man, solidly built and broad-shouldered, dressed with homey elegance in expensive chinos and a cashmere cardigan, but he stooped as if life had defeated him somehow, and under his thin white hair, his features were sagging and careworn.

His voice was careworn, too, thin and weary. "You're Professor Winter?"

"I am, yes. Thank you for allowing me to come."

Wasserman stood back to let him in. Winter was standing on the top stoop of an elegant brownstone in a row of brownstones. He didn't know Chicago well. He had followed his GPS to get here. But he could see with his own eyes that he was in a well-to-do and well-established neighborhood. Isaac Wasserman was a dentist. Like his brother, he was a prosperous man.

Winter followed him up a short flight of stairs.

"You've been injured," Wasserman said over his shoulder as he climbed.

"I was in a car accident," Winter said. "A fender bender really. But the airbag deployed. It's not as bad as it looks."

They rose into a finely furnished sitting room. It was stunningly fine, in fact. A gilded chandelier was reflected in a gilded mirror, shedding light on maroon-and-white flocked-velvet furniture and intricately carved antique chairs. There were Chinese vases and statues placed here and there. An antique silver menorah on the mantelpiece above the large fireplace. A wall of bookshelves with leather volumes of Jewish literature and Asian art.

Winter noticed the Jewish theme. He had noticed the little Jewish prayer capsule—he couldn't remember the proper name for it—attached to the frame of the door outside. He was so used to the secular life of his university town that it only now occurred to him that he had seen nothing like this in the ruins of the house in the Tulipwood community. There were no religious objects there that he noticed, not even secular objects relating to Jewish heritage.

"Harriet, my wife, is getting Bobby ready. They'll be down in a minute," Wasserman said.

"This is a lovely room," said Winter.

"Thank you. We've been collecting Asian art for years. Can I offer you something? Coffee?"

Winter shook his head. "I don't mean to pry . . ."

Wasserman waited for him to go on.

"Your brother. He didn't seem to have your religious interests."

Wasserman answered with a soft puff of air through his nose. It lifted his stooped shoulders and changed the expression on his face. Winter thought he detected a trace of—what?—regret? Disdain? Disapproval maybe. Some negative feeling. "He wasn't interested in that, no. Not even when we were kids."

Winter tried to meet the man's eyes, but Wasserman turned away. Winter wondered: Did he know? About his brother's nasty habits with young girls? Winter suddenly suspected he did.

He turned back to peruse the books some more. Only then did Isaac Wasserman say to him: "We weren't close. Norman and I."

Winter glanced around at him. "No?"

"We weren't very similar. I'm older by almost ten years. We grew up in two different worlds in a way, or two different countries at least. But I love Lila and Bobby. I loved Lila, I mean. They used to come to visit often when my kids were still at home. Lila—you know, she was a little lost, confused, the way all the kids are nowadays, but she had a good heart." He paused for a moment. "There's a reason I agreed to let you talk to Bobby, you know."

Winter lifted his chin. He waited to hear more.

"It's because Ann Farmingham spoke highly of you," Wasserman said. "You've met Ann obviously."

"The police officer. Yes, I have."

"Of all the police I met in Maidenvale, she was the only one who impressed me as someone who wanted to find the truth about what happened to my brother and his family. I think that matters. To find the truth. To seek justice. I think we have to do that, no matter what. No matter what we find. Don't you think?" He made a wry gesture with one hand, pointing at Winter's face. "You don't have to answer me. I can see by your 'car accident' that you agree with me, Professor."

Winter couldn't help but laugh a little. He enjoyed the man's wry tone.

"I'm trusting you to be sensitive with my nephew," Wasserman went on. "He's been through a lot."

"Of course."

There was a footstep on a winding stair that led up from the hall to the townhouse's next story. Wasserman turned toward the sound. He was shaking his head. "Something terrible has happened to this country, in my opinion," he murmured.

Through the living-room entryway, Winter saw Harriet Wasserman descending with the boy. Bobby was, Winter thought, a handsome lad, with dark brown hair on a round, sensitive-looking face. He had warm, thoughtful eyes and seemed alert to the solemnity of the moment. He held his aunt's hand and kept his face ducked down shyly.

The boy sat on a plush chair. Winter perched himself on the chair's ottoman, hoping that would seem friendlier and less threatening than sitting on a chair of his own. Harriet, a fit, strong-featured woman with short silver hair, stood behind the boy and fretted. Isaac stood near with his shoulders slumped and his hands in the pockets of his chinos.

"You know why I'm here, Bobby," Winter said.

The boy nodded gravely. "To talk about when my mom and dad were killed, and Lila and Agnes."

"Yes. I'm very sorry that happened. I read in the news that you heard your sister's boyfriend in the house that night. The police said you heard Mateo talking. Is that true?"

Bobby frowned, surprised. He shook his head. "No. I didn't hear Mateo. I didn't hear anything except . . . You know . . ."

"The gunshot."

"Yeah. The gunshot. That's all I heard."

"And you didn't tell the police you heard Mateo?"

Bobby hesitated, but then shook his head no. Winter wasn't sure whether to believe him or not. He wasn't sure whether the child remembered or not.

"Can you tell me what happened after you heard the gunshot?"

"I was in bed," the boy said. "I was kind of asleep but kind of awake too. It was almost time for Agnes to come and wake me up to get ready for school. Then I heard this loud bang. I sat up. And right away, Agnes came in with my jacket. She told me to put my jacket on. She said I had to go out the window and run away. I said, like, 'What's happening?' And she said, 'Well, I'll tell you later.' But now she said I had to get up."

"What happened then?"

"I got up. And Agnes gave me the jacket to put on. And she opened the window and she knocked the screen out. She kicked it with her foot and it fell out. Then there was another bang."

The boy stared blankly a moment. Then his expression changed. A depth of horror opened in his eyes. He blinked once, hard, and the horror went away. It had occurred to him what that bang was, Winter thought. Another member of his family dying. He had chased the realization from his mind, as children can do.

"Then she made me climb out the window," he said, staring into space. "She made me climb out while she held onto me. She held onto my arm." He rubbed his wrist where she had gripped him, as if he could still feel her fingers on him. He spoke now in a hollow voice, as if he were no longer listening to himself, as if he could no longer bear to listen to what had happened. "She said she had to hold my wrist, but I couldn't hold hers. She kept saying that. 'Don't hold me. I'll hold you . . .'" Then after a pause, he said very softly, almost in a whisper, ". . . sweetheart," and his lips trembled.

For a moment, the word left Winter confused. But before he asked the boy to explain what he meant, he understood and kept silent. Bobby was remembering what Agnes had said exactly, her exact words, her gentle, patient tone. *Don't hold me, sweetheart. I'll hold you.* He was remembering that Agnes loved him, and how much he loved her.

"She climbed out the window too," said Bobby. He said it with emphasis, looking right into Winter's eyes. "She climbed out too."

Winter was a hard character in many ways, but he was not without a heart. He understood what the little boy was telling him, and it moved him. Agnes Wilde had climbed out the window as far as she could, had hung on to the sill with one hand while she clung to the boy's wrist with the other. She had wanted to lower Bobby as close to the ground as she could to make sure he would not hurt himself when she dropped him. In doing that, she had not only risked falling herself, she had offered herself a fair chance of escape. It would have been nothing for her to release her grip on the sill and drop to the grass below. She might have sprained an ankle or even broken an ankle, but she would have gotten away from the house, from the murders, from the booming gun.

The boy continued in his dreamy, hollow voice: "She said, 'Run, sweetheart. Run into the trees and stay there till the police come. Don't look back,' she said. 'Just run.' Then she let me go. So I fell to the grass and I started running. I didn't look back. I thought . . ." His voice grew thick. His lips trembled. His eyes filled. Harriet Wasserman stepped forward and squeezed his shoulder, looking over him to give Winter a warning glance: *Not much more.* "I thought she was behind me," Bobby said. "I thought Agnes was running behind me the whole time."

Harriet Wasserman leaned down to put her lips close to his ear. "Agnes loved you very much," she told him. A tear spilled down the boy's cheek.

Winter frowned, fighting down his own emotions. This was the very moment that had drawn him into this story in the first place. Agnes had let the boy go—and then she had struggled to climb back up through the window. She had had time to escape, time and opportunity. But she had climbed back into the house. Gone down the winding stairs. Faced the killer.

Because she knew he had come for her.

That was the revelation he had had in his apartment. That was the idea that the doorman's buzzer had chased away. It had come back to him after Lori had left. After he had had time to sit alone and think and not think. To let Margaret's words play through his mind again: *It's our inner lives that form our bonds . . .*

This was why he had come to Maidenvale. More than anything else, he had wanted to understand why Agnes Wilde had come back into the house, had come down those stairs, had stepped out into that hall. Now—now he thought he knew.

She had done it because she believed she was the one the killer really wanted. She had done it because she thought the shooting would end with her. Maybe she thought she could talk him down from his insane fury. She probably hoped so. But she knew what she was risking.

How odd it was, how mad it seemed, sitting here in this luxurious city home, with the elegant Asian vases around him and the silver menorah on the mantelpiece above his shoulder, with the boy reciting his dreadful narrative, and the Wassermans hovering over him protectively—how odd and mad it seemed to imagine her in that moment of incomprehensible transcendence.

He saw her now, in his mind's eye. He dressed her in his imagination in a white nightshirt. He saw the white of it glowing in the predawn shadows, her figure glowing white as she hurried down the winding stairs into the red blackness of murder. She was to him a bright thing stepping fearlessly into the dark. And if his literary sensibilities were offended by that cliché or by the simplicity of the image, he let the offense pass over because it seemed to him still true—true and yet also incomprehensible—that she had done what she had done.

How could it be? he wondered even now. How was it possible that that house of death could have been, at one and the same moment, a house of such sacrificial love?

Winter leaned forward on the ottoman, pressing urgently toward the little boy. He needed to hear the rest, to hear everything, whatever there was to hear. It felt urgent to him, but he knew he had to speak slowly, gently, or the boy might become too upset to go on.

"Bobby," he said. "Agnes was a wonderful person, and she must . . ." Hard as he was, he had to pause to swallow the thickness in his own voice. "She must have loved you very much. The doctors who examined her said that someone had hurt her. Not then, not during the shooting. Before the shooting happened." The boy was already nodding as Winter said: "Do you know who did that? Do you know who hurt Agnes?"

Now the emptiness—the mesmeric hollowness—of Bobby's voice was suddenly gone. He broke out in tears and anger, "It was the person who came to watch her!"

Winter took a brief glance at Harriet Wasserman's ferociously protective expression, but she let him continue. They both knew this was the heart of the matter.

"The voyeur. The person who watched her through the window you mean," Winter said.

"So he could see her naked," the boy answered with furious disdain.

*Yes,* Winter thought, *because without our inner lives connecting, sex is just a predatory pleasure. It reduces our partner to a drug, living pornography.*

The boy sniffed and rubbed his nose with the back of his hand. "She slapped him right in the face!" he said.

"That's right. She chased him across Tulipwood and slapped him, didn't she?"

"Right in the face. She told me so."

"That's right. Agnes wasn't afraid of anyone, was she?"

"She wasn't afraid of anyone!" the boy echoed proudly.

"But the watcher came back, didn't he?" said Winter. "The person who looked through the window. He came back that night."

The boy nodded again, still sniffling, but bringing his tears under control. "It was my bedtime. Agnes was going to read me a story. One of the stories from a book she had about knights of the round table. It was my favorite. She was bringing the book to my bed, only then she looked out the window."

"This was the night before the shooting happened."

Bobby dragged his sleeve across his face to dry his tears. He nodded again. "Agnes looked out the window and she said a bad word. Because she was angry. She said a bad word, and she put the book down and ran out."

"Because she saw the person watching her through the window."

"And she ran out to slap him again," said Bobby.

"And what happened?"

The boy had calmed himself now. He spoke more clearly. He looked at Winter directly, fiercely, as if mentally clinging to him. Something about Winter's intensity seemed to hold the boy steady.

"She didn't come back for a long time. I think I fell asleep. When I woke up, she was there again. I saw her walking past my door to go to her room. I called out to her. She stopped and looked in and she said, 'I'll be right there.' I could see that her clothes were ripped. Her lip was bleeding, too. But she said everything was all right and she would be right there. When she came back, she had other clothes on, not the ripped ones anymore. I asked her what happened, but she just told me to go to sleep. I asked her to read me a story about the knights. But she said it was late now and I had to go to sleep. But she stayed with me. She sat on my bed and sang me some of her songs. And I guess I fell asleep. And then I woke up and there were gunshots."

For another long second, Winter's face and Bobby's, the boy's face and the man's, were close together as Winter leaned toward him. Then Winter knew that he had what he wanted. He drew back, sitting upright on the ottoman. The boy seemed to relax, as if a cord that had been holding him and Winter together had now been severed.

Winter vanished for a few seconds into his own meditations. He pressed his eyes shut, and opened them and returned to the moment.

"Did you tell this to the police?" he asked the boy. "Did you tell them about the watcher?"

He knew what Bobby would answer before he answered. "They didn't ask me."

Winter nodded, still looking into himself, into his own mind. He remembered to smile kindly at the boy only as an afterthought.

When they were finished, Isaac Wasserman led the way downstairs to the front door. He opened the door to let Winter out, but Winter paused to face him.

"Thank you for that," he said. "For letting me talk to him."

"It's a terrible thing," said Wasserman. "He will never get over it."

Winter sought for a comforting response, but couldn't find one. He remained silent.

"I don't know what's happening to our country," Wasserman said. "A thing like this . . . And no one seems to care. Where are the honest men? Where is the law? Where is justice?" He shook his head sadly. "Well . . ."

He put his hand out. Winter shook it. Their eyes met.

"There'll be justice," Winter told him. "I know what happened now. I'll make sure there's justice. For what it's worth."

# 25

By the time the afternoon began to shade into the autumn evening, he was in Maidenvale again, outside the Community Center. He was waiting for the killer there. For the killer and for the cops.

He had called Ann Farmingham on his way back from the city. He had told her what he knew. They had discussed the options together. They both agreed there was no point in trying to enlist the aid of Inspector Strange in making an arrest. Officer Ann said she would use her contacts at the state police and would try to bring the staties in to do the job. She had called back after only a few moments. She said the troopers were on their way. Winter had headed to the Community Center expecting to find the arrest in progress. Now he had been there for thirty minutes, and the police had still not come. He called Ann again but received only her recorded answering message.

He waited.

He had parked his Jeep SUV in the lot and was leaning against the back of it. He was calm, but aware of a weight of melancholy too. If all went well, there would be justice, some justice at least, as he had promised Isaac Wasserman. But he doubted there'd be much satisfaction in it for him or for anyone. He doubted whether this arrest would touch the corruption that, to his mind, was at the source of these killings. There was too much corruption for that. It went up too high, and down too deep. Whatever happened, this would likely be a sad day all around.

He had positioned himself so he could see the bicycle rack by the back door, and also the path that led to the lot from the front entrance. He looked toward the road, hoping to see the cruisers coming. He looked back to the bike rack and counted the bikes to pass the time. There were nine of them.

He shivered. It was cold: the end of the season of mists and mellow fruitfulness. He was wearing a thick cord sweater beneath his windbreaker. He had his ivy cap on, pulled down low. As he leaned against the Jeep, he kept his hands in the pockets of his black jeans. Still, the chill worked its way into him.

The recent rains had washed the leaves from the trees. Whichever direction Winter turned, he saw branches that were all but bare. The outlines of naked sycamores, elms, and oaks were stark against the deepening gray of the overcast sky. His eyes moved from these to the center's ground-floor windows. Dimly, he could see people moving within, adults and children both. He checked his watch. Soon, the afterschool program would be over, and the kids would come out.

He looked toward the road again, impatient for the police. But instead of cruisers, he was startled to see a figure coming toward him on the walk—startled to see who it was: Gwendolyn Lord, the head of the center's counseling program.

He had made an effort to put Gwendolyn out of his mind. There was no point thinking too much about her—her with her wedding band and her pictures of her two children on her desk. But the sight of her had an effect on him sure enough: a small electric jolt of tension that straightened his spine. He stood up off the Jeep to greet her.

She was as attractive to him as he remembered. Small and graceful, with that elevated, ladylike presence that seemed to bring all his senses to the surface. She was wearing a skirt that fell below the knee, dark with an orange floral print, a white sweater, and a black cardigan thrown over her shoulders for warmth. His thoughts crowded each other as she walked briskly toward him. He was sorry for the trouble he was about to bring to her workplace. He was also happy to see her, happier than he wanted to be.

She came nearer. Even as his purpose here weighed on him, he found the sight of her captivating. The elfin features and those witty green eyes—they entranced him out of his deep mood for a moment. She came close and saw his bandage and his purple bruises. The expression of tender concern that crossed her face—that captivated him too.

"Mrs. Lord," he said.

"What on earth happened to you?"

"I was in a car accident," he said.

"Oh no! Really?"

"No. I was beaten by a couple of Mexican gangsters and your Inspector Strange."

He could not read her reaction to this. He wished he could. He thought he saw some admiration in her eyes. He would have liked that: if she admired him. But whatever was there, she kept it to herself. She only nodded. Then licked her lips nervously. He liked her lips. Then, she went on—haltingly, he thought: "I saw you out here through the window. I thought . . . Well, I didn't . . . I mean, why are you here? What . . . ? Why are you here?"

She was flustered. He didn't know why. Again, he couldn't read her thoughts. Again, he wished he could. He hesitated before he answered her. He didn't like to tell her the truth. He did not want to tell her the murderer was in the building and the police were on their way.

Before he could fashion a reply, she went plunging on.

"I just wanted to come out for a moment. I just wanted to tell you . . ." She gestured helplessly, looked helplessly off into the surrounding trees.

"What? What is it, Mrs. Lord?" He really could not imagine what was on her mind.

Then those green eyes met his eyes directly. "I just wanted to say . . . I don't mean to presume but . . . Well, I am a therapist. I'm trained . . . I mean, I watch people. I'm trained to watch people. I do it automatically. When you were here before, I saw the way your eyes moved . . . Maybe I'm jumping to conclusions. If I'm speaking out of turn, I'm sorry . . ."

She gestured with her two hands, rolling her eyes. Winter thought she looked like a flustered schoolgirl—adorably like. "What is it?" he said again. "You can tell me. I won't be offended. It's all right."

"I just wanted to correct any impression you might have . . ." she went on. "I saw the way you looked at my hand when you were here before."

The woman was practically babbling. Winter could only wait politely, confused into silence.

"I'm not married," said Gwendolyn Lord at last. "Not that you have to care. But I thought . . . Because of your eyes. Looking at my left hand. The way men do sometimes. I'm a widow . . . I know I should take the ring off. It's been three years and I need to, you know . . . It's a problem for me. I just . . . Well, he was a marine. My husband. I lost him in the wars. It just feels disloyal to . . . But that's probably too much information.

I just thought I should say something. Now I feel like an idiot. Maybe I was wrong."

Winter stood there, blinking. He could not seem to arrange his thoughts. He said, "I'm sorry. About your husband. That must be difficult for you—you and your children."

"I'm sorry? What children?" said Gwendolyn Lord.

"The girl and the boy. In the photographs. On your desk."

"My niece and nephew? For heaven's sake, they're thirteen and fifteen. How old do you think I am?"

"I . . ." said Winter stupidly.

But then he glanced up—and there were the police. Four cruisers in a row, sirens silent, but their blue flashers whirling. Gwendolyn saw his change of expression. She followed his gaze, looking over her shoulder. The first car was already turning into the lot.

She looked back at him. She understood.

"What is it?" she said. When he hesitated, she said: "Here? He's here?"

"He is," said Winter. "I'm so sorry."

"Oh no . . ." she began. "Excuse me please." Shaking her head, she hurried away to meet the invaders.

All four cars had pulled in now. They'd stopped at the bottom of the path, and the khakis were climbing out. They had come ready for trouble, bulked up with Kevlar, some carrying shields and some rifles. Their leader was an older lieutenant with a gray mustache. Gwendolyn approached him but he brushed her back with his arm impatiently. She could only stand helpless while the riflemen marched into the building.

Winter waited too. He had no role in this. He had told Officer Ann everything he had found out or guessed. He had only come to make sure that someone, somewhere in this town was honest enough to make the arrest. He waited where he was, watching the police go in.

It was not a long wait. A minute, then another. Then the riflemen came out again, slack now, the tension gone out of them. The killer was not in the building.

The riflemen spoke to the lieutenant. He gave orders Winter couldn't hear. Then he spoke briefly to Gwendolyn Lord. She stood aside as the whole small army of them climbed into their cruisers again. A moment more, and they were heading away—not back the way they'd come, but out along the rows of shops and government buildings, past the local police station, and down the open road toward Maidenvale and ultimately, Winter knew, out toward the Hollow and the Hernandez house.

Winter and Gwendolyn Lord exchanged a glance. He could not read her expression. He was only now beginning to take in what she had said to him. She was a widow. Those weren't her kids. She had made the effort to come out and tell him, even though it embarrassed her. He wanted to say something to her now, to respond, but he couldn't think how.

She turned away and walked quickly into the building. He sighed. What bad timing it all was. He lingered there another moment. His eyes traveled over the scene, the building, the window, the parking lot, all of it. Something troubled him, but his mind was so full, he couldn't name it. Maybe it was just Gwendolyn Lord, what she'd said.

He climbed into his Jeep and went after the police

# 26

By the time he made it to the end of Maidenvale's Main Street, he had lost sight of the police motorcade. They had pulled away from him, speeding through the stop lights where he had to pause. Winter had to pause again as Inspector Strange came up behind him. Winter pulled his Jeep to the curb while Strange's Crown Victoria and two other local cop cars rushed past, their sirens screaming. When Winter finally got going again, all the cops were gone. When his Jeep reached the two-lane that led to the Hollow, the road stretched ahead of him, deserted.

He hit the gas, hoping to close the gap with the law, hoping to be on hand to witness the arrest. The light of day was beginning to die. The cloud cover was turning from a still, pale ceiling into a brooding leaden weight troubled by night and a coming rain. The forests that lined the road were winter forests now, stark and ghostly. The wind was intermittent. It made the bare branches sway.

Winter's thoughts drifted. Gwendolyn Lord. She was not married. She had come outside specifically to tell him. Her lips. Why did he feel so troubled about it? Or was he troubled about something else? Yes, he thought, something else. Something was wrong. He felt it in his stomach. What was it? His thoughts were a jumble of images. Gwendolyn. The killer. The mobster Del Rey. Inspector Strange . . .

When he came to himself, he noticed his Jeep had slowed down. He had eased off on the gas without realizing it. He was no longer chasing the cops. His eyes were scanning the eerie, tangled, and darkening reaches of the woods.

*Eight*, he thought.

He knew at once that's what it was that was bothering him. There had been nine bicycles in the rack when he had counted them, when he was idly passing the time until the police arrived. Then, when the police had left, his eyes had passed over the scene again. He had seen the change without quite registering what it was. But it was this: there were only eight bikes remaining. At some point, probably when he was distracted by Gwendolyn, entranced by her face, confused by her confusion, someone had gotten on one of the bikes and ridden away.

Winter groaned aloud as the meaning of it came to him. He could see what was going to happen next—the worst version of it played itself out in his imagination, step by step. His phone was linked to his car. He pressed the button and called Ann Farmingham. He got her recorded message again, her voice mail. She was avoiding him, he thought. This was police business now, and she did not want him butting in.

He left a message. He did not think it would help to dial 911. He did not think he could get a dispatcher to believe him. Ann would believe him. "They're going to the wrong place, Ann," he said. "If they don't hurry, he'll be dead. Or I will. Tell them to come to the caverns."

Even as he spoke, he spotted the turnoff to his left. Without thinking, he worked the wheel. A moment later, the Jeep was off the road, bouncing over the rutted trail that led into the forest.

Winter cursed to himself as, once again, the trees and shadows closed around him. He didn't want to be here. He didn't want to do what he knew he was going to have to do.

Dusk was near, but it was not full night. All the same, once the woods surrounded him, the light of day was nearly gone. The darkness deepened. He snapped his headlights on just in time for them to draw the sign out of the gloom: "Baptiste Woods. Trails close at sunset."

He reached the small lot. As he turned in, his headlights passed over the bicycle where it lay on its side at the edge of the pavement. He parked the Jeep and stepped out into the chill of sundown. That strange, whispering, rustling forest presence was all around him again. That creepy, haunted atmosphere, full of foreboding. It made him feel that only the worst could happen now.

He glanced over at the shape of the bike. Instinctively, he pressed his fingers to his windbreaker where the inner pocket was. He felt the knife still there—Ted Caesar's knife. But what good would that do him? He should have brought his gun. The killer had a gun. The killer would be carrying his .38. Why else would he head back to the caverns if not to blow his brains out rather than face the law?

That was why Winter couldn't wait for the police. There wasn't time. He clicked on the flashlight in his phone. He went to the trailhead. He took a breath. He plunged into the lowering woods.

He followed the weak beam of light as fast as he could, but it wasn't fast enough. Every step he took, he expected the sound of the gunshot. Moment after moment, the explosion did not come. There was nothing but the wind in the dead branches all around him, the wind like a chorus of whispering voices, the voices of spirits swirling in the air. He could not help but peer into the obscure reaches of the forest around him. He could not help but wonder if maybe the killer and his pistol were among the tangled vines and branches, peering back at him. Taking aim.

He reached the caverns, mountains of white stone. The cold had well and truly eaten through his sweater—not just the cold but the damp too because the air had grown thick with the coming rain. His cheeks stung and his hands felt brittle. He could no longer tell the difference between the chill that made him shudder, and the fear that made him shudder just the same. Second after second after second, he was still waiting for that gunshot.

He returned to the cavern where he had found Mateo's body: the large black entranceway like a gate into a dark tower. He stepped to the edge of it, shining his flashlight in. The beam played over a landscape of bizarre stone shapes before the deeper blackness swallowed it.

"Tomas!" he shouted.

There was no answer and there was no echo. The cave seemed to swallow his voice as it swallowed the light. The wind and the whispering forest were at his back, but all ahead of him was darkness and silence.

"Tomas! It's me. Professor Winter. I'm alone."

Again, nothing. No answer. No echo. Maybe he had the wrong cavern. But he didn't think so. Maybe the boy was already dead. But he didn't think that either.

He stepped into the cave.

As before, when he was here the last time, the wilting yellow light of his flashlight played off the weird formations of hanging rocks and rocks growing up from the rocky floor, a forest of silent stone. He made his way slowly and carefully among the obstacles.

He called out again: "Tomas!"

For a moment, he thought there was still no answer. But there was. There was a high-pitched noise, from deep in the cavern. Was it a bat? he wondered at first. But then he thought: No. It was the sound of a boy weeping.

"Tomas," he said again.

"Leave me alone," the boy shouted back. His voice was furious and tearful. Winter quailed at the thought of that gun in his hands, the trembling hands of a despairing child.

Still, he moved forward slowly. "Tomas, this is no good," he said as the cavern walls closed in around him. "What good will it do? It will only cause more pain."

"Stay away!" the boy shouted. "I'll kill you!"

"Don't kill me. I'm alone. Unarmed. There's no reason to kill me."

"I'll kill you anyway! I don't care what happens anymore."

Winter believed him and his chest felt hollow, windy as the wood. He came into the narrow passage he remembered. He had to turn sideways to edge through it.

"I'm coming in, Tomas," he said.

The boy screamed, high-pitched, wild: "I'll kill you, I'll kill you! You don't believe me? I killed them all! I'll kill you too!"

"I believe you," he said. "I know what you did. But there's no reason to kill me. I'm alone. I have no gun. I just want to talk to you. Let me talk to you, Tomas. You don't want to be on your own right now."

He came to the threshold of the final chamber. The beam of his flashlight broke through into the dark of that last space. It was answered by rapid, tear-washed breathing. He could imagine the .38 aimed in his direction, the boy's finger tight on the trigger.

"Please don't shoot, Tomas," he said. His voice quavered. He felt certain sudden death was coming. His fear was almost over-whelming. He had always been one of the braver sort of men, a cool hand in moments of danger. But no one is immune to fear.

He hesitated just a moment. He tried not to think about Gwen-dolyn Lord. He tried not to think he had something to live for. He steadied his breathing. He stepped into the chamber.

It was just as he'd imagined it. The boy sat on the cavern floor, pressed against the wall as if cornered. He sat right on the spot where he'd murdered his brother, the brother he'd admired and loved.

He gripped his father's .38 in both hands—both trembling hands—and pointed it at the narrow passage where Winter stood. That first moment, that first step he took into the chamber, struck Winter as the most likely moment for the boy to fire.

But he didn't fire. Winter stood above him, shining the flash-light down on him, anticipating the blast that would blow his guts out. It didn't come in that first second, or in the next. The second after that, Winter said, "See? I'm alone. You don't have to kill me. There's no reason. I have no gun, nothing like that. I can't stop you from doing whatever you want to do. You have all the power."

The boy continued to huddle where he was, breathing fast. His eyes burned darkly in the beam from Winter's flashlight. He kept the hell-black bore of the .38 trained on Winter's chest. Looking down at him, Winter could picture him in the Tulipwood house, rushing madly from room to room with his father's rifle. Mrs. Wasserman on the stairs. Mr. Wasserman near the bed. Lila in the hall. Agnes—Agnes coming down from the third floor because she knew it was him. *Boom. Boom. Boom. Boom.* And then coming here, coming for his brother. Mateo must have thought it was Lila's footsteps he heard, Lila coming for their reconciliation. Then when he saw it was his brother, he let him get close. *Boom.*

Now here was Winter, and there was the .38, and he could feel his own death stuck in his throat.

The boy shook with sobs. The gun slackened in his hands. Winter drew breath. He felt as if he hadn't breathed for hours. Could he dare to hope that maybe he would live through this, after all?

But then, baring his teeth fiercely, the boy tightened his grip on the pistol and swung the barrel around and jammed it up under his own chin.

"No, don't," Winter said helplessly.

"I'm going to kill myself!" said the boy. "I am."

"I believe you," said Winter. "I wouldn't blame you either. It's a terrible thing you did, son. Hard to live with. But you've got to live. It's the only way. Hey, look, do you mind if I sit down? My legs are a bit wobbly here."

It was a calculated question. He hoped it would focus Tomas's attention away from himself. The boy didn't answer. He sat as he was, pressed to the wall, his chubby figure was pitiful in his little-boy outfit, a fluffy blue coat and a watch cap. He was trembling and crying, the gun barrel pressed deep into the flesh under his jaw.

Winter slid down the wall opposite. He sat on the cold stone. He was shuddering, both with the chill and with the tension. He could see the boy's finger was white on the trigger.

He couldn't blame the kid really. He knew the guilt of killing. He knew the stain it left on the spirit, the deformity it caused in the soul. He knew the loneliness of living with it too. If it had been himself with the gun, he wasn't sure what he would do.

Still, he had to say something. If there was a way to keep the boy alive, he had to try.

"So," he said slowly. "I guess that was your pornography on Mateo's computer, wasn't it? It took me a while to figure that out, but I guess it had to be. You looked at it on his computer in case your folks checked on yours, which they probably did from time to time, right? You being only thirteen."

At first, the boy didn't answer. His whole body shook. His teeth were bared. His eyes were gleaming. He was trying to do it. Right then, right there, he was trying to pull the trigger. He couldn't quite work up the courage. Not yet. Winter thought he would eventually. If the police showed up too soon, that might push him over the edge right there. This could all end any second.

"Turn the light off," said Tomas, his voice tearful and shaking. "I don't want you to look at me. Turn the flashlight off."

"Tomas . . ." Winter didn't want to do it. He was afraid the darkness would give the boy the cover he needed to do what he wanted to do. "Let me just talk to . . ."

"Turn it off! Turn it off! Don't look at me! Turn off the light!"

"All right," Winter said quickly. "I'm turning it off. All right. Hold on."

He did it. He turned the flashlight off. Everything was suddenly blackness, a dark beyond dark, cave dark. Winter sat staring at absolute nothing. His heart was hammering. He thought the gunshot would come any moment, killing the boy or killing him. How could he know? In that absolute dark. How could he know which way the gun was pointing?

He had to force himself to speak. His voice floated bodiless in the blackness. "You know, it's a funny thing about those pictures. Those videos," he said. "The pornography, I mean. The girls in the pictures. They're just shapes, aren't they? Shapes on a page, shapes on film. You can't hurt them. Not really. Not like real people. They're just shapes. You know what I mean?"

He waited. There was no answer. Nothing out of the unfathomable depths of the unfathomable dark. There was only the gunshot—the gunshot hanging in the air of possibility—the gunshot that did not come and did not come.

Winter pushed on.

"I mean, we all have fantasies like that, fantasies like those videos you watched. But fantasies—they're just shapes, too, aren't they? Just shapes in your head. They don't have any emotions. They don't have any inner life. Not like real people. It's kind of confusing when you think about it. If you're a guy, you're made to like that shape, the shape of girls, you're made to like the way girls look. So, you look at those pictures, those videos, and they're exciting, right? They get you going. But they're not real. They don't have an inner life like real girls have."

He paused. He listened. The silence was uncanny. The darkness—uncanny. He felt he was floating in black nothingness, alone. Alone except for that gunshot, the silent gunshot hanging in the dark, hanging in the air of possibility.

He could not judge the effect of his words. He had no choice but to go on.

"I think that's what would bother me most," he said. "I mean, if I ever tried to do something to a real girl like the men do in those videos—I think what would bother me most would be to see her emotions, her inner life. I mean, that's what you like about a girl in the end really. It's not just her shape. It's who she is inside. And to see that she was afraid, that you were hurting her, that wouldn't be like the pictures at all, would it? It wouldn't be exciting like your fantasies. You can do things to a shape—to a picture, to a fantasy—but it's no good with a real person. Is that how it was for you, Tomas? Is that how it was for you with Agnes?"

He had to force himself to stop. To wait. To listen. He was afraid of the dark and the silence. He was afraid the blackness would ignite with the flash and the bang of the gun. He was afraid of the blood in the darkness. The death in the darkness, hanging in the air of possibility, waiting to become suddenly real. He had to force himself to wait for an answer. In the absolute black. In the absolute silence. Second after second after second.

"Yes," Tomas said then. His voice was small and high.

Winter swallowed hard. He forced himself to wait for more.

"I thought I'd want to do it, but I couldn't," said the boy. He was crying again.

"Of course not," Winter said. "Of course you couldn't. Why would you want to hurt a nice girl like Agnes? You loved Agnes. You didn't want to hurt her."

"It wasn't like in the pictures at all," the boy cried.

"Of course not. Of course it wasn't."

"They were just shapes, but she was Agnes."

"That's right. That's right."

In the bottom of the blackness, the boy sobbed harder. "I tried to stop looking at them," he said, in anguish. "They weren't so bad at first. They were just girls at first. Everybody looks at girls. But they got worse. They got worse and worse. Meaner and meaner. I tried to make it stop, but I couldn't."

"Sure," said Winter. "Because they were just shapes. Sure."

The darkness went silent again, so silent; uncanny. In the depth of that nothingness, it felt to Winter like a pause in the pulse of the world. For a moment, he dared to hope that he had reached the boy, that he had connected with him, given him a way to think of things and to endure them and to live.

But the very instant he dared to think so, everything changed. It was so sudden it was terrifying. With no warning, the boy's voice altered utterly. It became a spoken fire of rage. The voice of the child who had stormed through the house in Tulipwood, pulling the trigger again and again.

Tomas hissed like a cobra out of the absolute cavern night. "Why should I stop? Why should I?"

The sound made Winter shiver helplessly. It was cold here too. It was cold, but he was drenched with sweat. He had the agonizing sense that his next words would determine everything, life and death, the boy's, maybe his own. If he said the wrong thing, or if he waited too long, or if he did not speak at all, the gunshot would come. And who knew anymore which way the pistol was pointing?

He had to make a guess and go.

"I was thinking about your dad," he said. He paused—just a second. But there was no blast. Not yet. "I forgot that you worked at the storage place on weekends too. Your father told me that. He said you and Mateo both helped out. But I forgot you were there too. You saw what happened, didn't you? With those gangsters and your father. It wasn't just Mateo who saw it. You saw it too."

"He took their money," the boy said with strangled fury. "He can't say what I should do. He can't say anything. He took their money. He let them laugh at him." Then he cried: "Why did they ever have to come here?"

"Right. You knew it was no good: looking at those pictures, watching those videos. But why should you stop? If your dad was doing bad things, why shouldn't you?"

"He can't say. He can't say," the boy hissed. But the hiss broke. He sobbed. Winter hoped the flame of his rage was dying. "They were just girls, at first. Everybody looks at girls."

"Right. Just shapes. You can do anything to shapes. Not like real people. Not like Agnes."

*Without our inner lives connecting, sex is just a predatory pleasure. Living pornography*, he thought.

"Agnes was nice to me," said the boy.

"You really liked her, didn't you?"

Tomas sniffled, like the child he was. "She was nice to me. At the center."

"So you went to her house to watch her."

"She slapped me," said Tomas in the pitch blackness. "She yelled at me. She slapped my face."

"Well. You know. Looking at a girl through a window is not the same thing as looking at a picture of a girl."

"She didn't have to slap me. You can't let a girl do that. That's why I went back. I wanted to show her what I could do to her."

"Only you couldn't do it. Of course you couldn't. It was Agnes. She was nice to you."

Tomas sobbed. "I was afraid she'd tell. She'd tell I couldn't do it."

Winter didn't answer, but he nodded in the dark. He had figured it was that. That was why Tomas had had to kill all of them. Father, mother, daughter, Agnes, Mateo too. The whole house. *Boom. Boom. Boom.* Their dreams, their loves, their sins, their guilts, their inner lives. He had to erase them all. Because he was afraid Agnes had told Lila, and Lila had told Mateo, and everyone would know he was not a real man, not man enough to do to Agnes what the men did to women in the pictures.

Sweating, exhausted, Winter leaned back against the cave wall. He felt he should say something else, but he could not think of what, not a single thing. He stared into the nothingness. The blackness, the silence, the invisible gun pointing at the boy or at him. The blood in the darkness. The death in the darkness.

And now, in the distance: sirens. They were faint and far away, but he could hear them. The police had gotten his message. They were pulling into the parking lot. They would soon be coming down the path.

Tomas must have heard them too. He gasped. He groaned like a slave in chains.

"Tomas . . ." said Winter.

"No! I can't!"

"You have to, son. You have to face this."

"I can't," the boy said frantically. He was crying again. "I can't. I can't."

*Thirteen years old*, Winter thought. *Christ on the cross!*

"You have to live," he said. "You have to live to get past it. There's no other way. We all have to live to get past the things we've done."

"Go away," said Tomas. "Get out of here."

"Tomas . . ."

And then it seemed the silence shattered like glass. The blackness was pierced by the boy's blinding shriek.

*"Leave! Leave now! Just leave!"*

Again, Winter struggled to find words, but he couldn't, or maybe there were none to find, nothing more to say.

*"Right now!"* shrieked the boy. *"I'll kill you! Go! I'll kill us both! Leave right now or I'll kill us both!"*

There was no doubt in Winter's mind that the boy was about to pull the trigger. "All right," he said. "I'm going. All right."

He fumbled with his phone until it lit up. When it started to glow, he made a sound, an involuntary sound in his throat, a sound of relief because he was so glad to see the light, any light. He pressed the button for the flashlight. He looked up.

The boy was pointing the pistol straight at him, straight at his chest. He had been pointing it at him, Winter thought, all this time.

*"Don't look at me!"* Tomas said. *"I'll kill us both! Go! Right now!"*

"All right," Winter said.

He held up his hand as if to fend off the bullet. He pushed slowly to his feet. He fought the urge to hurry away. He paused another moment, looking down at the boy, down into the barrel of the gun.

"Go on living, Tomas," he said. "It's the only way to get past it."

"*Get out!*" the boy shrieked. "*I can't do this! I can't!*"

The boy's grip on the pistol tightened. Tears streamed down his cheeks. His finger whitened on the trigger again.

Winter felt he had no choice. He left the chamber.

# 27

Sick to his soul, Winter made his way out of the cavern. He pushed through the narrow corridor, stumbled through the maze of bizarre rock formations, reached the great arch of the entryway, still stumbling. With every step, he wondered whether he had done the right thing in leaving. He had felt he had to, but had he? Or had he been a coward? Should he have made a leap for the kid's gun? Had there been one more word he might have said to talk him down?

He knew—he felt certain—that if he had stayed even another moment, the boy would have killed him and then killed himself. But though he felt certain, he tormented himself with doubts. Had he really done everything he might have done?

He emerged through the cavern archway out into the woods. The wind was stronger now in the naked branches of the trees. The hiss and whisper of it was all around him. The calls of the damned in the vortex of desire. The release of the pressure on his mind—the release from his fear of death in the absolute darkness—had left him dazed, his thoughts scrambled, his mind disordered. Some portion of his brain was still waiting for the gunshot, waiting to hear it echo out of the cave's inner chamber.

With the beam of his flashlight zigzagging over the chaotic tangles of the forest, he stumbled to the nearest tree, and leaned against it.

He became aware of voices. Heavy footsteps. The police were coming down the trail. He gathered himself as best he could. He stood straight to meet them. He shone his flashlight down the path.

"It's me! It's Winter here," he called. "Don't shoot."

He saw the bright beams of their flashlights first. Winter raised his hand to shield his eyes from the glare. The state lieutenant with the gray mustache led the way out of the darkness. To Winter, half-blinded, the rest of the troopers were shadow-figures arrayed behind their leader. The men with shields and rifles looked like enormous insects amidst the trees.

"You're Winter?" the lieutenant said.

"Yes. Yes," said Winter, still confused. "The boy's in the cave. He has a gun. He's distraught. Be careful."

The older man nodded. He gestured toward his riflemen. They moved toward the cave entrance.

"He's only thirteen," Winter called after them.

Then he gave out. He leaned against the tree again, exhausted.

For the next several minutes, he retreated into himself, leaning there with his eyes cast down. Moment by moment, his attention seemed to narrow until there was only the wind around him and the whispers in the wind and the gunshot in the cave that was surely coming. The boy would kill himself or fire on the police and the police would kill him, and the story of the house in Tulipwood would be over, the last life gone. Winter was not sure how he would be able to live with himself, knowing he had not found the words to say to the boy, knowing he had left him there alone to face this moment. But it seemed obscene to think about himself now, so he tried not to. He leaned against the tree and listened to the wind and waited for the gunshot.

Just before the end of it, there came a second or two when the wind died out almost completely. The hisses and whispers settled into a stillness of creaking branches. He could hear the murmured voices of the nearby police, the ones who hadn't gone into the cave, who were waiting like he was. An owl hooted. Something scrabbled through the duff, a squirrel or a raccoon. The forest was full of life, he thought. He waited for the gunshot. He did not know if he could ever forgive himself.

At last, a stir of movement caused him to stand straight and look up. Flashlight beams danced in the cave entrance. The police were returning. Where was the gunshot? Had he missed it?

The men like giant insects appeared at the cave mouth. Two of them were holding the boy between them. The boy's hands were cuffed behind him. His tearstained face turned this way and that. His eyes were misty and distant. They paused for a moment when they found Winter. Winter opened his mouth, but still there were no words. The boy looked back at him over his shoulder as he was taken away.

Winter's legs went weak. He felt his body relax like ropes had fallen from him, as if ropes had held him upright and now released him. He put his hand out blindly until he found the tree. He leaned against it. He stared after the police as they led the child away into the depths of the forest. He did not know how to feel.

The boy had lived! He had never expected that. The boy had lived. That was something. Wasn't it? Somehow the boy had not pulled the trigger. That was a good thing. Wasn't it? Life—life was better than death at least. Wasn't it?

In fact, he didn't know. He leaned there, dazed, and he found he couldn't decide. Was life better for someone like Tomas? How did it help? What good could it do him to go on living? The child had done such terrible things. Tomas had. Winter had. How could they ever get past them?

He turned to gaze again at the mouth of the cavern. It was dark now. He thought of those minutes he had spent with Tomas in the blackness, with the gun trained on him. They had both done such terrible things.

After a moment or two, he found he was thinking of something else. He was thinking of Agnes Wilde. He was seeing her as she came down the spiral stairs, her white figure in the gunshot-riddled darkness. She came downstairs hoping she could stop the murder. She knew it was Tomas. She knew he had come for her. Maybe she thought she could talk to him. But really, Winter didn't believe that. He believed Agnes came down the spiral stairs simply to offer herself. Tomas had come to kill her and she hoped if he killed her, it would be over. It would end with her and anyone who survived would be saved.

Winter hung his head. Shook his head. What good had it done? She was too late. There was no one left. It was all for nothing. She could have escaped. Instead, Agnes died and saved no one.

He found the strength to push himself upright. He turned on his flashlight. He began making his way back along the trail to his car. The ghostly forest bent and swayed all around him. His footsteps crackled on the autumn duff.

Maybe she still could though, he thought. Agnes. Maybe she could save someone yet. Maybe over time, Tomas would think about her, as Winter had thought about her. Maybe Tomas would wonder, as Winter had wondered, why she had done what she'd done. Maybe he would realize the truth of it, as Winter had. Maybe he would come to see, as Winter had, that there was so much love, so much love even in the house of death.

Winter walked on through the night forest.

The boy had done such terrible things, he thought. As he himself had done such terrible things.

Maybe it would help the kid somehow to think about Agnes. To think about what she'd done.

Maybe it would help them both.

# EPILOGUE

"I've been reading the news lately," Margaret Whitaker announced.

This came as a surprise to Winter. He had just come into the brown therapy room, just settled himself into the tan armchair across from her brown leather swivel chair. Their sessions usually began with little more than a gesture from her, at most an invitation to him to tell her what was on his mind. Maidenvale was on his mind. The events in the cavern, the events in the days that had passed since. It was all still troubling and strange to him. He was just about to let it all come bubbling out of his mouth. But Margaret spoke first.

"I've been following the news very closely lately."

"Have you?" he said. "You don't always do that, do you?"

"I try not to. I find it too upsetting. I try just to skim over it and get a sense of things. I'm past worrying about all the politics and so on. If the world can hold itself together another ten or fifteen years, it won't be my problem anymore. Meanwhile, my clients are enough to entertain me."

"I endeavor to amuse," said Winter with a wintry smile.

"But I was interested in these murders of yours. That family in the house. A terrible thing. Such a young boy doing something like that. How awful."

"It is awful, yes."

"I would have thought it would be a bigger story. In the news, I mean. There wasn't really very much about it at all. Even on the Chicago sites. You would think something as sensational as that . . ." Her voice trailed off.

"Yes, I noticed that too," said Winter. "I'm not sure why they didn't make a bigger deal of it. Maybe the wrong people were to blame. Or maybe it was just hard to turn it into a proper fable. The press does like a good fable. A good, neat moral. Maybe pure tragedy doesn't make for clickbait. I don't know."

"You were mentioned in one story I saw."

"Was I? I didn't see that."

"Yes. Someone with the state police said you had provided him with information—'essential information,' I think he said—to assist them in their investigation."

"Well, that's gratifying. I guess. The truth is, it was you who put me on the right track."

Margaret's eyes widened. "Me?"

"Something you said. About sex and pornography. It made me think about voyeurism and pornography. Murder and pornography. It's all sort of the same thing in a way. Losing sight of the inner life of others. I'm not sure how to put it into words exactly. But what you said—it helped to connect everything in my mind."

"Well," said Margaret Whitaker, pleased. "Now I really do feel like Sherlock Holmes."

Both of them sat silent for a few moments. It was not the awkward silence of strangers. It was comfortable between them, as it is with good friends. Margaret's eyes were warm on him. It gave him an odd feeling, partly pleasurable but partly . . . something else. He had been feeling somehow unworthy of her lately. He felt he hadn't lived up to her expectations in some way he couldn't quite name. Maybe he just felt unworthy in general, and her tender gaze brought the feeling to the surface. He didn't know. He wasn't sure.

He opened his mouth to speak, to end the silence. But before a word came out of him, Margaret said: "But that's not what I want to talk about today."

Surprised again, Winter said, "All right. I thought I was supposed to start the discussion. That's the way we usually do it."

"Yes, well, today we're going to do it differently," said Margaret Whitaker primly. "Today, I get to choose the subject."

Winter shifted uncomfortably in his chair. "All right," he said again.

"I know," she said. "You like to tell me stories. About your past. The Division and so on."

"Isn't that helpful?"

"It can be helpful," she said. "It can be very helpful. But it also lets you filibuster. Dominate the conversation. The stories hold my attention, and they take up almost all our time."

"You make me sound diabolically clever."

"Oh, I don't know. 'Diabolical' may be a bit much."

Winter smiled again.

"But as I was looking at the news stories about these murders in Maidenvale, I was led to another story there. Very dramatic. Gunfire. Death. A federal investigation. All involving a local police detective. He had a wonderful name—like in a Victorian novel. Inspector Strange."

Winter broke eye contact, looked down at the tan carpet. He was still smiling, but it was not the same smile. The humor had gone out of it. Just a little shift in the affect of his eyes, and the smile had become wistful, even sad.

"You're not saying anything," Margaret said.

"I don't want you to accuse me of any diabolical filibustering."

"Go on. I'll stop you when I've heard enough."

⚬━━⚬

Two days after he had returned from Maidenvale—a Saturday—Winter had realized he was being followed. A large Hispanic man in a corduroy bomber-style jacket and jeans was trailing lazily along on the sidewalk behind him. The man was working hard at looking causal.

Winter caught on to him almost at once though. He spotted him almost as soon as he stepped out of his building to go for a morning coffee. Maybe it was his old instincts kicking in, or maybe the tracker wasn't very good at his job. Maybe it was a bit of both. In any case, Winter pretended not to notice him. He kept his pace steady. Walked a block. Turned a corner down a side street. Then he stopped short and waited.

Sure enough, a moment or two later, the tracker came around the corner and nearly smacked right into him. Startled, the man pulled up short. He was taller than Winter, wider at the shoulders and thicker at the waist too. Winter grinned at him. It was not a nice grin. It was a grin that said: *Got you. I got you.*

After a startled moment, the tracker grinned back, also not nice. He drew his right hand slowly out of his jacket pocket. He shaped the fingers like a gun, and pointed the gun at Winter. He dropped his thumb—like dropping the hammer, firing the gun.

Then he put his hand back in his pocket and went on walking, brushing past Winter, giving him a bit of bump, shoulder to shoulder, as he passed.

⚬━━⚬

Winter paused after telling this.

Margaret Whitaker said, "Your face is looking better. The bruising has gone down fairly quickly."

"I told you, it looked worse than it was."

"Mm," she murmured. She was studying the wound from her chair. He had taken the gauze off. The gash was just visible beneath the semi-transparent butterfly bandages the doctor had used instead of giving him stitches. "So," she said. "I don't mean to be dense or anything, but I am just an old lady."

"Oh, you're not so old, Margaret."

"I am very, very old. And I just want to make sure I understand you. This man who was following you. Your assumption is that he worked for the same gentleman who did that, who banged you on the head there. Is that right?"

"Well, it wouldn't surprise me if he did."

"And he was following you in order to—what?—kill you?"

"I suspect this was more of a preliminary visit. Scoping out the territory. Learning my behaviors. The killing would come later. But it would come. A man like Del Rey doesn't forget a personal slight."

"Del Rey," said Margaret Whitaker.

She pressed her hands together and put them to her lips as if she were praying. This made it hard for Winter to read her expression, and that was the way she wanted it. His story about the following man had made her heart rate rise with anxiety. She didn't think her client needed to know that.

"All right," she said. "Go on."

❦

The next day, Sunday, when Eduardo Hernandez came home from church to the Hawthorn section of the Hollow, Winter was waiting for him. His Jeep was parked across from Hernandez's house and he was leaning against it, his hands in the pockets of his jeans, his windbreaker zipped over his sweater, his ivy cap pulled low.

He watched as the Hernandez minivan, a dented gray Dodge, pulled into the driveway. The engine died and there was a moment of silence. Winter watched a gentle breeze move over the sparse lawn behind the diamond-link fence. The American flag by the front door shuddered and flapped.

Hernandez saw him as he stepped out from behind the wheel of the van. Mrs. Hernandez and their daughter emerged from the other side at the same time. Hernandez stood frozen where he was, considering Winter. His wife followed his gaze and she saw Winter too. She exchanged a somber glance with her husband. He gestured at her to take the child inside. Mrs. Hernandez took her daughter by the hand and they both hurried in.

Winter stood straight as Hernandez walked toward him. He didn't know if the man was angry at him or not, whether he blamed him for Tomas's arrest or not. He didn't know whether he would attack him or not. It was as it so often was around this place: he was never quite sure whether he was going to get punched in the mouth.

As Hernandez came closer, Winter saw with a small shock how diminished he was. One son was dead, the other was in jail awaiting trial for killing him. His daughter had been molested, and he himself had been corrupted. His life was a catastrophe. It was not that he had lost any of his bulk or substance. He still filled his black church suit at the waist and shoulders. But something within him had withered. Winter could see it on his suddenly narrow face, and in the sallow skin beneath his silver hair and mustache. His eyes were mired in pools of darkened flesh. They were bright with inward agony.

Winter waited to see what he would say.

"My boy Tomas," Hernandez began. His voice cracked on the words. He looked away, along the street of modest homes. He fought down his emotions. "My boy Tomas says you saved his life."

Relief swept over Winter. He lifted his chin and drew a deep breath as the feeling hit him. He had not been able to convince himself that he had done the right thing when he left the cavern. The father's words soothed him. "He said that?"

"Yes. He said the way you talked to him made him feel human again. He did not feel human because of what he did. The terrible thing he did to that family . . ." The father shook his head at the thought. "All those people. His own brother. Ah, it was my fault."

Winter made a lame gesture. Hernandez faced him again and said, "He saw me with those mafiosi. His father. He cried when he told me. I went to talk to him in the jail. He kept saying, 'Why did you do that, Pa?'" Hernandez's voice cracked again, and this time he couldn't control himself. He lowered his head and tears fell from his eyes onto the pavement at his feet. "I said to him, 'What could I do? Call the police? It *was* the police who brought them to me. Call the government? They sent them here.' I tried to explain it to him. Ah, but my poor boy . . . My poor boy."

A sour feeling came into Winter's stomach. He had come here for a reason. Hernandez's anguish would make it easier for him to accomplish his purpose. He did not like himself much for taking advantage of such an opportunity. But that wasn't going to stop him.

"Listen," he said. "At your facility, your storage place."

Hernandez didn't seem to hear him. His head was still bowed. His shoulders shook. His tears made dark spots on the macadam as they fell between his black church shoes.

"You have security cameras," said Winter.

Hernandez drew a deep breath. He wiped his face with his hand. He lifted his eyes. "Cameras?" he said, in a daze of grief.

"I saw them," said Winter. "You have cameras that watch the lockers."

Confused, Hernandez answered helplessly: "Yes. I have them."

Winter breathed away his own misgivings. He looked up and down the street. It was quiet. Deserted. Sunday morning.

"Inspector Strange steals from them. From the mafiosi. Del Rey and the others. He lets himself in when no one's there, takes product from the bags. Sells it for his own profit. Your cameras must have caught him on video."

Hernandez opened his mouth, lowered his brow. The expression made his shrunken features seem even more depleted, more gutted, like the features of a starving man. "What? What are you saying? Strange? He steals? From Del Rey? That's crazy. Del Rey will kill him. Police or not. He doesn't care. How do you know this? How can you know this?"

"Strange bragged about it to his lover. She wrote it in her diary. And yes, they might kill him. But then, he got you into this. There was no one you could call because of him. Because he was dirty. He got you into this and your boy saw it."

Hernandez stared at him. "What do you mean? What are you telling me to do?"

Winter didn't answer. He met the man's stare silently. He saw Hernandez's lips part as he began to understand. After a moment, he opened the door to his Jeep and climbed inside.

As he drove away, he looked up in the rearview mirror. He could see Hernandez standing in the street, watching him go.

Winter paused again. He wanted to give Margaret a chance to respond. But she didn't. Not right away. She knew he was expecting something. A rebuke maybe. Or a mournful shake of the dead. Disappointed Mommy. That's what he was waiting for, she thought.

But in fact, she already knew this story—had already guessed it in outline anyway. She nodded once and said, "Go ahead, Cam. I'm listening."

He lifted his eyebrows, surprised. But he obeyed her. "The next day, I went to see Strange," he said.

○━━●━━○

He had found the dirty detective at work at the cop shop, the police station out by the Community Center. It was a modern setup with a glass security booth in the lobby. Winter gave his name to the receptionist and waited. He didn't have to wait long.

It was Ann Farmingham who came to fetch him. The burly patrolwoman pushed the inner door open and beckoned him inside. She gave no sign that she recognized him. He took the hint and followed her silently as she marched down a white hall of office doors. She knocked on the last door. It was marked "Inspector Strange."

"Come in," Strange called.

Even when Officer Ann held the door open for him, even when their eyes met, she gave him nothing. Winter understood. It would cost her her job if Strange knew how she had gone around him to the staties. Winter thanked her politely and stepped into the office.

Inspector Strange had himself all but enthroned in the cushiony leather swivel chair behind his gunmetal desk. Two flags against the wall behind him flanked him right and left. The stars and stripes were to his right, the state flag to his left. There were framed photos on the paneled wall. Pictures of Strange receiving plaques and ribbons. Shaking hands with luminaries, including the governor.

Strange didn't rise to greet him. Didn't offer his hand. The last time they had met, Winter had held a knife to his throat. Humiliated him in front of his gangster pals. He could still see some of the wound above the white collar of his shirt. Now Strange played his authority boldly, with open hostility. Erect on his throne, he royally gestured Winter to a lesser chair.

Winter sat before the desk. The two men sneered at one another, no love lost.

"What do you want?" said Strange.

"Del Rey knows," said Winter. Strange was about to ask: Knows what? But Winter said: "About you, skimming his product. You bragged to Marion Wasserman about it. She wrote about it in her diary. It's on video. You stealing. Del Rey has a copy of the video."

The blood drained from Strange's face. It was very dramatic. As Winter sat and watched, still sneering, the color went out of him forehead to chin, like a white blind being pulled down over a red window. It was as if Strange had been transformed into a corpse in front of Winter's eyes.

"You did that?" Strange said hoarsely. "Did you send him the video?"

Winter stood up. "You're a dirty son of a bitch," he said. "I don't care what happens to you."

Strange's corpse-colored face gaped at him, mouth open.

Then Winter was gone.

⚬—✦—⚬

Margaret studied him, one hand to her chin now, one finger laid across her lips, her expression hidden. She had her emotions more or less under control by this time. Her mind was engaged. She was interested. Working her work. Thinking it through.

"Well," she remarked mildly. "The Recruiter would be proud of you, wouldn't he?"

Winter made a short sound something like laughter.

"No, I'm serious," she said. "This is what he taught you, isn't it? How to arrange for things to happen. How to build the machine that makes things happen, automatically, without your fingerprints on them."

Winter shrugged. "I suppose it is what he taught me, yes."

"Which is why you came here to begin with. Came to me. All those assassination machines you built. All those deaths. Roy Spahn. Madeleine Uno. Even the other one. Snowstep, bad guy though he was. You lost—what did you just call it?—you lost sight of the inner lives of others. And you ended up alone, locked in your past, locked in your guilt and solitude. That's why you came to me, isn't it?"

Not for the first time, Winter was startled by a wave of warm affection for her, helpless affection, like a child's. He was startled, too, by how much he wanted her affection in return, and her approval as well. The mother he never had. It was a cliché, but it was also true.

Still, he had to go on with this. He had to tell her the rest of the story. He had to tell her everything. Her approval was no good to him unless she knew the truth in its entirety.

"You're interrupting my diabolical filibustering," he said.

Margaret's nod was almost imperceptible. "Pardon me. Go diabolically on."

⊶✦⊷

Federal Agent Stan "Stan-Stan" Stankowski was still undercover as a mentally ill homeless man. After a brief search, Winter found him sleeping under a freeway overpass, a shapeless bundle of clothing sprawled on his back atop a sleeping bag on a raised strip of concrete at the structure's base. There were five or six other homeless people in nooks around him. Winter brought a box of sandwiches for them. He dropped one sandwich beside each sleeping bag. He dropped the last sandwich on Stan-Stan's belly. He crouched down beside him.

"Not now. I'm schizophrenic," Stan-Stan growled under his breath.

"And I'm a charitable soul who brings food to the homeless," Winter answered in a low tone. "It was this or go undercover as a serial killer who sets homeless people on fire. You'd have been my first victim."

"That probably would've killed me quicker than whatever you have planned."

"There's a cop in Maidenvale named Inspector Strange," said Winter.

Stan-Stan lifted his head. Lifted the sandwich off his belly till he could see it. "What is this?"

"Roast beef on rye."

"With Russian dressing?"

"Of course. What do I look like, a barbarian?"

His head still lifted, Stan-Stan peeled open the white butcher paper that was wrapped around the sandwich. He frowned appreciatively. "Inspector Strange, huh. What the hell is he, a limerick? 'There once was an Inspector named Strange, whose habits were somewhat deranged . . .'"

"He's fallen in with a nasty Mex gangster named Del Rey. I believe your *federale* masters let Mr. Del Rey into the country as an act of benevolence or corruption. It's so hard to tell those two apart these days. Anyway, they shipped him to the Midwest to keep him from being cruelly deported. And so he fell in with Inspector Strange in a joint enterprise sometimes known as the Homeland Highway."

"Sad story."

"What people you work for, Stan-Stan."

"But the benefits are amazing." Stan-Stan lifted his head even further until his chin touched his chest. That allowed him to take a nibble of his sandwich. He chewed and frowned appreciatively again. "Rye bread is a wonderful thing, isn't it?"

"A great blessing, yes," said Winter. "Strange has been skimming Del Rey's product. He was caught on video. Del Rey found out about it. Strange found out that Del Rey found out."

Stan-Stan stopped chewing. He looked balefully at Winter, squatting there beside him. "You know, I was kind of hoping you were a hallucination."

"But you're only pretending to be schizophrenic."

"Oh yeah, I forgot. Damn it."

"It's your people's mess, Stan-Stan. You ought to clean it up," said Winter.

As he walked away from the encampment, he heard Stan-Stan screaming at whatever phantoms were supposed to haunt his supposedly diseased mind.

He screamed: "A hooker named Schlector, said Strange would inspect her, then leave her a dollar and change!"

○─━─○

"So we come full circle," said Margaret Whitaker. "Back to the news story I read."

"I thought this might get us there," said Winter. "What was the story exactly?"

"I suspect you already know. I read that this Inspector Strange and his officers made a raid on the hideout of a drug gang," said Margaret.

"Do tell."

"The gang's leader, a man known as Del Rey, was killed in an exchange of gunfire with the police."

"The drug trade is a dangerous business."

"Oddly, the very next day, federal agents brought Strange in for questioning because they suspect he is corrupt and involved with interstate drug traffic."

"What a disappointing world it can be," said Winter. "You never know who to trust anymore." When she neither smiled nor answered him, he said: "Well, don't look at me like that, Margaret."

"How should I look at you, Cameron?"

"Del Rey whacked me in the head with his gun."

"Well, I think we can certainly agree that was a mistake on his part."

"He threatened to kill me. He sent a man to scope the hit."

"I suppose that won't be a problem now."

"No. It won't. And Strange—he kicked me in the stomach."

"Foolish of him."

"It was. It's no fun to be a cop in prison."

"Yes, I get the general idea," said Margaret. "But then, what were you doing in Maidenvale in the first place? Investigating murders. Solving crimes. You're an English professor. You teach the Romantic poets. Why should you even involve yourself with people like Del Rey and Strange?"

Winter's mouth opened and closed but he had no answer, not really. Margaret had to fight down a self-satisfied smile.

She had been more or less ready to hear all this even before the session started. The moment she stumbled on the news story about Strange and the gangsters, she had begun to put the pieces together. It shocked her when she first thought about it, but it didn't shock her anywhere near as much as she thought it should. She was pretending to be stern with Winter now. But she did not feel very stern. In fact, if she was honest with herself, she was harboring a secret pride in him. She had no love for this Del Rey person. She had been holding a grudge against him ever since he had laid violent hands on her boy. And, well, if this gangster had gotten himself killed in a gun battle with the police, so be it. It was ta-ta and too bad, as far as she was concerned.

Margaret knew she ought to be ashamed of herself for feeling this way. She had scolded herself for not being ashamed. What was Winter turning her into with all these violent stories of his? If this kept up, she thought, she would not be surprised if she started her own side business as a hit woman. That would be a fine therapeutic outcome!

"Tell me something, Cam," she said. "What really happened in Maidenvale finally? The end of it I mean. How did the boy come to be arrested for the murders?"

Winter told her. About the interview with Bobby at Isaac Wasserman's house. About the raid on the Community Center. About how he got distracted there and how, when the police went inside, the boy was gone. He told her how he and the boy ended up together in the cavern. About those endless minutes plunged into absolute blackness with nothing between them but the gun and the sounds of their own voices. He spoke for a while about the guilt he felt when he left the boy alone. How he wondered whether he had failed him or run out on him to save himself. He told her how relieved he was when Tomas told his father that their conversation had convinced him to go on living.

"It seemed to me there had to be so many failures before a thirteen-year-old kid would do what he did. So many things had to go wrong from the top down, if you see what I mean. Even the fact that a kid that age can lay his hands on that violent pornographic garbage is a kind of failure. I was just glad I wasn't one last failure on the list."

Finally, he told her about Agnes Wilde. He told her about what Agnes had done during the murders and why he thought she had done it.

Margaret sat up straighter in her chair. "That's remarkable," she said.

"It is, isn't it? I can't get it out of my mind," he told her. "I find myself going back to it again and again. I keep picturing her going down the spiral stairs, this white figure in the darkness on the stairs. It's a clichéd image, I suppose. But I find it comforting somehow. I think about the dark in that cave. How complete it was. How black it was. Nothing there but death waiting to happen. Am I making any sense?"

"I think so. Yes."

"I'd hate to think that everything was like that. You know? Just darkness. Just death."

"Agnes certainly didn't think so."

"No. No, I guess she didn't, did she? Maybe that's why I keep thinking about her."

He fell silent, gazing into space. Margaret Whitaker's eyes flicked to the clock on her desk. Their session time was almost over. She was sorry for that. She had a sense that this story was unfinished. Something was missing. Something had been left out.

Then she realized what it was.

"When you were at the Community Center, waiting for the police, you said you were distracted, that that's how the boy slipped away."

Winter began to smile ruefully even before she finished.

"Was it the woman you told me about? The therapist? The one who was married and had children. Was she what distracted you?"

"Really, Margaret," said Winter. "How *do* you do that?"

"Did you actually speak with her?"

"I did. She saw me waiting there and came out of the building to talk to me."

"*She* came out. While you were waiting for the police to arrive? Why would she do that? And what could she possibly have said that would have distracted you at such a moment?"

A faint touch of color came into Winter's cheeks. Was it possible he was blushing? Margaret wondered.

"She told me she wasn't married," he said. "I didn't ask her about it. I didn't say a word about it, I swear. She just saw me waiting outside and she came out specifically to tell me. She had been married, but she was widowed. She was reluctant to take the ring off. It was a problem for her, something she knew she had to work on, I guess."

"What about her children?"

"It turns out they're her niece and nephew. She's too young for them to have been hers. I should have thought of that really."

"Well, you saw her wedding ring . . ."

"Exactly."

Margaret sat back in her chair. She was surprised—surprised and abashed—at how sharp the pang of jealousy was. She supposed she should really feel gratified instead. After all, Winter was a man in the prime of life, desperately isolated inside himself, desperately lonely. He had come to her to help him solve that problem, and she had worked very hard to give him back his access to his soul. Now that work was beginning to come to fruition. She should feel pleased, even proud. This was her job. This was what she was here for. Everything else was just an old woman's daydreams.

She detached herself from her feelings. She managed to regard him with a look of gentle generosity.

"So basically, you panicked," she said.

"What do you mean? That's ridiculous, Margaret. I didn't panic."

"Oh, please! The woman went out of her way to let you know she was available. She obviously wants you to call her. Ask her out. It scared the living daylights out of you. That's why you went through all your Recruiter nonsense with this Del Rey and, what's-his-name, Strange. You wanted to make sure you were still a cold-blooded assassin, still doomed to solitude. Still the antihero and not suddenly some hero who might win the princess after all."

"Oh, you're talking nonsense. Del Rey whacked me in the head with his pistol, Margaret. Strange kicked me in the stomach."

"Oh yes, yes, yes."

"Del Rey threatened to kill me. He sent that man to watch me!"

"Our time is up, Cameron."

"Damn it. I hate you," he said.

"Nobody cares. Get out of my office."

She stood and marched to the door. Opened it for him. That was their ritual. That was the sign that it was time for him to leave.

Muttering darkly, Winter got up out of his chair. Yanked his windbreaker from the coatrack. Jammed his arms angrily into the sleeves. He snapped up his ivy cap and yanked it down over his eyes with near violent force. He shuffled sullenly to where she stood waiting.

Normally, Margaret would have said nothing else. With the door open, their therapeutic seal of confidentiality was broken. But she could see that the waiting room was empty. So, as he came up alongside her, she said, "Well?"

He stopped. "Well, what?"

"Well, are you going to call her?

Winter glared at her—glared at her with hollow, frightened eyes.

"Well?" she said again. "Are you going to call her or not?"

Winter continued standing there a long, long moment. Then he fled. There was no other word for it. He charged past her into the waiting room, flung open the outer door, strode swiftly into the hall.

Margaret laughed as he slammed the door behind him.

# ACKNOWLEDGMENTS

My thanks to firefighter Tony Torres for explaining how to fight a house fire. And to Neal Edelstein, friend for life, who has helped me with research any number of times. Also thanks to Mark Gottlieb and Robert Gottlieb and everyone at Trident Media. Likewise, the mighty Otto Penzler and everyone at Mysterious Press, including Charles Perry and Luisa Cruz Smith. And to Jeremy Boreing and Ben Shapiro of the Daily Wire for their friendship and continued support.